JELLYFISH HAVE EYES

A Novel

Joram Piatigorsky

To Adela –

I hope you enjoy my first
efforts at becoming a novelist!

Joram
11/22/2014

Edited by NY Book Editors
nybookeditors.com

Copyright © 2014 Joram Piatigorsky
and International Psychoanalytic Books (IPBooks),
25–79 31st Street Astoria, NY 11102.
Online at: http://www.IPBooks.net

ISBN: 978-0-9895622-6-3

Library of Congress Control Number: 2014947088

The time is the near future when an economically stressed government threatens academic freedom of basic scientists. In *Jellyfish Have Eyes*, an award-winning scientist pays a heavy price for his breakthrough discoveries that jellyfish interact and visualize evolution. Piatigorsky's imaginative account of Dr. Ricardo Sztein's path from discovery to condemnation gives a chilling warning that is sure to stimulate debate on the role of government in dictating the direction of scientific research.

—Joseph Horwitz, Ph.D.,
Distinguished Professor,
UCLA School of Medicine

In memory of my mother, who always believed in me, and for my wife, Lona, who gave me her love and our treasured family.

"...well, the fact is the heart has its reasons that the reason knows nothing about."

Antonio Tabucchi, *Pereira Declares*

Author's Note

Ricardo Sztein's adventures in La Parguera were influenced by my trips to the Marine Station of the University of Puerto Rico—Mayagüez at La Parguera, Puerto Rico, where I collected jellyfish in the mangrove swamp and performed research on the jellyfish eye. Jellyfish do have eyes, remarkable ones that are embedded in dangling structures called rhopalia. The brief descriptions of the jellyfish eye and rhopalia in this book are scientifically correct, however Ricardo's experiments and scientific interpretations are fiction. The various statements and digressions on science are correct to the best of my knowledge, and I take responsibility for any errors that they may contain. Any resemblances of the characters to known persons or of the happenings to known events are entirely coincidental.

PROLOGUE: Mid-21st Century

Ricardo Sztein tossed restlessly dreaming that he was treading water in the mangrove swamp of La Parguera. Jellyfish pulsated through the tepid water in small clusters. Crabs, tubeworms, sponges, sea urchins and other colorful invertebrates decorated the muddy bottom.

Lillian's ghost, gaunt and riddled with cancer, whispered, "I told you to be careful, Ricardo."

Yes, she had. So had Benjamin. But Ricardo hadn't listened to his wife or his best friend and colleague.

"If you had been there and seen the jellyfish, Lillian. They have eyes and minds. We have so much to learn from them."

"You're a dreamer, Ricardo, a dreamer."

Benjamin faded and Lillian, now young and beautiful, floated into his dream wearing a pearl-ivory wedding dress. "Poor baby," she said to Ricardo with tenderness, awakening him.

5:13. Too early to rise. The trial didn't start until nine, so he drifted off again, dreaming this time that he was in a small boat gliding through the tropical lagoon lined with lush mangrove trees. He luxuriated under the golden sun. A noisy speedboat with a ringing motor broke the silence.

7:15. It was time to face the music. The jury would determine his fate.

PART I

Chapter 1

Ricardo Sztein's life changed forever on January 15, 2047—a gray, icy Tuesday morning—when Lillian announced at breakfast that she had felt a lump in her breast. "When?" he asked, clearly shaken. "This morning," she said, "in the shower." Ricardo didn't need to tell Lillian how frightened those words made him; she didn't need to elaborate. A lump in her breast was a lump in his. She was 69, he 70. They had hoped to soon retire: he from the Vision Science Center and she from social work. They were resurrecting forgotten plans and exploring new ones. But now there was a lump in her breast, like her mother had when she was 68. Her father was a widower the following year.

Ricardo met Lillian Shields the day after he had emigrated from Buenos Aires some fifty years ago to be a graduate student at George Washington University. He had responded to an advertisement to share an apartment with three graduate students. Two of the prospective roommates, both men, had interviewed him at the dining room table. They were sipping lukewarm coffee when Lillian, the third roommate, bounded into the apartment with a cheery "Hi!" carrying groceries and perspiring heavily from the July heat of Washington DC. She was lean and firm, five-foot four with short, curly auburn hair and dazzling blue eyes. Oh, how she glowed and sparkled. Ricardo, pudgy, five foot six, with a receding hairline, couldn't take his eyes off her.

After almost forty-four years of marriage, Lillian was his foundation and conscience. He took her for granted in the same way that he never doubted that his heart was a part of his body. She was always there for him when he returned home after a long day in the laboratory. She celebrated his successes and empathized with his disappointments, and never complained when he buried himself in the laboratory on weekends. Their lives were a complementary mosaic. When he made a scientific discovery Lillian had a sense of accomplishment; when she found a promising foster home for an abused child he felt virtuous. When he squeezed her gently around her waist, she'd say light-heartedly, "You're my other half." He'd respond, "You're my other three-quarters." She was his myth of an eternal present.

Maybe the lump would be benign.

"Try not to worry," he told her behind a mask of optimism. "Let's get a biopsy right away and be done with it. Thousands of women have false alarms."

They had no such luck. The biopsy showed a grade 4 malignancy. Lumpectomy and radiation followed. Despite enormous scientific advances in the treatment of cancer in the preceding years, there was still no cure. Lillian's cancer didn't submit to a barrage of promising pharmaceuticals.

Ricardo and Lillian, thin as a bamboo stalk, sat in the oncologist's office eight months after surgery. "Is there anything more to try?" Ricardo asked.

The physician sighed. "I'm sorry." Lillian's team of physicians—surgeon, internist, endocrinologist—had all said the same thing in different ways. How was it possible that cancer could still defeat Lillian in the mid-twenty-first century? Her genome had been sequenced and scrutinized for mutations in cancer-associated genes. The tests revealed nothing. The current experimental anti-cancer drugs were equally unsuccessful. Genetic studies and pharmacology had promised to revolutionize medicine and personalize medical treatments, yet early promises remained only that. DNA was still a foreign language.

Discouraged, Ricardo scanned the framed credentials on the wall in the physician's office: he saw a Bachelor's degree from Yale and MD degree from Harvard, certificates for completion of internship and residency at the finest hospitals, membership to elite professional organizations, a signed photograph of the surgeon general. This oncologist was the best and the final word on what was possible.

Ricardo looked at Lillian and forced a smile. Confronting the death of friends, colleagues or even family didn't compare with Lillian's impending loss. He had transformed her from wife to patient in his mind, perhaps to protect himself emotionally. His great challenge was to remain well and stable himself so that he could be supportive.

As the months passed Lillian became progressively weaker and Ricardo increasingly lonely and frightened. Her body withered. He was scared that she might break if he hugged her too tightly. When they talked about shared experiences—the Greek Island tour, the visits to Papi in Argentina, the surprise seventieth birthday party she threw him—the words seemed hollow. Without a future the past lost significance.

Shortly after midnight on Sunday morning during the second week of Lillian's hospitalization, Ricardo received a phone call from the nurse in the cancer ward. "I'm sorry to call at this hour, Dr. Sztein, but your wife has taken a turn for the worse. Her blood pressure is low and her pulse is weak. She's falling in and out of consciousness. I thought you should know. You may want to come to be with her."

Unlike his visits during the day, few cars populated the parking lot at night. Ricardo's footsteps echoed in the hospital lobby. Iron bars barricaded the gift shop, the newsstand was empty, and the flower shop closed. A solitary attendant listlessly turning pages of a magazine at the information booth looked up at the wall clock. It was 2:32 in the morning.

"Can I help you?" he asked.

"My wife's a patient in the cancer ward. I just received a phone call that she's not doing well. I've come to see her."

"Of course. I'm sorry, sir."

Their many years of marriage seemed no more than a dot in space as Ricardo entered the elevator. How quickly the time had passed. Was he really 70 and almost a widower?

Ricardo got out of the elevator at the fourth floor cancer ward, which was somber in the eerie quiet of the night. The brown cloth-upholstered couch and the empty porcelain vase on the small table in the nook by the elevators looked like props for a screen set. But this wasn't theater; it was real life and death. The patients slept behind closed doors on both sides of the hall. A crayon drawing of a bedridden woman with long red hair and gold earrings under a yellow sun was taped to the door next to Lillian's room. "Git wel soone grama!" was written in a child's hand at the bottom of the picture. Ricardo wondered what his life would have been like if they had had children and grandchildren. They had tried—fertility clinics, in vitro fertilization—but that's just the way it was.

The rhythmic click of the mechanical heart monitor greeted Ricardo when he entered Lillian's room. Her eyes were open.

"Hi," he said as he touched Lillian's emaciated arm.

"I guess it's time," she said.

Ricardo glanced at his wristwatch remembering the importance of promptness to Lillian. It was 2:40.

"You must be tired." She always thought of him first. He loved her for that.

"I'm fine," he lied.

"I'm sorry," she said.

"Me too."

An awkward silence followed. Ricardo wanted to lie down next to her and comfort her, but he also wished he were back in his bed away from this horror.

"You've got to learn to cook."

He nodded. "I will." Ricardo's fear of the future became mingled with resentment for all the times she had implied that he couldn't take care of himself. But she had a point. "You never know, I may become an expert chef and start a catering service. And kings and queens will want my services," he said trying to be light-hearted.

"No more stories, Ricardo." Lillian coughed, her face twisted in pain. "Life isn't a story or a dream."

She's right, he thought. It's a nightmare.

She motioned with her fingertips for him to move closer to hear something important, something she wanted to be sure he heard and understood. Even in death, Lillian was watching out for him, advising him.

He placed his ear close to her lips and covered her hand with his. "What is it?" he asked.

"Be careful, Ricardo."

"I'm always careful."

"Not enough. Watch yourself. You're impulsive. It's who you are. Be careful."

Ricardo remembered Papi's belief that you are who you are and that's all anyone could be. He nodded and kissed her cheek.

Her thumb pressed his hand. She twisted a few inches. "Remember me, remember my pain."

Ricardo stroked her forehead. Her pain was the last thing he wanted to remember.

"I love you," she said. "Thank you."

"Thank you too."

"Do something so that other people don't have to go through this," she said with more energy than Ricardo thought she had left. "Do something, anything, please. You're a scientist."

"But I'm not a physician."

"Poor baby," she said and closed her eyes. Then she whispered, "Be compassionate."

"I am," he said, somewhat hurt.

"Look for treatments. Cure cancer. If not cancer, other diseases. Blindness. Help people. Promise me. It's what I want."

"Rest now," he said. He stroked her forehead. If only he *could* help Lillian, or anyone for that matter. As much as he'd tried to focus his research on medicine, he wasn't a physician.

Lillian looked at him with imploring eyes. "Promise me," she demanded again.

Ricardo squeezed her hand. Was that a promise?

Her brow wrinkled, her eyes still closed as if looking inward; her shoulders clenched and then let go.

He moved his cheek to her mouth to test for her breath. He took her wrist searching for a pulse. Tears dribbled down his cheeks. He held her limp hand, her skin more leather than flesh.

"I promise," he said, too late for her to hear.

She never felt the final, gentle kiss he gave her parched lips.

Ricardo sat by her body for a few moments, then he rose slowly. The illusion of eternity had evaporated. Lillian was beyond pain, the ending an anticlimax.

He dragged himself towards the door and went to the nurse's station at the end of the hall. His feet felt heavy on the floor.

"She's gone," he told the nurse. "Thanks for calling and telling me to come. At least I was with her at the end." But did that comfort her? Also, if he hadn't been there he wouldn't have heard her plea for him to devote his research to medical issues. He wondered whether she died thinking that he had made a promise.

"I'm so sorry," the nurse said.

"What should I do?" he asked the nurse as much as himself.

"You don't have to do anything right now. The hospital will get in touch with you tomorrow to make arrangements."

"Thank you." He walked slowly to the elevator.

Back in his car, Ricardo collapsed behind the steering wheel, deadened by fatigue and grief. He reran a mental tape of Lillian's sickness. His spirit had crumbled when she'd felt that fateful lump, not hers. She'd met the biopsy report with strength while he'd felt terror. He never was as brave as she. Following the fragile hope of surgery, the opaque shield of her optimism transformed into a clear window through which he'd seen her despair. Finally, they had both surrendered to the last stronghold of the human spirit: acceptance of the unavoidable. And then she died. Less than an hour ago.

With daylight on the horizon, he drove home. It was another day.

Chapter 2

When he returned from the hospital Ricardo removed his shoes and flopped on the left side of the king sized bed. The right side was for Lillian's ghost. He shut his eyes but couldn't escape from her ghostly image on her deathbed. He hated for that image to displace the memory of the woman he loved. He had wanted to experience everything in their life together, but that ending had been too much. He wrapped his arms around Lillian's pillow and slept until noon. After his ritual cup of coffee, he called Benjamin Wollberg, a Professor at the University of Minnesota, and his closest friend and colleague.

"She's gone, Benjamin," he said in a monotone, struggling to speak. "Lillian died last night."

"I'm really sorry, Ricardo. Were you with her?"

"The nurse woke me up around two in the morning and said that Lillian was doing badly. She said I should come."

The receiver was silent.

"Benjamin? Are you there?"

"It was a privilege to be her friend." Benjamin's voice was weak.

"She looked peaceful when I left her."

"Did she suffer at the end?"

"She was doped up pretty well with morphine. Oh, god Benjamin. It was awful. She begged me to…" His voice dropped off.

"Begged you to what?"

Ricardo recovered his composure. "Nothing. I can't believe she's dead."

"Mattie's here beside me. She's so sad." Lillian had been close to Benjamin's wife, Mattie, until she started having children. Lillian only had miscarriages. "Lillian was lucky to have you, Ricardo."

"She wanted kids. We should've adopted. It was my fault."

"Don't think of fault, Ricardo. She loved you more than anything."

Lillian had four miscarriages before they stopped trying. Benjamin was right. It was not his fault.

Suddenly Ricardo's heart skipped a beat when the note on the door of the room next to Lillian's in the hospital flashed through his mind: "Git wel soone grama!" The loss of their babies had created such a void in Lillian's life, and what had he done about it? Nothing. Why did he place his work above all else, even her?

Benjamin rescued the pause. "She really did, you know, love you."

"I know," he said.

After they hung up, Ricardo visualized Lillian's drawn face and heard her frail voice in his mind before she died: "...cure cancer...help people...be compassionate." Of course Lillian had begged him to direct his research towards curing cancer and other horrible diseases. Not only was she suffering, she had been a social worker with a strong social conscience. But he was a scientist, and science was motivated by the mind, not the heart. Why then had she told him to be compassionate? Did she think he wasn't compassionate?

No! Impossible. Even sick as she was, she knew that compassion wasn't measured by a research project. He had received awards for his genetic research on Fuch's dystrophy, a degenerative, hereditary pathology that rendered the cornea opaque and could lead to blindness, and on his biochemical studies of lens cataracts, still a major cause of blindness throughout the world. Wasn't that proof that his research contributed to the greater good and well being of mankind? Wasn't that a form of compassion?

He spent the rest of the day moping around the house. Sitting down with his third cup of coffee, he scanned the *Washington Post*. A headline caught his eye. The Maryland legislature had cut funding for the arts in public high schools because taxpayers didn't want their money "wasted on entertainment."

"What morons," Ricardo muttered under his breath, thinking that expenditures for art represented a minuscule sum of no real consequence. "Why cut art?"

Ricardo glanced at Papi's painting of an abstract sea animal hanging on the wall. Ricardo's father had been a butcher to earn his keep, but he had loved to paint and had the spirit of an artist. Papi had signed his name on the bottom of one of his bloodstained aprons calling it "expressionistic art," and he had often cut meat in amusing shapes for display in his shop. He had made oil paintings of marine creatures, both real and imaginary, and had boasted that his make-believe critters were examples of what he called "premature realism," species not discovered yet.

"No matter how fanciful an idea," he used to say, "it holds some truth."

Ricardo hadn't taken Papi's romantic notions seriously, for what would a butcher know about complex scientific ideas and theories? However, he had been impressed by the idea that what is only imagined could foreshadow what is real. He had daydreamed of foreshadowing the future himself—of being ahead of the pack—ever since he was a little boy. Now, he foresaw a bleak future as an aging scientist lost in a faceless mass. Despite years of research he had found no cures or even treatments for any disease, and his scientific publications stagnated with empty promises and ended with "more research is warranted."

Why hadn't he dared to search for new principles of vision by investigating unusual light receptors that fascinated him, such as those in the single-cell *Euglena* or other protozoa? Few investigators even knew these specializations existed within a single cell. What secrets might they hold?

Instead, he had buckled under the pressure of performing goal-oriented research directly related to human disease. He had joined the herd as it were, in deference to his prestigious position and the need to maintain sufficient funding from the government. How different his career path appeared years ago when the road stretched before him, rather than now near the end of his travels. Had he mistaken climbing the professional ladder for bold exploration?

Ricardo called his secretary to tell her that Lillian had died and he wouldn't be in until next week. He had many matters that needed attention, Lillian's cremation among them.

"Be sure to tell Pearl too," he said. He had no energy to deal with Pearl Witstein, the only postdoctoral fellow in his dwindling laboratory.

Later in the afternoon, Ricardo needed a nap. Although nothing had changed in the bedroom since Lillian had gone to the hospital three weeks ago, it now seemed more barren, as if she had taken all her belongings with her when she died. The wooden "tree" upon which they perched their clothes for the night held only the shirt he had worn yesterday. He would have to get rid of Lillian's clothes in the closet, but that could wait. Should he offer them to her friends or just donate them to charity? Every small decision seemed momentous and exhausting.

He opened the top drawer of Lillian's dresser and saw the edge of a piece of frayed paper, yellowed from age, protruding from underneath a sweater. He pulled it out and found in her handwriting a short list of names. The list was labeled "just in case," with Samuel and Devra underlined. She had never shown him that list.

He lay down on the bed to rest. Chilled after a few minutes, he went to increase the temperature on the thermostat located in the hallway. He clicked on the television as he crossed the living room and was greeted by the familiar voice of Randolph Likens, a vitriolic, aggressively ambitious reporter in mid-career who had started the popular public interest program, "Your Money/Your Health." The voice from the television said, "We are rotting with sickness while researchers, rolling with taxpayer dollars, promise cures they don't deliver." Rolling with taxpayer dollars? What's he talking about? thought Ricardo. "We must demand more," continued Likens. "It's Your Money/Your Health." When Lillian was alive Ricardo had dispensed with Likens as an opportunistic rabble-rouser; now, he thought of Lillian's dying plea for him to help others not to suffer her fate. Maybe Likens had a point. Maybe Lillian would still be with him if he had thought more like Likens. Maybe he could have saved many other lives as well.

That night Ricardo awoke at three in the morning. He sat on the edge of the bed restlessly wanting to go somewhere or do something, but he had nowhere to go and nothing to do. He listened to the thin patter of rain on the copper roof of the porch. If Lillian had been there he would have nudged her to wake up and they would have trekked to the kitchen to munch on nuts or yogurt or cereal or chocolate. What wonderful nights they were, munching and gossiping, then returning to bed to make love or hug and be covered by the warm blanket of sleep. But all that was past; it was another life. He made his way to the bathroom and swallowed a Valium that his physician had prescribed for his anxiety when Lillian was in the hospital. "Be gentle with yourself," the doctor had said. Ricardo translated that to Papi's philosophy of: "Accept who you are." The Valium helped. He was grateful for pharmacology.

At times Ricardo awoke at night dreaming of Papi in the distance saying, "It's not fair." Lillian dying was certainly not fair. What *was* fair? Was it fair that his mother died giving birth to him? Was it fair that he immigrated to Washington DC, leaving Papi by himself in Buenos Aires? Fairness had nothing to do with it. Things happened; life moved on. Bad luck was just the mirror image of good luck. Did anyone question the fairness of good luck?

Not taking over the butcher shop, as Papi had wanted, had been difficult for Ricardo. It was still painful when he remembered telling his father that he had secretly applied to George Washington University and had received a scholarship as a PhD candidate in biology.

"Well, good for you," Papi had said, though sadness had projected from his forlorn look.

Ricardo, conflicted by guilt, had responded, "I'll be *someone* when I get a PhD. I'll become a famous professor. You'll see. You'll be proud."

"What would make me prouder than I already am, Ricardo?" Papi had asked.

Ricardo hadn't said that he wanted to win the Nobel Prize. That would have been too honest, too vain to admit, even to Papi. So he had said instead, "Oh, I don't know, that I do well, earn good money, marry and have lots of kids to carry on our genes?"

He had married, but he was not rich. Now he was a widower with no offspring—an orphan with no siblings or kin. How rapidly life changed, although it seemed still from minute to minute. Ricardo's last visit to Papi in Buenos Aires, already some ten years ago, seemed like yesterday. Papi, eighty-five and in a nursing home, was battling partial dementia, having suffered a stroke that had made communicating with him trying and emotionally painful. Leaving had been the most difficult part.

"I'm sorry we can't stay longer, Papi," Ricardo had said the day they were going to return home, his voice artificially cheerful.

"What? You're staying longer?"

"No, Papi," Lillian corrected him. "We have obligations back home. Ricardo has to give a lecture next week in Philadelphia, and I need to find foster homes for two little girls."

"Leaving already, Renya? That's okay," said Papi, which Ricardo interpreted as, "That's not okay. I miss my wife. I'm always alone. Where are my grandkids?"

"She's Lillian, Papi. My wife, not yours. Remember."

Papi's eyes turned away. "I'm sorry you never had a brother or sister."

"I had you, Papi, and now I have Lillian and our dog, Raffle. You would love him. He's very cute."

"We had Mulligan," Papi said.

Ricardo nodded. "Remember how Mulligan used to purr when I stroked him and then for no reason at all slap my hand as if he were furious? I still have a scar next to my left thumb to prove it." Ricardo held out his hand.

Mulligan had been an ordinary Tabby cat, overfed, golden brown with stripes like a miniature tiger, a white chest and green eyes. Mulligan's bewildering behavior had fascinated Ricardo when he was a boy. Mulligan retreated from invisible enemies, stalked nonexistent prey and disappeared for hours at a time. Occasionally he would leap from a chair and bolt into the next room like a rock hurled from a slingshot. Often he pranced about looking satisfied. He would settle down on a chair and groom himself with his scratchy tongue as he scanned the Persian rug with the royal demeanor of a king. At other times Mulligan looked bored, almost depressed, and slithered under the couch in the living room where he would remain for the better part of a day.

Ricardo had often wished that he, too, could hide in a hole. Animals seemed to have a freedom that he longed for. As a kid, Ricardo had obsessed about what was in Mulligan's mind, or in the mind of any animal for that matter. Ricardo's preoccupation about what animals thought and felt had not changed over the years, and he often wondered how it would feel to be Raffle or a squirrel darting up a tree, and Mulligan's mysterious ways still came to mind whenever he saw a cat.

Suddenly Papi looked more alert and said, "You're not a cat, Ricardo. You can only be who you are."

"I know, Papi. But wouldn't it be amazing to creep into the mind of another animal, to *be* that animal, for a short stint?"

Lillian put her arms around Papi's neck and hugged him. "I love you," she said. "You're right. We're all stuck with ourselves." She kissed him on the cheek and he gently put his shaking hand behind her head to hold her close.

Ricardo watched Papi and Lillian and wondered if it would be possible to discover when and how the ability to think and feel emotion evolved and how one might identify thought in an animal. Did fish think? Did any invertebrate think?

"Does your leg still hurt?" Ricardo asked, returning his attention to Papi.

"Everything hurts, but I'm fine. You're leaving now? Go. I'm going to have dinner in a couple of minutes."

It was two in the afternoon.

Ricardo looked at Papi's shriveled, shaking hands that could no longer chop meat or hold a paintbrush. There was no use trying to discuss politics or literature or any other topic that used to excite him. Ricardo feared the day that he too would be ravaged by age. What was the point of learning anything new if it would be forgotten in a few years? Also, he abhorred the idea of being patronized, like he was patronizing Papi.

He glanced at himself in the mirror on the wall and saw wrinkles on his sixty-year-old face.

Lillian came to his side and took his hand. "Kiss Papi good-bye. He'll like that. We have to go," she whispered.

Ricardo obeyed.

"I love you, Papi," he said, his voice strained, when he leaned down to kiss his father on the forehead.

Papi looked up and blinked both eyes several times.

Ricardo and Lillian waved good-bye as they walked out the door. They heard Papi saying, "Bye, Ricardo. Bye, Renya," as they proceeded down the hall.

"Do you think we'll be back soon?" Ricardo asked.

Lillian didn't answer. She was crying.

Now Lillian was dead and it was Ricardo's turn to cry.

The following Monday Ricardo went back to work. Returning to his office after a quick lunch at the cafeteria, Ricardo found Marcus Topping, the Director of the Vision Science Center, in the hallway. Dr. Topping was in his mid-forties and had been the Director of Research for almost ten years. A quirky man who wore bright ties that clashed with his colored shirts under his pristine, white lab coat, he was often brusque and inconsiderate, which made him less than popular among the staff. But he was a model of efficiency.

"I was so sorry to hear about Lillian, Ricardo. I wanted to come personally and express my condolences." He put his hand on Ricardo's shoulder. Ricardo had never seen this side of Dr. Topping: warm, expressive, caring. The only other time Marcus had ever touched him was to shake his hand. "Will there be a service for Lillian?"

"Lillian was cremated," Ricardo said. "She didn't want a memorial service."

Marcus nodded. Then, in a different, business-like tone of voice, he said, "We depend on your excellent research, Ricardo. In fact, I was hoping that when you feel up to it we might organize a conference here on corneal diseases. When you're ready. You could highlight your studies on Fuch's dystrophy. Are you interested in that?" He hesitated. "I hear that Pearl's research on the cornea is moving along. She could make a presentation at the conference. Let me know if you need anything more for your laboratory."

Ricardo shifted his weight from foot to foot as if trying to catch his balance. The line between personal and professional suddenly seemed thin. He had no idea what new laboratory equipment he could use now. He had to speak to Pearl about what she might need, since he had no plans to initiate a new research project. And even the thought of organizing a conference made his shoulders sag, like a thousand pounds had been dumped on him. It would involve dozens of emails, phone calls, hotel reservations, bureaucratic forms, travel arrangements, scrounging for funds, scheduling decisions. It was more posturing than science. And when the conference did come about, then what? More obligations: enduring rambling lectures, organizing a banquet, hosting colleagues and accompanying spouses, dealing with issues relating to publication. He'd rather train another dog than organize a conference.

How could he make any plans for the future now? Just getting through the days was an uphill battle. He wasn't even sure of everything he had to do now that Lillian was gone. She had paid the bills, cleaned the house, cooked the meals, watered the plants—a never-ending list of chores that he had yet to incorporate into his life. In a word, Ricardo felt lost. He would need to keep a "to-do" list and conscientiously check off one chore at a time when it was completed, like Lillian had done. For now he clung to Lillian's advice in the early days of their marriage when he had difficulty juggling his beloved basic research driven by curiosity and the continual pressures to focus on eye diseases to meet the expectations of the Vision Science Center.

"You're smart, Ricardo," Lillian had told him. "You'll figure out what you want. Something will click. You'll see."

If only it were so easy. He didn't feel smart then, and nothing was clicking now.

Ricardo looked Dr. Topping in the eye and thanked him. After a few more minutes of small talk Dr. Topping excused himself to return to his work.

Ricardo went into his office. He had always relished sitting quietly in his office with the door closed, reading articles in the latest scientific journals, thinking about new experiments to do, and preparing manuscripts for publication. For all his complaining about the silly regulations and bureaucracy mandated by the Vision Science Center, he was grateful for his job and the support he received, and proud of his accomplishments. He had always loved science above all else and felt he was where he belonged. But now his quiet office seemed like a cemetery for a past life. He felt more like weeping than anything else.

Courage, he told himself, as he turned on his computer. He deleted a barrage of junk emails. One especially irritating advertisement said, "Buy Now/Cure Disease". Ridiculous, he thought. Why not "Buy Now/Understand Health"? He thought of Randolph Likens: Your Money/Your Health. Gone were the good old days when colleagues exchanged information and marveled at their discoveries because of the new questions they created, not because of the revenue they might generate or the immediate, practical use they might have.

A lot of Ricardo's emails needed a response: editors of three scientific journals wanted him to review manuscripts submitted for publication; two scientists asked for DNA clones made in Ricardo's laboratory (at least he could delegate that to a technician); a student with the ink still wet on his PhD diploma wanted him as a postdoctoral mentor; a colleague pestered him (again!) to be nominated for an award from the American Vision Association; and two former postdoctoral fellows requested letters of recommendation. There were also reminders about the promotion committee's meeting the next day, and about a conference on gene expression next month that Ricardo thought he should attend. He imagined himself trapped in a glass box with no escape, a volcano rumbling furiously within him unable to erupt.

Ricardo leaned back in his chair, his mind drifting to his youthful daydreams of roaming in Nature's mysteries as an explorer. How impressed he had been when he first read the famous last sentence of Darwin's *On the Origin of Species*. What a magnificent blend of science and poetry. He still remembered it by heart: "There is a grandeur in this view of life, with its several powers, having been originally breathed into a few forms or into one; and that, whilst this planet has gone cycling on according to the fixed law of gravity, from so simple a beginning endless forms most beautiful and most wonderful have been, and are being, evolved."

Reciting Darwin's sentence to himself reminded him of the last sentence in his application essay to George Washington University: "Anyone who has ever smelled a lily, caressed the velvet skin of a skate or watched a colony of ants at work would understand my obsession to devote my life to the endless beauty of biology." He had wavered between writing "my obsession" or "my desire," but "obsession" seemed more truthful at the time.

Ricardo trudged to work regularly as the months dragged on. He spent much of his time on administrative matters and committee meetings, activities he had always dodged. Now they kept him busy. "Scut work to fill my empty barrel," he said to himself. He tried to keep abreast of advances in science but felt discouraged by the technology that seemed to be passing him by. The few departmental seminars he attended didn't interest him, though he never skipped a lecture on Fuch's dystrophy, Pearl's research topic. Mentoring Pearl was an effort despite the fact that she was following up on Ricardo's own research.

"I seem to be going in circles," Pearl said one afternoon when she was going over her data with Ricardo. "Sometimes I see this strange protein popping up on my gel which would suggest that it's involved in Fuch's dystrophy. Other times it's not there. Sometimes I feel like...I don't know...that my research isn't going anywhere. What do you think I should do?"

Despite his reservations, Ricardo replied, "Stick with it. You've got some interesting results that will attract medical schools. You do need a job, after all."

Pearl sighed and nodded her head slowly. "I know."

Ricardo was disappointed to see a worried look replace the open, enthusiastic smile she had when he hired her a couple of years ago. He had originally encouraged this project because he thought its medical relevance would attract potential employers. But he knew even then that it was not consistent with her curiosity and passion for Nature. Her frustration now felt like a mirror reflecting his disillusionment.

Time marched on. Ricardo especially dreaded the weekends. With Lillian they had whizzed by all too quickly. They often went to a movie on Friday or Saturday night. Ricardo loved stories of any kind—documentaries, fiction, fantasy. If not a movie, they read quietly together, sharing passages and thoughts. How sweet those times were. That they had a future when they could fulfill their dreams was taken for granted.

As the months rolled past, Ricardo's spirits improved. He took leisurely walks—"little journeys" he called them—after sunrise. He befriended the neighborhood dogs; they would wag their tails when he approached them with small treats. He paid attention to his neighbor's yards and decided that he preferred a more rustic aesthetic to highly pruned landscaping. He inhaled the fresh morning air with a new appreciation of what it meant to be alive and began to accept the irony of having the grandeur of life defined by the inevitability of death. He read the morning newspaper after his early morning jaunts. He even checked out the style section and gossip columns, both firsts for him. He enjoyed learning new recipes, and grocery stores became interesting repositories of delicacies rather than places to check items off lists. On occasion he bought lilies for the crystal vase that Benjamin had given them on their thirtieth wedding anniversary. Lillian had always favored roses. "Lilies are pretty," she had admitted, but then she sneezed and added, "but they smell too strong." He enjoyed the freedom that allowed him to submit to small temptations and began to think that past dreams may not have to be lost forever. Wasn't he the same person, just a little older, a little wiser (hopefully) and a little freer?

But as Ricardo's fog of misery thinned it also exposed the turbulent, anti-intellectual world of the times. During his "little journeys" in the morning he saw posters in the streets agitating for cuts in government spending on art and education and basic science. Signs like "Keep the Military Strong" and "Kill Sickness" and "Down with Academic Waste" were commonplace and on bumper stickers of the cars. One poster, its edges lined with dollar signs jutting wings, showed Randolph Likens's face. Your Money/Your Health was written under his image in bold, stark black letters on a white background: black and white. There was nothing ambiguous about the message. These signs made Ricardo worry about the future of basic research even more than he had in the past and to think about Lillian's agonizing death and the victory of cancer.

Randolph Likens: despot or savior?

Chapter 3

One Sunday six months after Lillian's death, Ricardo felt especially lonely. At times like this he often called Benjamin, but this particular weekend his friend was giving the keynote address at a scientific conference and couldn't be reached. Benjamin had a full life anyway, with Mattie and his kids and grandkids, not to mention his active laboratory and host of professional commitments. Ricardo didn't want to become an albatross around his friend's neck. He decided to go to his office and read scientific journals.

The building was deserted and unnervingly silent. When he entered his office every tick of the clock on his desk sounded like a metronome setting the pace for a monotonous song that went on and on regardless of whether anyone was listening. In the past most of his postdoctoral fellows—at least half a dozen at any one time—worked through weekends and created a bustling atmosphere in the lab. Ricardo chuckled as he glanced at Papi's painting on the wall of two abstract creatures that looked like jellyfish covered with eyes and ears and a prominent mouth. They appeared to be conversing. "Anything interesting happen while I was gone?" Ricardo asked them.

Ricardo looked through the pile of recent journals on the floor next to his desk. One had a picture of a platypus on the cover. Since his graduate research involved the platypus he pulled the journal from the stack, opened it to the article and started reading. He was delighted to run across a reference to one of the four published articles on platypus vision that he had co-authored with his mentor, Vincent Salisbury, when he was a graduate student.

Dr. Salisbury wasn't Ricardo's mentor when he started graduate school. Richard Winelly had been, but that was short-lived. Winelly, an eager assistant professor and rising academic star, did research on anemic patients and had attracted the brightest graduate students. He was publishing regularly in prestigious journals and seemed like a good choice for the ambitious Ricardo to help advance his career rapidly. He joined Winelly's laboratory; however, he became disheartened soon after he had discovered a mutant hemoglobin gene. Winelly was excited with Ricardo's discovery, but in order to hasten publication he had insisted that Ricardo collaborate with a postdoctoral fellow to perform a barrage of experiments.

The idea of collaborating on his discovery had threatened Ricardo and turned research into a race, which didn't sit well with him. He kept thinking of Papi's art. Whether Papi's abstract images

turned out to be premature realism or not, they were *his* expressions
of *his* imagination. This had been Ricardo's first encounter with
competitive science, and although ambitious, he questioned whether
he wanted to focus so intensely on the professional ladder.

Ricardo's immediate conflict was resolved by accident. One
day, he was eating a turkey sandwich at the cafeteria and overheard
another student who was unhappy with his mentor speaking to a
friend. He overheard the disgruntled student say, "The guy just
rambles on about the platypus and complains that no one is
interested in the beauty and mystery of science anymore. I've got to
build a career. Nobody cares about the duckbill platypus. I have to
worry about a job and funding after I get my degree."

Ricardo had read about Dr. Salisbury and his platypus
research in the annual report of the department and correctly figured
that he must be the person they were talking about. Since the two
students spoke softly Ricardo only caught a few more words here and
there: "...the guy's a fossil...change mentors..."

The next day Ricardo went to speak to Dr. Salisbury about
switching mentors. Ricardo felt comfortable as soon as he walked into
Salisbury's office, which was in a state of disarray: articles and
journals were stacked haphazardly; a large print of a platypus hung
crookedly on the wall; a glass octopus was perched on a small table in
the corner; the two bookcases were crammed with biology books and a
few novels; and a stained rug covered the floor. The old professor
behind the desk looked tired. He removed his glasses, exposing
wrinkles at the edges of his eyes.

Ricardo and Dr. Salisbury talked, and then talked some more.
When Salisbury gave Ricardo a staccato briefing about the platypus,
he spoke his heart. "So few people study the platypus that almost
everything one finds is new and exciting. It's an evolutionary link
between reptiles and mammals, and filled with mystery and wonder.
Salisbury paused and then added as if he were speaking about his
own child, "It's a treasure."

When Salisbury had called the platypus odd, Ricardo heard
"odd" like one of Papi's premature realism paintings. Suddenly the
elderly professor had become a kindred spirit and the unheralded
platypus now glowed like a lighthouse in the fog.

Salisbury had no Winelly in him.

But there was also a certain sadness about Salisbury, a sense
of shattered dreams that gave Ricardo pause. Ricardo didn't want to

take the easy path to mediocrity or to surrender fierce battles for a grand career.

Ricardo asked Salisbury what project he would be assigned if he became his student, and that was when Ricardo learned an important lesson. He always remembered Salisbury's precise words: "One of the most important challenges a researcher faces is deciding what to study. I can be your mentor, but not your conscience or your imagination. What excites you, Ricardo?"

That had been the key question then, and it was still the key question today as Ricardo sat alone in his office. Exactly what project would satisfy his long-frustrated desire for adventure now that Lillian was gone and his time was running out? As he pondered this question, Lillian's plea—devote your research to helping others—felt like a splinter under his fingernail that he couldn't remove.

Salisbury had pressed all the right buttons for Ricardo by putting biology first and never mentioning career. Everything he had said about the platypus was fascinating to Ricardo, even how the weird animal foraged for small prey in the water by swimming with its eyes closed and its ears and nostrils covered with flaps of skin.

"How does it find its food then?" Ricardo had asked.

"Ah, yes. Biology is counterintuitive," Salisbury had answered. And then he explained in his eccentric manner of punctuated phrases: "The platypus detects prey by nervous responses in its porous beak—the duckbill—that it sways from side to side as it swims. The duckbill has thousands of receptors to detect small electrical fields and mechanical water movements. The electrical signals reach the brain first and these are followed by the mechanical signals. The difference in timing allows the platypus to fix on the depth of its victims."

That was the kind of thing that excited young Ricardo: unpredictable, surprising, and counterintuitive. Encouraged by Ricardo's interest, the old professor had rambled on with verve. Now, fifty years later, Ricardo listened as his mental recording of Salisbury's low, gravelly voice expounded on a stream of biological gems: "Animals see...perceive that is...by all sorts of ways invisible to humans. Pit vipers use infrared radiation to outline images in their brain by the difference between the warm body of a rodent and the cooler ambient air. Birds and bees perceive magnetic fields. Some insects, dragonflies for instance, see things we can't by using ultraviolet radiation. Barn owls locate a mouse in the dark by the difference in time that the mouse's squeak reaches its two ears with the same pinpoint accuracy that an eagle spots a tiny meal from a great distance in bright light using its densely packed photoreceptors. Bats navigate by the reflections of emitted sonar. We are all—man and beast—hopelessly locked into our own senses. When we think of eyes, all we think of is seeing images in our own way. Yet the blind mole rat has small eyes with functional retinas buried under thick, furry skin, but they can't use them to see images."

"What do they use their retinas for?" Ricardo was bubbling with curiosity. All this was new to him. How wondrous Nature was!

"It's not known for certain," Dr. Salisbury answered. "The photoreceptors may regulate how the animal perceives night and day—maybe—by being sensitive to slightly more or less light penetrating the fur and skin. A kind of clock." Dr. Salisbury stopped for a moment to take a breath. "My goodness, the diversity and complexity of living forms are endless. We don't even know what to study until we discover what phenomena exist. And each time we make a discovery by poking around, which is how so many important discoveries are made, new possibilities arise, and a new priority is born."

"A new priority is born," Ricardo muttered softly in his office as he reflected on his graduate student days with Salisbury. That's what he needed now: a new priority. That was what life was all about, changing priorities, adapting to new circumstances, refocusing. He needed to fill his empty heart with renewed meaning.

Ricardo's priority—interest—when he had first learned about the enigmatic platypus was whether a platypus *thinks* in terms of electrical signals instead of images. Dr. Salisbury had furrowed his brow and looked confused. Ricardo, flushed with insecurity, apologized for thinking out loud, yet asked, "I wonder what it would be like to sense the world like a platypus."

Ricardo never forgot the expression on Salisbury's face at that moment. His eyes had widened as if someone had just lit a candle in a dark cave, and then he smiled ever so slightly with no hint of ridicule. And so Ricardo, encouraged, told him about Mulligan and how he had always wanted to get into the mind of that bizarre cat, to sense what Mulligan sensed.

As Ricardo now remembered those days long gone, he heard Dr. Salisbury's voice in his mind again: "What interesting questions," he had said. "Why don't you go for it and try to figure out what's in the mind of a platypus? Yes, I love that question! It's so off the wall."

That had been a scary challenge: put your money where your mouth is! Ricardo had no idea how to determine whether a platypus "thought" by electrical and mechanical signals or through images, but Salisbury—what a kindly old man he was—suggested that Ricardo could start by using electrophysiology to analyze the platypus brain. He could test whether the regions of the brain activated by stimulating the duckbill were the same or different from the regions of the brain activated when the creature saw an object with its eyes.

"Great idea," Ricardo had acknowledged.

Their initial conversation had not been restricted to the platypus. They exchanged thoughts about the impossibility of absolute knowledge, the role of storytelling in science, the relationship between art and science, what constitutes courage in basic research, the difference in personalities between basic researchers and goal-oriented researchers, and the social obligations of a research scientist. They were surprisingly on the same wavelength on most topics.

The following day Ricardo told Winelly he was switching to Salisbury's laboratory. This had made little impression on Winelly, who immediately replaced Ricardo with another student.

As Salisbury had suggested, Ricardo mapped the platypus brain regions that were activated by stimulation of the duckbill and those that were activated by vision. Despite overlap of activated brain regions, he wasn't able to shed much information on how a platypus "thought," though he did consider the issue in the Discussion section of his PhD thesis. He published his findings and this led to the opportunity to establish his own laboratory at the Vision Science Center.

Now almost fifty years later, both Salisbury and Lillian were dead, and neither Ricardo nor anyone else knew yet what went through the mind of a platypus or any other animal. He closed his eyes for a moment as he sat in his office and wondered whether a platypus saw an image when its duckbill was stimulated or whether a fish thought about anything as it moved gracefully through the water. Then Mulligan's antics came to mind.

The sound of distant thunder snapped Ricardo out of his trancelike state and his questions crystallized. The ability to think couldn't have evolved in a single step. What *was* the evolutionary history of thinking? What species first thought, and exactly how did that "thought" differ from a reflexive action? He wondered what his career would have been like if he had pursued his research on the evolution of thought. He scratched his head and looked with some pride at the numerous certificates and honors framed on the wall of his office. Postdoctoral fellows from around the world had applied to his laboratory, and most of the lucky few he selected had gone on to prominent scientific positions in academia and industry. There were many reasons to be satisfied, even proud of these accolades. But, something was missing. What was the hole that remained unfilled?

Nightfall approached and Ricardo gobbled a few jellybeans to put off his hunger. His mind drifted to the Baltimore aquarium he and Lillian had visited a few years after they were married and how mesmerized he had been by the moon jellyfish. "Look, they're friends," he had said about two jellyfish that were close together. "Lovers," she had corrected him, and then she pecked him on the cheek and said, "You're cute."

Wouldn't that be something if they did attract each other, he thought now. He remembered objecting when Lillian had called jellyfish primitive because they were ancient. "It's the opposite, Lillian," he had said. "Jellyfish have been around for seven or eight hundred million years, so they may be more sophisticated than species that have evolved more recently. Who knows?"

Yes, who knows, he repeated to himself in his dark office.

Chapter 4

Two weeks later Benjamin called to tell Ricardo that he had decided to accompany Mattie to Washington to visit the Mark Rothko exhibit at the National Gallery while she attended a workshop on graphoanalysis. She believed that a person's character could be deciphered in their handwriting. Benjamin thought it was bunk until she analyzed his handwriting and said it showed an ambitious person with high goals and an excellent memory.

"How does she know that?" Ricardo asked Benjamin on the phone.

"It's the horizontal line crossing the t's and the dot over the i's. My t-bars are long and near the top of the vertical line, which apparently shows enthusiasm and goal orientation. I dot i's directly above and close to the vertical line, and that indicates attentiveness to details. At least that's what Mattie says."

"And you believe that?"

"Well, I am enthusiastic and goal oriented and have a good memory and am attentive to details." Benjamin was not the most modest man.

"Okay. I often cross my t's with long horizontal strokes above the vertical line and almost never hit the bull's eye when I dot my i's."

"My god, she may be right after all," Benjamin said.

"Why?"

"If I remember the rules right, that makes you an enthusiastic dreamer who is not concerned with details. That sounds right. What about the loops on your l's? Are they high or low?"

"Wait, let me write a few." Ricardo wrote a few l's on a piece of scrap paper. "Three are low, one a little higher."

"Hmmm. If I remember correctly, the low loop denotes creativity and imagination, and the high loop denotes capacity for abstract thought. I think she's got you nailed!"

"Interesting how we believe interpretations that fit our expectations or wishes," said Ricardo.

Benjamin laughed. They decided that was enough amateur speculation about a subject that neither knew much about. They planned to meet for lunch the following day at the Silver Diner, a local restaurant that they had frequented for many years.

Ricardo arrived early and ordered a Diet Coke. When Benjamin walked into the diner ten minutes later, his trim elegance reminded Ricardo of the first time they had met some forty years ago at the American Society for Eye Research. Benjamin's quiet confidence and regal bearing had made the stocky, balding Ricardo self-conscious.

Benjamin gave Ricardo a big hug. "Great to see you. It feels like old times."

"Same here. Maybe it's the ageless Silver Diner."

Whether it was the Silver Diner or Lillian's death or simply aging, both Ricardo and Benjamin were in a nostalgic mood, and they started bantering memories back and forth. They teased each other about the ravages of time on their bodies, although except for his silver-gray hair, Benjamin looked remarkably the same. They reminisced about the lectures that each gave at the symposium where they first met.

"Yours was a model of clarity," said Ricardo, and then he thanked Benjamin for how much biophysics and technical know-how he had learned from him.

Benjamin reciprocated. "Listening to you was like inhaling fresh mountain air," he said. "Your talk on how a platypus sees with his beak was a thing of beauty."

They agreed on how much they had complemented each other over the years. Ricardo had always been flooded with ideas, wonderful ideas, and Benjamin had fed on Ricardo's enthusiasm and imagination. Ricardo had envied Benjamin's skill with technology, which had been invaluable for him. Ricardo's mind flowed like poetry, while Benjamin's clicked like machinery. They fit like lock and key.

Ricardo and Benjamin also had a personal rapport. They were both immigrants. Neither had siblings, and both had fathers who wanted them to take over the family business. For Ricardo it was the butcher shop in Buenos Aires; for Benjamin it was an electric car battery company in Tel-Aviv. Both had followed their dreams for careers in science and regretted disappointing their fathers.

"Well, we've had good times together, eh?" Benjamin said as he put his hand on Ricardo's arm. Ricardo nodded and smiled, but Lillian's image passed through his mind and he felt a little lost.

"What'll it be, gentlemen?" the waiter asked, pulling the two friends out of their nostalgia. "The special today is cactus soup."

Benjamin looked surprised. "Cactus soup? Really? What kind of cactus?"

"I've got no idea. It's the chef's creation."

Ricardo ordered a turkey sandwich and Benjamin the soup. "I wonder if this soup is really made from a cactus," Benjamin mused. Ricardo asked Benjamin why he was so concerned about that, and that's when Benjamin revealed experiences in the Israeli army that he'd never spoken of before.

"I was nineteen and stationed in the West Bank," he said. "Finally we had reached some kind of temporary peace with the Palestinians. I was bored so I started making lists of the wild life I saw to keep me busy. Bats, rodents, snakes. Then I got interested in the prickly pear cactus called *Opuntia*. It's famous for its sweet meat. You can't judge the inside of anything just by looking at the outside."

Ricardo nodded in agreement.

"But it was the sharp thorns of the cactus that were the most interesting for me. Every time a thorn pricked me, it really, really hurt..."

"What's weird about that? It probably had toxins to keep animals from eating the plant."

"That's the theory," agreed Benjamin, "but when the pain dissipated I felt alert...alive...it's hard to describe...connected to people and even to objects. It was strange."

"I think I read somewhere that some cacti have narcotics in them." said Ricardo.

"True. Some cactus have mescaline. So once I got out of the army I was able to get hold of some mescaline and try it—as well as pot and LSD and cocaine."

"So you're a druggy. I knew it!"

"Not quite." Benjamin's voice lowered a notch. "The feeling I got after being pricked by the cactus thorns was much more personal than any feeling I got from any of those narcotics. It reminded me how the immediate sting of the spankings my Dad gave me was followed by a hug. Crazy, wouldn't you say?"

Ricardo couldn't say anything about that; he'd never been spanked. Sometimes he wished he had been. He might have felt less guilty about abandoning his father.

Benjamin was on a roll. "After being pricked I talked freely to my comrades about everything that crossed my mind. I noticed details such as the weave in the fabric of a shirt, or extra fine scratches in tabletops, or specks of dirt on the floor that I would never see normally. I talked one of my army buddies into taking the 'cactus trip', as I called it, to see if others were affected like me. It turns out that I wasn't the only one to react that way. The 'cactus trip' became the rage in the barracks. Soldiers punctured themselves and even jabbed each other. Conversations became intimate, secrets revealed and new friendships forged. But no one ever seemed out of control in any way. They were just very observant and bonded with each other."

"So you think those cactus thorns have some stimulant that's different from the usual psychedelic drugs?"

"Absolutely! It's something new and different. It's not hallucinogenic. I'm convinced that it taps an unexplored functional compartment in our brain. And although this is just a guess I think it may be important in some way for treating psychiatric problems." Benjamin's eyes brightened in a way that Ricardo had never seen before.

Benjamin stopped speaking abruptly as if he'd been caught doing something illicit. "Sorry, Ricardo. I got carried away."

"Amazing, Benjamin. You've never told me about any of this." Ricardo was impressed, but for the first time in their long friendship he felt excluded from something important in Benjamin's life. "Have you followed up on this in any way?"

Benjamin shook his head. "Not really," he said cautiously, but then continued in a controlled voice. "Well, actually a little, on nights and weekends when I have time. I brought a bunch of the *Opuntia* paddles when I came to the United States from Israel and kept them frozen for years so that I might be able to figure out what's in those thorns and how it affects the brain."

Ricardo, still hurt that Benjamin had never told him about the cactus, asked, "How the heck did you get them through customs? I thought that no biological materials were allowed into this country."

"I told the customs official that the closed bag is stuffed with sentimental things from my childhood to remind me of Israel."

"And he believed that?"

"He looked skeptical, so I volunteered to open the bag, but I had tied it up with so many knots that he didn't think it worth the trouble. I was counting on that."

"Smart!" said Ricardo.

Benjamin was shrewd.

"I guess he just saw me as an ordinary foreigner. He wished me good luck in my new life in the United States."

"Really," Ricardo said, without even considering the possibility that Benjamin's cactus-filled bag would be a link in the chain of events that would shape history and that the future hides in ordinary details.

PART II

Chapter 5

Ricardo's first wedding anniversary—it would have been their forty-first—after Lillian's death fell on a Sunday, making that weekend especially lonely. He had planned to go to a movie with his neighbor, but the neighbor had cancelled due to a bad cold. Ricardo didn't want to go by himself. Doing things alone made him miss Lillian even more than staying at home. He also felt self-conscious going to events that most people attended with family or friends. So that Sunday afternoon he went for a brief walk and spent the evening ambling restlessly from room to room. Lillian and he had always celebrated their anniversary at Leo's, a local restaurant famous for freshly baked bread and sinful desserts. Despite being slightly overweight he had always indulged on their anniversary. Now, without Lillian he had no appetite for dinner.

"What's this?" he mumbled to himself as he picked up a book in his library in the evening on a survey of vision in invertebrates that he'd never found the time to read. He placed it on the table next to Lillian's picture as a young woman dressed in gym attire. Her irrepressible smile of good health made him feel lazy and overweight. He lit logs in the fireplace, turned on the small lamp next to the photograph and sat in his favorite armchair that they had bought shortly after they were married. He loved its worn leather skin.

"Time to discover something new," Ricardo said quietly to Lillian's picture before opening the book. She had always loved jumping into anything new—traveling to places they hadn't been before, eating food they had never tasted, learning expressions in foreign languages.

He skimmed the first few chapters, which were filled with diagrams and classification schemes. A number of chapters were devoted to the compound eyes of insects, especially the famous fruit fly, *Drosophila*. He grew sleepy as he turned the pages and dozed off. Chilled once the logs had burned to ashes, he awakened, threw on fresh wood and returned to the book.

And then came the great moment, not announced by trumpets or fanfare but by the quiet turning of a page to the chapter on Cnidarians, the invertebrates that included corals, sea anemones and jellyfish.

Seeing the jellyfish pictures transported Ricardo back to that Sunday afternoon many years ago at the Baltimore aquarium. "Imagine that," Ricardo exclaimed to himself now when he saw the diagram of the jellyfish eye in the book. An eye! He turned his head to

Lillian's picture and asked, "Can you believe that jellyfish have eyes?" He said, wondering whether Lillian would have been as amazed as he was, "Yes, she would have."

The jellyfish eye had a large cellular lens for transmitting light, a retina with photoreceptors and black pigment in the back to dampen scatter. It looked like a variation of a human eye, except the cornea in front of the lens was reduced to a single layer of cells. Despite the fact that he'd studied eyes for almost half a century, he had no idea that jellyfish had eyes. He doubted whether any of his colleagues knew either, although he read in the book that the jellyfish eye had been described already in the nineteenth century. He smiled at the irony of a vision scientist not knowing that jellyfish have eyes. He looked at Lillian's photograph once again and said, "I guess we all live in the proverbial black box of ignorance."

He suddenly had an urge to break out of that box.

The pictures in the book showed one large and one small jellyfish eye situated at right angles to one another. These sophisticated eyes resided on specialized structures called rhopalia. The jellyfish species described in the book had four rhopalia equally spaced around its cuboidal body, called a bell, which Ricardo found strange for such a silent, non-musical structure. Thus, each jellyfish had eight complex eyes. Each rhopalium dangled from a stalk and nested cozily within a cavity open to seawater. Jellyfish saw all around, as well as above and below, at the same time. Their vision was much more encompassing than that of fish and other vertebrates, including humans, and remarkably adapted for the three dimensional, liquid niche of the jellyfish. In addition to the eyes, each rhopalium had a balancing organ, a statocyst, which jellyfish used for orientation as they swam.

Ricardo marveled at how the jellyfish squeezed the complexity of vision and orientation into tiny rhopalia only about two hundredths of an inch long. The jellyfish eye seemed much more than an evolutionary stepping-stone on the path to the human eye. It was already highly evolved. Jellyfish, often considered mere nuisances, were remarkable visual creatures. How misleading to call them "jellyfish"—jelly—sweet stuff spread on toast. And they certainly weren't fish.

Ricardo could hardly believe that such complex eyes existed in jellyfish, almost on a par with the lowly sponge. Of course, it was possible that jellyfish were eyeless for much of their history and evolved eyes relatively recently. If that were the case, human eyes might have been a much shorter evolutionary hop up from jellyfish eyes than imagined. But still, jellyfish and humans were so different. Evolutionary distance could be illusive, he thought, and what seemed remote might be much closer to humans and medicine than realized. Wouldn't it be ironic if jellyfish could teach him more about eye diseases than could rodents and other commonly used research mammals? Lillian's plea for medical research and his desire for curiosity-driven, basic research were tugging against each other in his chest.

Ricardo's wonder at the mysterious universe of jellyfish vision reminded him of his excitement when he first learned of the duckbill platypus. The notion of probing the shadows of human knowledge for camouflaged treasure tingled his curiosity and made him feel important again. Jellyfish have eyes! His poetic Lord Byron self collided with his analytical Louis Pasteur self and merged: he saw jellyfish as a poem and their eyes as a laboratory.

In jellyfish he saw a future, a story to develop. Benjamin had cactus; why couldn't he have jellyfish? In that moment of discovery Ricardo no longer felt like driftwood passively floating downstream; rather, he foresaw himself leaping precariously from rock to rock across a rushing stream. The jellyfish eye was one of those rocks. Excitement overwhelmed his depression. He wanted to open the lid of his black box. He had forgotten Lillian's warning to be careful and to restrain his impulsive nature.

Chapter 6

After a lengthy breakfast and immersed in editorials in the *New York Times* on disease and cuts in basic research, Ricardo arrived in his office later than usual on the Monday following his discovery that jellyfish have eyes. There had been a new outbreak of a life-threatening respiratory infection believed to be a mutated flu virus in Texas and Oklahoma. The editorial pointed out that this was the seventh new epidemic in the United States in the last four months. Scientists were baffled. The diverse geographical distribution of the outbreaks made the same environmental toxins an unlikely cause.

It was the syndicated article by Randolph Likens that most disturbed Ricardo. Likens, who had been increasingly outspoken against taxpayer dollars being siphoned to academics, now questioned the relevance of studying evolution to treat present diseases. He wrote, "Does it really matter how snails are related to clams or snakes to birds? Are such esoteric research projects the best use of hard-earned taxpayer dollars? How do such research expenditures protect us against the deadly diseases which are popping up everywhere?"

Ricardo was furious. How could anyone in this day and age not understand that evolution depended on mutations, and that mutations affected both the resistance to disease—sickle cell anemia being the classical example—as well as the outbreak of new microbial diseases?

Ricardo was in a bad humor when he arrived at the office to go over Pearl's research project with her.

"Is everything okay?" she asked, sensing his irritability.

"Yes. No. Have you read any of the ridiculous articles by the journalist Likens? He blasts studies on evolution without knowing anything about biology."

Pearl listened and after looking serious, she gave Ricardo one of her winning smiles. She could charm a lizard. They went over her experiments, which were designed to detect the appearance of new proteins in the corneas from a deceased patient who had Fuch's dystrophy. There were small clues that she had some interesting results, but much more work was needed. The leap from research findings to clinical relevance was daunting. Nonetheless, Ricardo felt that it was necessary for her research have a medical slant to facilitate her getting a job when she left his laboratory. Since he wasn't a physician, he struggled to find the best way to tilt her research towards the clinical side.

His bigger problem at the moment, however, was that images of jellyfish kept intruding in his mind. What did jellyfish see? Why did they have such sophisticated eyes? He glanced at Papi's painting of jellyfish on the wall in his crowded office, and he suddenly felt confined. He was tired of having science being strictly an intellectual experience. He yearned for a physical connection to Nature. Then the telephone rang.

"Hi, Ricardo. Marcus here. Do you have a few minutes to spare? I'd like to speak to you about next week's lab review."

"Is there a problem?" Ricardo asked.

"Nothing of that sort. Can you come to my office?"

"Right now? I'm going over Pearl's research with her at the moment. I'll come as soon as I can." Marcus Topping was not what Ricardo needed, but he would go to his office immediately after his conference with Pearl.

Maybe due to the multiple cups of coffee he had consumed that morning or his aching back, Ricardo had little patience to sweet talk Dr. Topping. Marcus's voice on the telephone had been a far cry from the consoling tone he'd had the day after Lillian died. What had become of the conference he had promised Ricardo that day? Nothing. There had been no further mention of a conference, and his request for a new DNA sequencer had been turned down because of insufficient funds. "I'd love to oblige you, Ricardo, but it's this damn economy," Marcus had said. Maybe it had been for the best. Ricardo hadn't had the energy or desire to plunge into administering a conference, nor did he care about receiving new equipment. Everything connected with his research at the Vision Science Center seemed oppressive.

"Hello. I'm here to see Dr. Topping," Ricardo said to the secretary when he arrived at the office. She continued tapping the keyboard, ignoring him. A long fifteen seconds or so later she said, "Have a seat, please, Dr. Sztein. Dr. Topping will see you shortly."

Ricardo leaned back on the plush chair and rested his sore back. He looked at his wristwatch: 11:10. It felt later, like the day was escaping. He checked his email on his cell phone. Nothing new. Ricardo picked up the latest *Science* magazine from the coffee table, its pages crisp and unread, unlike the journals in his office, which were dog-eared and coffee-stained. A short report on a black hole captured his interest. Astronomy was humbling and as impossible for him to grasp as infinity or eternity and made him feel insignificant, like whenever he pondered the immensity of evolution. He wondered whether the earth and all its wonders would be sucked up by a black hole one day.

11:20.

"Is Dr. Topping with someone in his office? He asked me to come right away." Ricardo tried to control his mounting anger as the secretary kept typing.

"He'll be back soon," she replied, never taking her eyes off the computer screen in front of her.

Ricardo grumbled to himself. She suddenly looked up and smiled at him. "Sorry. Dr. Topping is very busy today. It's the upcoming review."

Ricardo sighed for her benefit. "Okay," he said, not meaning it. He looked at the photographs of Marcus's Wyoming summer home that were on the walls of his outer office, which was palatial by Ricardo's standards, and then he picked up the *Washington Post* from the coffee table. He turned to the obituaries as he did regularly since Lillian had died, paying special attention to the age of the deceased, the cause of death and whom the *Post* decided to feature. Ricardo couldn't help comparing the lives of these dead strangers with his own. The comparison often depressed him. He saw an obituary with the following title:

"Sir William Smiling, Nobel Laureate, Dead at 71."

Ricardo was 71.

After perusing the many accomplishments of Sir William, an eminent Australian scientist, his eyes slid down to the smaller type lower down the page, which listed the less majestic souls now gone from this world. At first he thought he misread it, but upon more careful inspection, Ricardo confirmed what he understood initially:

"Dr. Frank Miles, 83, passed away after suffering a stroke. Dr. Miles, a research scientist at the Rockefeller Institute for forty-three years, leaves his wife, Martha, of fifty years, two sons, Adrian and Todd, a daughter, Elizabeth Randall, and six grandchildren."

The Frank Miles was dead? The scientist who had pioneered quantum biophysics? His research had given many insights about communication networks within cells. Ricardo had never understood why Miles hadn't received greater recognition. Perhaps Miles ruffled too many feathers. Ricardo thought of his own abrasiveness on occasion and worried that he had sounded arrogant at times, although he had never meant to. Or had he?

Smiling and Miles were two giants in the field, though one received big type, while the other small type. It seemed that their importance was an editorial decision. No, it was the Nobel Prize. External factors decided importance. Ricardo thought of Papi, the butcher/artist of premature realism paintings. His art had never been appreciated. Life had many ways to be unfair.

11:32.

Still no Dr. Topping. Impatience inflamed Ricardo's anger. Just as he was ready to return to his laboratory—a passive aggressive act, he knew—Dr. Topping bounded into the office. As always, Topping's white sweat socks and scuffed, overused, canvas athletic shoes—an affectation that Ricardo believed meant to show that he was a regular fellow—irritated him.

"Hello, Ricardo. Let's go in my office." Dr. Topping was unapologetic for keeping him waiting. Ricardo was annoyed for allowing himself to be rattled. Topping was always late; that was part of the game, and he set the rules.

Ricardo forced a smile.

Dr. Topping's office wall was littered with diplomas, pictures of him receiving awards, and framed letters from important people, including a President and two Vice-Presidents. Ricardo thought of the wall between the bathroom and the exercise room at his home that had a few photographs of his colleagues and some certificates of his honors and professional services. They didn't seem to measure up. It helped that Lillian never cared about honors, or at least never let on if she did.

Ricardo waited for Dr. Topping to speak.

"Your laboratory is being reviewed next week by the Scientific Priorities Committee. These SPC evaluations are open to the public and reach Congress. An outstanding review helps us receive funds, while a poor review can damage our chances for being funded. In view of the scarcity of money these days, I thought it would be helpful to go over what you are going to share with them. Which of your studies are you planning to emphasize? You're a star, you know."

Star? That seemed gratuitous.

Dr. Topping must have sensed Ricardo's ambivalent reaction. "I mean it, Ricardo. You're a star." And he probably did mean it.

"We're proud of your accomplishments. You have been extremely helpful in attracting funding to the Center."

Ricardo couldn't help but feel happy with the recognition.

After a short pause, Marcus continued, "Jim Lazaar made a big hit with the SPCs last year when he described the connection between protein 451 mutations and multiple sclerosis. He received the LeBlanc Prize for that work, you know."

"I was on the award committee, remember?"

"You were? Oh, yes, of course. Could you please give me a rundown of what you intend to present?" It was more a command than a question.

Ricardo scratched his left hand next to the scar that Mulligan had inflicted on him, a nervous habit when he strained to control his anger.

The SPCs evaluated each laboratory in the Vision Science Center every five years. The Directors—and there had been several over the years—had never tried to influence his presentation before. He was outraged that Dr. Topping would try to supervise him in this manner now, but he was also worried. The Director relied heavily on the SPC reviews for apportioning funds to the different laboratories.

Although Ricardo had received excellent evaluations in the past, the review committee noted last time that his research tended to wander from its stated goals. Although he'd fashioned his research in politically acceptable ways—the gene expression studies were designed to advance genetic therapy; the protein function studies stressed finding treatments for intractable disease—he was aware that he often disregarded criticism. Now he was concerned that he might have acted too independently, even arrogantly, though that was never his conscious intention. As he confronted Dr. Topping face to face, Ricardo remembered Benjamin warning him to take care. Benjamin knew Ricardo resented "living with intellectual blinders," as he'd called it, and to be coerced to orient his research to specific aims. When Benjamin reminded Ricardo that he hadn't been invited to be a speaker at a scientific conference for several years it had hurt because it was true.

Was he "losing" it? Ricardo didn't think so, but he knew that he wasn't striving to build a career as he had been before, even though he was still publishing articles and managing an active research laboratory. Ricardo didn't like the way things smelled. The Director had flattered him, yet implied that he—an old pro—needed guidance for his presentation to the review committee.

Ricardo felt a weight on his shoulders, though truth be told, Dr. Topping did have a point. He needed a positive SPC review of Ricardo's laboratory to convince Congress to continue flowing money to the Vision Science Center. Lillian, always the realist, would have agreed with him in that respect. Black and white was really gray.

The telephone rang, which gave Ricardo a moment to organize his thoughts.

"I don't know which dress you want me to pick up on the way home, dear. I never saw the one you wanted. I'll ask the saleslady. I can't speak now. Dr. Sztein is in my office." The Director placed the receiver back on the phone and looked sheepish. "Sorry."

Ricardo wasn't sorry. The short break had allowed him to prepare his spiel. "No problem. I'll give the review committee a synopsis of our work on corneal opacity, stressing Pearl's—"

"She's a very smart young woman."

"Yes. Anyway, as I was saying, I'll stress her evidence for the existence of two new proteins in corneas with Fuch's dystrophy. Corneal opacities remain big medical problems."

"They certainly do," Marcus agreed, looking pleased with Ricardo's emphasis on disease.

Ricardo continued. "We need to be able to replace diseased corneas with artificial corneas like we can replace cataracts with lens implants." Ricardo tried to give the impression that he was genuinely involved in this corneal research, or perhaps he was trying to convince himself that he was committed to the work. It wasn't that he didn't think that it was important, but it seemed more technical than adventuresome. His mind wandered for a moment as he looked at the office's enormous plate glass window and thought how nice it must be to have an office with the outside leaking in.

"Artificial corneas would be a major advance," Dr. Topping said.

After a moment of silence, Ricardo spontaneously decided to mention his ideas regarding jellyfish. "I thought I would tell the SPCs about a new project, still an idea, but…I think it's important to try to push the conceptual frontiers of knowledge a bit, don't you? Try to be bold, ahead of the pack." Ricardo didn't give Marcus time to answer. "Do you know that jellyfish have eyes?" There, he'd said it.

"Jellyfish?"

"Exactly. Neither did I."

"So what?"

"Well, these aren't just puny, primitive eyespots that sense light. They're complex eyes with lenses and retinas that in many ways look like human eyes, with some differences of course. I wonder what jellyfish actually see—perceive that is—and how that affects their behavior. Jellyfish eyes may be used only for simple functions like detecting light in order to regulate breeding cycles, or to detect the shadows of predators. I don't know."

"Jellyfish eyes?"

Ricardo felt his face flush and was angry with himself for having spoken so freely on something that he hadn't thought through. Exactly *what* was he looking for in jellyfish eyes? He didn't know. Perhaps that was the fascination, the dense fog of the unknown, where no one could see more than anyone else, where no one could judge him. Wasn't asking a question that no one could yet answer a reasonable and sufficient justification for a research project? He wasn't really planning to talk to the review committee about jellyfish, but for some reason he felt compelled to challenge Dr. Topping. He didn't consider it arrogance; it was foresight, or perhaps his retaliation for being kept waiting.

"From what I gather, no one is studying jellyfish eyes," Ricardo continued, trying to regain his composure.

"I bet hardly anyone even knows that jellyfish have eyes," said Dr. Topping, raising his eyebrows.

Ricardo's mind drifted to Papi and how he had free-associated in his butcher shop about art and politics, giving his customers more to chew on than just meat. It wasn't the choice of subjects that had made Papi interesting; it was how Papi injected vitality into the subjects. Yes, it wasn't just jellyfish. It was him, Ricardo, and that realization gave him the courage to speak his heart.

"Perhaps, Ricardo, jellyfish eyes aren't being studied today for a reason," Dr. Topping retorted with irritating calm.

"Perhaps they *should* be studied, however. And, with such terrific eyes, jellyfish might even have brains." Ricardo added with flair.

"Brains?"

"Yes. I wonder if jellyfish have brains," Ricardo asked. "If they have highly evolved eyes, they should have some kind of brain to process the visual information, to make a type of memory trace of it." Recognizing his mouth was working faster than his brain, he smiled self-consciously and slowed down. "I know it sounds unusual these days when we're expected to deliver treatments for diseases, but jellyfish are very interesting. I think Congress would understand that, if the argument is presented well." Ricardo wasn't speaking to Dr. Topping anymore; he was addressing Randolph Likens.

Dr. Topping tensed his jaw muscles.

Ricardo looked intently at him, wondering whether he had understood or agreed with anything he had said.

"Do you *believe* the SPCs will be interested in jellyfish?" Dr. Topping asked.

"I hope so," Ricardo said. "It's important to understand the full range of perception. Exploring other species would add a lot to our understanding of human vision." It sounded right to him.

"I see." The Director winked. "Perception is important, I agree. How then do you perceive our fiscal situation today?"

"That's not what I mean."

"I know. But how do you...*perceive*...jellyfish vision from a medical point of view?"

"That's up to the physicians to decide, once basic discoveries are made. We hardly know anything about jellyfish vision yet." Ricardo paused. "I'm a basic scientist, not a physician. It's like being an explorer and..."

STOP! Lillian's faced glowered in his mind.

Dr. Topping's eyes narrowed as if focusing on a target. "It's also up to me to convince Congress to fund us in a shrinking economy where medical costs continue to rise. And that's not quite as easy to do as you seem to think it is."

Ricardo glanced at the stacks of papers, bureaucratic forms, memos and medical journals on Dr. Topping's desktop.

Marcus glanced at his watch. "I have an appointment for lunch with the CEO of GlaxoSmithKline. Let's continue this conversation next week."

They never did.

Chapter 7

"Slow down, Ricardo," said Benjamin on the telephone the day after Ricardo had met with Dr. Topping.

"You don't get it, Benjamin. Jellyfish are amazing. Those eyes! Did you know that jellyfish have eyes that look like ours in many ways?"

"Well, not...."

"Me either. Nor does anyone else apparently. Don't tell me to slow down...we need to get..."

"Hey, Ricardo. It sounds interesting, but I've got a class to teach in a couple of minutes. Can we talk about this tonight? Call me at home."

"Okay."

Benjamin was always busy.

Ricardo called Benjamin after dinner, which was fine with him. He preferred talking about his new passion from home. Jellyfish eyes weren't just another potential scientific project to him. Keeping his interest in jellyfish separate from the office made it more mysterious and more personal.

"This afternoon, as I was saying, there's more to jellyfish eyes than meets the eye." Ricardo said to Benjamin.

"How's that?" Benjamin asked.

"I want to study jellyfish eyes. It's just that simple." He felt like a student again when he had told Lillian that he wanted to study platypus vision although he knew nothing about platypuses or eyes. Now it was jellyfish and their eyes, another tantalizing mystery.

"I'm not sure what I'm looking for," Ricardo continued. "It's like the old days when I was a graduate student and sat at my desk not knowing what to do. I was scared. But when I thought of it as an adventure, it became exciting. Funny, isn't it? Confusion is scary if you find it threatening, but exhilarating if you find it challenging. It all depends on your viewpoint. Do you think that eyes popped up in jellyfish when they first appeared seven or eight hundred million years ago?"

"I have no idea."

"Me either. There doesn't seem to be much known about jellyfish eyes. Hundreds of millions of years is a lot of time for jellyfish to learn a bunch of tricks. Isn't that reason enough to study them?"

"Maybe. But, Ricardo, you haven't got that much time. Do you really want to jump in the middle of the ocean?"

Ricardo was genuinely enthusiastic, but he was also trying to justify going on a tangent to study jellyfish eyes. It was true that he was not young anymore and it was late to start such a new, bold project that would require years of work. Even more troublesome was Lillian, who kept whispering in his ear, "be careful, Ricardo, you're impulsive." His mind drifted to the cruelty of cancer, her dying wish for him to do research on disease so others didn't have to suffer like she did and the promise he had never made, at least not to her before she died.

"Ricardo? Hello? Are you still there?"

"Yes. Sorry. My mind drifted for a moment."

"So, what are…?" Benjamin started to say something.

"Here's my plan," Ricardo interrupted. "I've checked the Internet for people doing research on jellyfish and a Harold Freeman came up. He works at a marine station in La Parguera, Puerto Rico."

"La Pa…what? From the Internet? Are you serious? Do you know anything about this guy?" Benjamin was being Benjamin, sincere, but sometimes a bit snobbish.

"La Parguera. It's in Puerto Rico. Freeman was a co-author on an article on jellyfish ecology about fifteen years ago. That's his only publication that I could find. You've never heard of La Parguera?"

"Nope."

"Neither had I. It's a small resort on the Southwest coast of Puerto Rico. The marine station is part of the University of Puerto Rico. The main campus is at Mayaguez, which is pretty close to La Parguera. Getting interested?"

"Not yet."

"I emailed Harold Freeman, and he replied quickly. At least he's responsive. I don't know much more about him. He's not Puerto Rican with a name like that. He said he would show me how to catch *Tripedalia*—that's the name of the species of jellyfish with eyes that lives in the swamps there—if I come to La Parguera for a few days. He doesn't have to be Einstein to teach me how to catch jellyfish. Getting interested now?" Ricardo knew that Benjamin loved new challenges.

"Go on."

"Well, listen to this. I checked up on what's been published on jellyfish eyes and found a few old articles, mainly in the late twentieth century and early in this century. I couldn't find anything recent. Ever since the economic crash in 2022 almost all science research has been focused on human disease. Is that smart?"

"You can hardly blame them. And times are piss-poor now, even worse than then," Benjamin said.

"Yeah, I know. A couple of articles a long time ago suggested that jellyfish eyes see images. What an image means to a jellyfish is another question. One article indicated that the biochemistry of jellyfish vision has similarities to that of humans. The differences between human and jellyfish vision are probably more interesting than the similarities, but people don't seem to appreciate that these days. Check out pictures of jellyfish eyes online. They're complex. Are you getting a little more interested?"

"I admit, it's intriguing, but...."

"Good! I bet that these jellyfish eyes are going to be interesting. It's important to look at all kinds of species because it opens new vistas of knowledge and new possibilities. Don't you get tired of so much research these days being on the same few species? Flies, a little on frogs and chickens, mice and rats of course. I have nothing against focusing, but come on, what about something new now and then?"

"Depth is important, Ricardo. A little knowledge can be misleading and difficult to exploit."

"I know the old argument. Put everyone to work on a common goal and you make real progress. But if national research priorities are always based on last year's discoveries, who makes next year's discoveries that lead to new priorities? Tell me that."

"I'm with you."

After a short pause Ricardo asked, "Do you think jellyfish think?"

"What?"

"Do you think that jellyfish think? They've got these fantastic eyes. I'm really curious as to how they interpret whatever they see. Whether there is a kind of brain activity, you know, perception."

"Now you're going too far, Ricardo. Jellyfish thinking? How could you ever test that?"

"You're right, as usual. But still...I've always wanted to know what an animal thinks about. Any species: a cat, a dog, a fish. Why not a jellyfish? When did *thinking* start in evolution?"

Through the window Ricardo saw a cat walk by on the sidewalk. He looked at the scar on his left hand.

"I want to go to La Parguera and get a feel for these jellyfish. I don't have a concrete research goal in mind. I just want a pilot look-see. It may give me ideas. And with Lillian gone..."

Benjamin sighed. "I'm really sorry, Ricardo."

"I could use something new in my life. Do you want to come? I've got to email Harold while he's still interested."

"You know what? Yes. Why not? I'll keep you company for a few days."

Ricardo couldn't tell whether Benjamin was interested in jellyfish eyes or whether he was just being a good friend. Maybe it was both.

"Really? Great! Dr. Topping seemed upset when I threatened to tell the Scientific Priorities Committee that I wanted to study jellyfish. I guess I went too far, but it was worth it just to see the look on his face. He turned green and got rid of me." Ricardo had a tendency to exaggerate. "I really do believe that exploring the unknown, figuring out how animals see the world is important and relevant...God I hate that word: *relevant*."

"It's too late to get into that topic again, Ricardo. Let me know when you plan on going."

"Will do."

The next morning Ricardo sent the following short email to Harold Freeman:

"Dear Harold—Thanks so much for your prompt response and willingness to help me collect jellyfish in the mangrove swamp. I am eager to come with my colleague, Dr. Benjamin Wollberg. We know nothing about jellyfish and would be very grateful for your help. I'll let you know dates that could work for us. Thank you again! With best regards, Ricardo"

As soon as Ricardo hit the 'Send' key on his computer, he turned his attention to requesting travel funds from the Vision Science Center. It was imperative that he justify the trip in a convincing fashion. He emphasized how the complex jellyfish eye resembled the human eye. Then he wrote a detailed paragraph stating that jellyfish first appeared about seven or eight hundred million years ago and are at the base of the evolution of higher animals, including humans. He preferred to think of animals as adapted for their niches rather than as higher or lower on an evolutionary scale, and so in his request he strived to elevate the so-called lowly status of jellyfish by emphasizing their evolutionary connection to humans in order to make his project more attractive. Finally, Ricardo proposed two objectives: first, to look for a jellyfish variant of the corneal growth hormone he'd discovered in mice, and second, to probe for evolutionary precursors of the genes he'd linked to Fuch's dystrophy. He believed that those research projects had clinical relevance, even if distantly, and that they linked the proposed jellyfish research to his past and present research.

Later that afternoon Harold emailed Ricardo and said that he would reserve a motel room for them as soon as he knew when they were coming.

A week after that, Dr. Topping approved Ricardo's request for travel funds.

"I'm all set, Benjamin. The travel request has been approved. Are you still good to go?"

"You applied for travel funds?"

"Sure. Why not? Since the Vision Science Center owns my research shouldn't they support it whether it's performed in house or elsewhere? I'm not allowed..."

"I know," Benjamin interrupted. He had heard Ricardo gripe about this for years. "It's Catch 22."

"Exactly. You can't win. If you work for the government they insist on supporting any work you do connected with your job, and then they complain that you're spending too much. It's like the perfect spouse that sticks by your side when you're having all those troubles you wouldn't be having if they weren't sticking by your side."

Ricardo suddenly felt sad, as if he had been that spouse by Lillian's side all those years.

"Well, I'll pay my own way," Benjamin said. "My research isn't even remotely connected with jellyfish. For me it's sort of a vacation. Anyway, my grant money is running low, and I don't want to waste any of it for this trip. It's not a big deal."

Six weeks later Ricardo and Benjamin set out on their jellyfish adventure, not sure what to expect.

Chapter 8

After landing in San Juan, Ricardo and Benjamin rented a car to drive to La Parguera. The tropical heat and humidity melted the obligations that pressured Ricardo in his daily life, and he felt an invisible vise loosen its grip as he drove through the lush vegetation of the rain forest pursuing jellyfish. Jellyfish eyes of all things!

They stopped at a stand where a young woman was selling mangoes and pineapples while her daughter played in the dirt with a filthy, one-legged doll. The little girl had lined up a series of small rocks, apparently pretending that they were friends of her doll. When Ricardo got out of the car, the girl threw one of rocks into the bushes and then made the doll dance as if finally freed from an enemy.

Ricardo turned to Benjamin and said, "Even dolls can feel oppressed."

"O'la," said the girl with a smile.

Ricardo smiled back at the girl but she had already turned her attention back to her one-legged doll. She reminded him of his childhood in Buenos Aires.

He bought a mango and joined Benjamin by the roadside. They cut into the fresh fruit with a penknife.

"Not bad." Ricardo rubbed juice from his chin.

"I'll say," Benjamin agreed.

Refreshed by the warm fruit, they headed on to La Parguera. Ricardo began to question his excitement. He didn't know whether it was that Benjamin viewed this trip as a vacation instead of a serious scientific endeavor, or Lillian's haunting plea to devote himself to medically relevant research, or even a feeling of guilt for escaping his responsibilities at government expense. But there was a difference between an idea and its reality. His goals were fuzzy at best. He didn't know how to locate jellyfish or dissect their eyes, and he had no idea if Harold Freeman was a serious scientist. This jellyfish adventure was a radical departure from anything he'd done before.

They passed a small group of run-down shacks. A few men with doll-like faces sat on porches; they rotated their heads following the car as it drove by. Ricardo wondered how many chances these individuals took on a whim, like he was doing now. Abandoned junk, used cars, spent tires and other trash brought Ricardo to a reality different from his normal life, and he liked that. He was on a grand adventure in a land that spoke his native tongue.

"What do you think, Benjamin, are we crazy to be doing this?"

"You worry too much. Relax. It's a beautiful day."

The houses grew more upscale as they drove, and soon a small sign with an arrow to La Parguera appeared on the side of the road.

"Looks like a metropolis," said Benjamin.

La Parguera was anything but a metropolis. Only a few small houses and a bakery marked their entry into the town. Ricardo turned right onto the main street and drove past some shops and a central square dotted with people. After a few blocks they found the motel that Harold had booked for them.

After settling in their shared room, Ricardo and Benjamin explored the town. Soon they were dripping with sweat from the oppressive July heat. Stray mutts, bone thin with dirty knots of hair substituting for fur, wandered aimlessly through the town.

"Pathetic, isn't it?" said Ricardo. "The dogs are like walking rib cages."

No one in the streets seemed bothered about the dogs or anything else. The open doors and windows of the shops distributed the heat democratically between the outside and inside. Air conditioning was limited to a few noisy window units here and there. Colorful graffiti decorated the walls of the buildings. There were several places for tourists to rent scuba and snorkeling gear.

Ricardo and Benjamin reached a fountain in the center of the main square where people congregated, ate food and socialized.

"This is certainly different from our busy life at home, wouldn't you say? Sometimes less is more," said Ricardo.

Benjamin nodded. "This place reminds me of Israel."

There were benches around the fountain and a large stone statue of some ancestral hero standing proudly, his chest thrust to the sky. The Spanish explanation attached to the base was too faint to read. Ricardo ran his fingers along the leg of the statue and muttered under his breath, "So that's what happens to big shots. They turn into stone."

Benjamin walked ahead and sat on a bench occupied by a young boy no more than eight years old licking an ice cream cone.

"Hey, Ricardo, want one of those?" Benjamin pointed to the ice cream. The kid smiled, exposing two missing front top teeth. Benjamin: everyone liked him.

Ricardo didn't answer. He was standing in front of a large mural of a seductive woman with an inviting smile. Ice cream was far from his mind as he gazed at the well-endowed image. He thought of

Lillian, but not really. The picture on the wall looked nothing like her.

"Ricardo!"

"What?"

"Want some ice cream?"

"Ice cream? Sure. Quite a picture, wouldn't you say?"

"Wishful thinking, Ricardo."

They both treated themselves to ice cream cones. The rich chocolate was sweet and cool in Ricardo's mouth. He winked at the young boy and felt free, as he felt when he was the boy's age and assumed an endless future. A slight breeze swept his face. Life could be good if given a chance.

Chapter 9

The sun beamed through the curtainless window of the motel room. Ricardo woke up and glanced at the alarm clock on the bedside table: 6:15. Early, he thought. He sniffed the sea air and heard gentle splashes of water from the bay. A rooster serenaded him from the street.

"Where did that rooster come from?" grumbled Benjamin, not yet fully awake.

"Beats me," said Ricardo. "He sure is loud. Since we're awake, let's grab an early breakfast and go see the lab."

After cereal and coffee, they headed down the main street to the other end of town to catch the small ferryboat that would take them to the marine station. The town was still sleepy.

"Good grief, are we in Jurassic Park?" exclaimed Ricardo when he stepped on the dock of the island and a large prehistoric-looking iguana waddled by. It was like walking backwards in evolution, which Ricardo considered a good omen for his plans to study the ancient jellyfish. Ricardo and Benjamin made their way from building to building until they happened upon the one in which Harold Freeman worked.

"It's quiet here," said Benjamin.

Ricardo agreed with a grunt. They went down the hallway until they found the laboratory with Harold's name on the open door and they walked in.

"Hey there! Ricardo? Is that you? Ricardo Sztein?" The voice came from the back of the laboratory. Apparently Harold Freeman was an early riser.

Ricardo and Benjamin entered the small office in the rear and saw a disheveled, gray-haired man, sixtyish, with a round face. He wore tennis shoes, oversized jeans belted with a rope and a sweatshirt with U of P in faded gold letters across the front. Ricardo breathed in deeply and liked the smell of humidity tinged with sea-air.

"Dr. Freeman?" Ricardo asked.

"Not doctor; just ole Harold Freeman. Good to finally meet you." He extended a broad hand with a silver ring on the middle finger and a leather bracelet on his wrist. A partially unwrapped chocolate bar on his desk caught Ricardo's eye.

"Nice to meet you just old Harold," Ricardo said. They shook hands. "You have an American accent. Are you from the States?"

"Yup. Nebraska. Married a Puerto Rican gal. I've been here for over thirty years."

Ricardo felt a bond with immigrants—people displaced from the land of their birth. He wondered whether any immigrant truly felt their adopted country as their own.

"I know what it's like, an American married to a Latino. I'm from Argentina and am...I mean was married to an American."

Harold looked slightly confused.

"My wife died a year ago. Cancer."

"I'm sorry."

"This is my colleague, Benjamin Wollberg."

Benjamin and Harold shook hands.

"Thanks for arranging everything for us," continued Ricardo. "The motel's perfect. We got in yesterday evening walking around the town. Cute little place."

"Cute? Maybe. They say a hurricane is brewing off the coast of Africa and may drift this way."

Ricardo glanced out the window. It was cloudy, but not threatening.

"Let's hope it changes its mind," added Benjamin, as he looked at the glass bowls that held aquatic specimens and the antiquated dissecting microscopes on a table in the corner of the laboratory. The shelves along the walls contained alcohol-filled jars of fixed invertebrates.

Ricardo's mind went back to jellyfish and the reason for their visit. He had many questions for Harold. How difficult was it to find jellyfish in their habitat? Was it hard to dissect the eyes? "Can we get started pretty soon?" he asked.

"Yup. Sure can," said Harold. "I've reserved an outboard motor boat to go catch a few *Tripedalia* jellyfish this morning and make sure we get some today, just in case the hurricane comes our way."

"You said it's just starting in Africa, didn't you?" asked Benjamin. "That's pretty far away."

"You never know, though. Things change fast around here."

Ricardo rolled his eyes at Benjamin and then was distracted by an open book on marine animals lying on the laboratory bench top. He skimmed a few pages as Benjamin small-talked with Harold with the ease that had won him so many friends and admirers, a social ease that Ricardo envied. Each page of the book contained colorful images of invertebrates. Some of the species were familiar—starfish, sea anemones and lobsters—but others were foreign to him. He was impressed with how many apparently related animals looked so different and how many of the invertebrates resembled plants.

"What's this little hat-like thing?" asked Ricardo.

"A limpet. It's a mollusk. Lots of different animals in the sea." Harold replied.

"It's getting dark outside," noticed Benjamin.

Within a few minutes the bay darkened, and ominous rolls of thunder rumbled in the distance.

"Like I said, things change quickly around here," said Harold. "I think this will blow over quickly."

The sky cleared as if by magic ten minutes later.

"Let's go." Harold tightened the rope holding up his pants. He snatched several bottles of water from his desk drawer and three small dip-nets with long handles and walked out the door more rapidly than Ricardo thought he could move. The two scientists followed.

Chapter 10

Harold skillfully guided the small outboard motorboat along the edge of town. A few people sitting on the decks of their houseboats docked along the shore basked in the sunshine peeking through the clouds.

"Who lives in those houseboats?" Ricardo asked Harold.

"Squatters mainly. People who don't pay taxes."

"And nobody says anything about that?" Benjamin inquired.

"Well, they don't make any money to speak of and they're not living on land, so technically they can't be touched by the government. They're enjoying life."

Ricardo was enjoying life himself. The wind caressed his face, the sun warmed his body, and the gentle bounce of the boat against the choppy waves comforted him. He closed his eyes. Drops of saltwater splashed against his arms and face, and he licked them off his lips. He filled his lungs with the moist, balmy air. "This sure beats my lab in Washington."

"Sure does," Benjamin responded, his fingers cutting the water beside the boat as it moved along.

After a few minutes the sound of the motor dulled. Ricardo opened his eyes and found himself in a tranquil lagoon surrounded by mangrove trees. Algae-coated roots projecting down from the branches penetrated the shallow water. Colorful life forms populated the water near the shore: sponges, tubeworms with their fan-shaped tops gathering microscopic food particles, and countless species that Ricardo couldn't identify. It was Nature's zoo. On the left Ricardo saw the passageway they had come through to enter the lagoon, and on his right he saw a narrow canal lined with mangrove trees. It was a visual paradise—an extended labyrinth of splendor—and so close to the town with its half-starved stray dogs and rundown houseboats. It was Nature's version of an elegant residential neighborhood situated a few city blocks from an impoverished ghetto.

"It's like a jungle here," said Benjamin.

"Yup," agreed Harold, unimpressed.

"Can you even remember the busy streets, the masses of people and the ridiculous rules we live by?" Ricardo asked Benjamin, who responded with a half-smile.

Both scientists absorbed the surroundings in silence.

"It can get nasty in here," said Harold. "Lots of mosquitoes this time of year. Hot too." He wiped sweat off his brow.

"It's fantastic," Ricardo said.

Benjamin scratched his neck.

Harold steered the boat directly into the mangrove trees along the shoreline. The men dodged sharp protrusions from the branches. Only the chug-chug-chug of the boat's motor disturbed the peace.

"This is the best spot to collect." Harold took one of the two buckets from the front of the boat and filled it with the brackish seawater. "This should hold our catch."

Harold taught Ricardo and Benjamin to recognize the jellyfish as they swam by the boat in jerky motions propelled by regular contractions of their muscular surface bell. The largest of them was only about a fifth of an inch in diameter. Ricardo felt like a clumsy newcomer next to the sleek jellyfish, which had inhabited the planet for six to eight hundred million years.

"You've got to have a kid's eyes to see these little guys," said Ricardo, discouraged by his failing eyesight with age.

"You'll get the hang of it," answered Harold. "You can see the jellyfish best when there is a bit more direct sunlight. Have patience."

Harold was right. The short tentacles of the jellyfish reflected the sunlight. Harold scooped out jellyfish one by one with the dip-net and dumped each into the bucket. Soon Ricardo and Benjamin were doing the same, but more slowly and with far less skill.

"Do you think these jellyfish have a destination in the lagoon?" Ricardo asked.

Benjamin, his eyes squinting, sat in the front on the boat scrutinizing the water for the tiny critters. "Got one!" he exclaimed, looking proud.

"Are you kidding? They're gobbling up food," said Harold, returning to Ricardo's question. "They may have evolved from sponges, or more correctly a common ancestor of sponges, but they're little predators. When you get back to the laboratory, put them under a dissecting microscope and you'll see tiny crustaceans or even small fish in their stomachs. Jellyfish eat whatever is in their path."

"Maybe," said Ricardo, thinking about what Harold said, "but sometimes they're heading down to the bottom, like they're going home, while other times they are going straight ahead full speed as if they're late for an appointment. Also, the little buggers often travel in groups, like they are on some kind of a mission. How do you know they're not going somewhere, whatever that means to a jellyfish?"

Harold looked at Ricardo quizzically. "Whatever you say."

Ricardo thought about the radical changes in behavior that accompanied each new species as it branched off Darwin's famous tree of evolution to occupy a new niche. There was a reason that jellyfish had survived hundreds of millions of years on this hostile planet. Maybe they did congregate in groups for a purpose, or had a destination in their travels.

As Ricardo watched jellyfish swim by he wondered whether they appeared as threatening to their prey as they appeared docile and delicate to him. It was satisfying to catch a cluster with one swipe of the dip-net, but there was also something sad, even immoral, about yanking these innocent creatures from their natural habitat and dumping them into a bucket. What had they done to deserve such a fate? He looked apologetically at his captives and wondered if they were scared or felt disoriented. He thought these animals must be more than reactive machines. They were beautiful small, complex beasts traveling in groups. What made them congregate like that? He also wondered what they saw as they cruised along. Did they notice him?

The stultifying humidity, the buzzing mosquitoes and the sharp branches of the mangrove trees jutting out over the shoreline were constant reminders that Nature does little to accommodate its inhabitants. Even so, it was special for Ricardo, the kind that he'd dreamed about in his dreary government office during the gray winter days. At La Parguera he had no interfering bureaucracy, no emails to answer, no interruptions by students and colleagues, and no seminars or committee meetings to attend. Dr. Topping could not command him to his office. It was glorious following his whim, finally, and merging with Nature.

Ricardo stared at his reflection on the water's surface. The sight of his gray beard and thinning hair jolted him back to the reality that he was the aging widower not fulfilling Lillian's plea, and that escaping his responsibilities as if on vacation smacked of retirement, which he'd sworn he would never do. No, he thought. This was a serious scientific project, an exploration, an effort to tease apart Nature's secrets.

A speedboat dragging a water skier through the lagoon created waves that rocked the boat and spilled water from the bucket holding the jellyfish. Iridescent gasoline glistened on the water behind the speedboat and loud metallic-sounding music disrupted the peace.

Harold glanced at his wristwatch. "Let's head back," he said. "We've been out here a long time, and I have a bunch of tests to grade at the office."

Benjamin agreed. His arms were scratched from the branches and his forehead was pockmarked from mosquito bites.

Ricardo nodded but felt pressured because of their limited time on the island. His knee bumped on the side of the boat as he moved to the center seat preparing for the ride back. "Damn," he said, feeling clumsy.

The irritating music from the speedboat dissipated. The scenery looked the same as it did before, but the serenity of a few minutes before was gone. Ricardo slapped away a nasty bug from his arm, scarlet from the intense sun.

"Have a good life," Ricardo said to a solitary jellyfish cruising by. His eyes shifted to the dense collection of jellyfish in the buckets. He'd acquired a new skill and become a collector of jellyfish—from novice to expert in only a few hours!

"Do we have time to take a quick look at other spots?" Ricardo asked. He wasn't ready to call it quits.

"I've never seen *Tripedalia* anywhere else," Harold replied.

"How's that possible?" asked Benjamin.

Harold shrugged.

Intrigued, the two scientists insisted on scanning the opposite side of the lagoon for jellyfish. They didn't see a single one. Skeptical that the jellyfish were confined to the one spot where they had collected, Ricardo persuaded Harold to go to a different area, and after that to yet another site. They didn't see a single jellyfish. Was the water different in some way from their original spot? What was going on? Harold had been correct: the jellyfish lived only in the limited region they had visited first.

"Strange," said Ricardo.

"I told you," Harold replied.

As they motored back to the laboratory, Ricardo puzzled over why the jellyfish swam in groups and why they didn't populate more than one location in the mangrove swamp. Little did he realize, while Benjamin half-dozed on the boat, the implications and danger in asking these questions.

Chapter 11

The three scientists returned to the laboratory at two o'clock. "I'm starved," said Harold. "I haven't eaten since breakfast."

Harold took them to a local diner with no air-conditioning and only a few dilapidated tables. The room smelled of grease.

"You like this place?" Ricardo asked incredulously.

"I've been coming here for years. Great hamburgers."

Harold spotted the owner of the diner, Juan, a heavy-set man with a big smile and the top three buttons of his shirt undone, exposing a hairy chest.

"Juan, meet Ricardo and Benjamin. They're from the States for a few days."

They all shook hands.

"How's Margo doing? She over the flu?" Harold asked Juan.

"Much better, thanks. But Alfredo and Eva got the bug now, however they're happy that they don't have to go to school."

"Do you think the picnic on Sunday will be cancelled? So many people seem to be sick."

"Maybe," said Juan. "I can't do it the following weekend. What if we postponed it until sometime in the middle of the week? How about Wednesday? I'll close the diner. Are you free?"

"No problem," said Harold. "The students would be happy to put off the test I have planned for next week. We can't let work interfere with life, can we?"

Both men laughed.

Ricardo turned to Benjamin and said in a low voice, "Imagine if we played hooky on a workday afternoon in order to attend a party?"

"Impossible."

Ricardo agreed, but wasn't happy about it. There was something attractive about giving equal weight to play and work. What's life about anyway?

The diner began to smell less greasy and seem less shabby to Ricardo. Rather, there was something human and intimate about the place. People counted. Pleasure had value. He wondered whether Harold would be more driven by professional ambition if he hadn't immigrated to Puerto Rico. Would he, Ricardo, be different if he lived here? How long would it take for him to like this greasy joint?

Juan came to their table to get their orders for food.

"Give us three burgers with fries and cokes." Harold turned to Ricardo and Benjamin. "Okay, guys?"

"Sounds good," said Ricardo. He especially wanted some French fries. He knew that Lillian would have disapproved and wanted him to order a salad. But Lillian wasn't there, and all her salads and exercising hadn't kept cancer at bay. Still, if only he didn't feel guilty about consuming all that cholesterol.

"I'll give it a try," Benjamin said with ambivalence.

The three sat at the corner table and listened to the burgers sizzling on the grill.

"What are you working on, Benjamin?" Harold inquired. "You don't seem to know much about marine biology."

"You're right about that. I work on eye diseases—mostly autoimmune problems in the retina. Right now I'm investigating birdshot retinopathy. Some patients go blind, and that's serious."

"I bet," said Harold.

Ricardo nodded in agreement.

"I also work a little on cactus, a diversion I picked up in Israel," Benjamin added nonchalantly.

Ricardo's eyes widened when Benjamin mentioned his covert cactus project. Perhaps the free, non-competitive environment had affected Benjamin as well as him.

"Benjamin's here to learn about marine biology, as I am. We've been friends for years," said Ricardo, trying to change the subject.

"That's right," Benjamin said. "And these jellyfish are certainly interesting."

"As interesting as cactus?" Harold asked, without realizing the importance of that question.

"Absolutely!" Benjamin exclaimed.

Ricardo found Benjamin's enthusiasm for jellyfish forced. What did Benjamin really think of this jellyfish project, that it was a vacation, or perhaps another "hobby," like his cactus experiments?

"I'm glad that Ricardo asked me to come here with him and do honest to goodness fieldwork. The scenery sure beats the dreary walls in my office. It's like a great vacation out among the mangroves, except for those damned mosquitoes."

"My whole life is a vacation of sorts," Harold said. "When I met Delores I knew that the career rat race wasn't for me. We've only got one life, haven't we?"

"Not for me."

"What's not for you, Ricardo?" Harold asked. "Having only one life? The rat race?"

"This isn't a vacation for me, as much as I may love it here. I want to learn about these jellyfish eyes. They're amazing. I want to know what they see and what..."

"...they *think* about," Benjamin said, completing Ricardo's sentence.

"That's right," said Ricardo with a defensive edge to his voice. "I want to know if jellyfish think and if they do, what they think about."

Harold laughed. "Jellyfish think? You're a hopeless romantic, Ricardo."

Ricardo tightened his jaw. "You don't need such sophisticated eyes like jellyfish have just to respond to light and dark. Even plants respond to light. Anyway, jellyfish rhopalia also have four simpler clusters of photoreceptors in addition to their complex eyes, and those should be enough to detect changes in light intensity. I wonder why, then, do they have such sophisticated eyes?" He paused. "Do you believe that only humans think and feel emotions and...well, cherish life? Does an animal have to look like us or a monkey or a dog to have...I don't know...a psychological life?" He told himself to slow down. But he really meant what he was saying. So he was impulsive and passionate and maybe off the wall sometimes. So what? That was who he was.

"Do you believe jellyfish think?" Harold asked Benjamin.

"Who knows? If they did, I'd have no way to figure it out. You can't ask the jellyfish. How do you determine if and when thinking occurs?"

"Isn't that the truth," said Harold. "I ask myself that sometimes about Delores! Just kidding. Who cares if a jellyfish thinks? They don't. Believe me."

Ricardo frowned. Juan brought the hamburgers and French fries, breaking the awkward silence that had fallen on the group.

"Greasy, but good," Benjamin admitted after he finished his hamburger. "I just hope I don't have a coronary tonight."

Ricardo picked up the check and paid the cashier before they left.

"Thanks," said Harold as they walked along the street. "If you two aren't tired, you might try to catch some jellies by the dock tonight."

Ricardo jumped on the comment. "Catch jellyfish at night? How do you see them in the dark?"

"It's not the same as going into the mangrove swamp. First of all, it's a different species called *Carybdea marsupialis*. Their eyes resemble those of *Tripedalia*, but the jellyfish are three or four times larger and have long, whitish tentacles. Just shine a light on the surface of the water and wait until they come to you. They're probably *thinking* about what the light is all about," he added, winking at Benjamin.

Ricardo ignored Harold's sarcasm, although he did wonder why the jellyfish were attracted to the light. Were the little predators, as Harold called them, looking for food? If not, what then?

When they returned to the laboratory, Harold gave them a lantern to shine on the water if they decided to go night fishing for jellyfish, and then he went home for a siesta. Ricardo and Benjamin stayed to excise the rhopalia containing the eyes of the *Tripedalia* they had caught for analysis later in their laboratories at home. Since Benjamin had no experience in dissection under a microscope, Ricardo took charge. He sharpened the ends of the forceps that he had brought and poked around the jellyfish trying to figure out how to remove the rhopalia containing the eyes. He discovered that he could stick the tip of his fine forceps into the tiny cavities, pinch off the rhopalia at their stalk and place them in a chilled tube. It was a quick procedure. Benjamin followed Ricardo's instruction, although more slowly since he lacked the hand/eye coordination under the microscope that Ricardo had. After several hours they had accumulated hundreds of rhopalia that they preserved in a portable tank of liquid nitrogen.

They returned to the motel for a short rest before going off to catch jellyfish at night. Ricardo was happy that Harold was busy that evening and wouldn't be overlooking his shoulder. He and Benjamin were on an adventure exploring Nature's secrets, uncertain what they would find, and not beholden to anyone.

That was wonderful!

Chapter 12

After sunset, the two scientists made their way down the sloping path from the laboratory to the dock. Benjamin carried the pail to collect the jellyfish and stared at the ground as he walked, concentrating on the work at hand. "It will be interesting to compare the eyes of these night jellyfish with those of *Tripedalia*. Harold said that *Carybdea* was several times larger than *Tripedalia*, so I guess their eyes will be bigger and easier to dissect."

"Not necessarily," said Ricardo. "Bigger animals don't always have bigger eyes. Whales are huge, but their eyes aren't proportionally bigger, at least that's what I've read."

As they walked, Benjamin rambled on about how size differences between the two jellyfish might affect the protein content of their tissues, how many jellyfish would be needed to do various analyses, and so on.

Ricardo lagged behind. The lush, humid air reminded him of summers in Argentina. He stumbled now and then on rocks as his mind wandered. He felt young again, not burdened with the pressures of funding and bureaucracy, of helping students find jobs, of tiptoeing past the demanding eye of Dr. Topping. Finally he was living his youthful dream of adventure. The moonbeam vibrated on the water, splitting the distant bay into complementary halves. From a distance, the tranquil tree-lined bay looked like a postcard. Well, maybe not that peaceful. He imagined drama beneath the soft skin of the sea: sharks hunting seals and turtles prowling for jellyfish. Nature's beauty often camouflaged the ugly reality of survival. Of course he couldn't enter the mind of another species, as he had wanted to since he was a boy, since he had Mulligan. Ricardo thought of the complex platypus that 'saw' prey with its eyeless beak. How could an animal that required eyes to see ever penetrate the mind of a different species that could visualize its environment without eyes? Evolution had made it impossible for one species to enter the mind of another. Survival strategies had to remain secret to maintain the tricky balance of life and death, which were sublime and cruel at the same time.

Ricardo mused that Nature solved problems without stated mission objectives and committees to establish priorities. Evolution progressed without morality or responsibilities. Beauty existed without a beholder. The idea of justifying his jellyfish adventure to Dr. Topping or anyone else—even to Lillian if she had been still alive—seemed ridiculous, like trying to explain a poem.

Flashes of brilliant bioluminescence danced on the surface of the water, reminding him of the jellyfish green fluorescent protein that had led to the Nobel Prize in chemistry in the last century. Such perfect merging of dispassionate Nature and human curiosity had led to being able to detect the positions and movements of proteins in cells, even to greater understanding of how cancer cells spread. Once again he reminded himself that great strides in medicine often came from unexpected places. Perhaps his basic studies *were* fulfilling Lillian's plea. He mustn't let his dreams and beliefs be trampled.

"Come on, Ricardo," urged Benjamin, who had already reached the dock.

"Coming," answered Ricardo, picking up his pace.

"Where can we plug in this lamp?" Benjamin searched for an electrical outlet for the light. "How do people do science under such primitive conditions?"

"Would you rather be back home?" Ricardo asked. He remembered Harold disparaging the rat race. Did Harold's life amount to less than his or Benjamin's? How did one judge a successful life? By counting the number of publications or honors received? Ricardo pondered, not for the first time, whether he had chosen the wrong career path. No, certainly not. If he'd been a poet or a novelist or anything else, he would have fantasized about being a scientist. There was nothing more remarkable than Nature.

"Here's an outlet," said Benjamin, plugging in the lamp. "Let there be light." And there was. "Now let's see if these jellyfish really swim toward the light."

Ricardo stared at the colorful reflections of the light beam on the water's surface. "I'll miss it here," he said.

"It *is* nice," Benjamin agreed. He looked around and inhaled the moist sea air. "It reminds me of Tel Aviv."

"I wish I could bottle La Parguera and take it home," Ricardo said.

"Wouldn't that be nice," said Benjamin.

Home continued to echo in Ricardo's mind: an empty house, solitary bed, pressures to meet the demands of his fund-raising-obsessed boss. Once he returned, would he even remember the La Parguera he was experiencing at the moment? He doubted it. To know La Parguera one needed to see the bay and mangrove swamp, watch the crabs crawling on the mangrove roots, feel the mosquitoes' sting, see the thin dogs scraping for food in the streets, smell the brackish water, and sense the hot sun burning one's skin. Memories were reproductions, not the real thing. They dulled and mutated and couldn't be trusted. But then Lillian came to mind. She hadn't changed in his memory. Or had she?

The small, empty boats along the dock rocked gently in the water. The locked boathouse looked like an abandoned shack. The night version of the marine laboratory was very different from its daytime version—quieter and as if a blanket covered Nature's mysteries.

The two scientists co-existing in the same environment yet their minds in different worlds sat down to eat their sandwiches. They engaged in small talk while keeping their gaze on the water for the jellyfish to come to the light. Dozens of small fish swarmed within the spotlight on the water. Squid darted by with astounding speed, visible one instant, gone the next. Their tentacles gave the illusion of a rotating propeller. Several hours passed, but no jellyfish.

"Too bad," said Benjamin. He didn't sound as disappointed as Ricardo felt.

"At least we got plenty of *Tripedalia* during the day," responded Ricardo. "Our plane leaves tomorrow afternoon, so we might as well go back and get some rest."

"Hey, what's that!" exclaimed Benjamin suddenly.

An angelic, translucent form with trailing white, lace-like strands—a single jellyfish—rose from the depths. Ricardo watched, transfixed by its majesty. Why had it taken so long to arrive? Did it live directly below the dock or had it traveled from afar? How far? What did it expect to find at the water's surface? And most importantly, what did the jellyfish see and what would it do with the information?

Ricardo dipped the net into the water and gently scooped it up as it was making a U-turn to head back to deeper water. Five more jellyfish followed within as many minutes, and the eager scientists captured each one. As with *Tripedalia*, these jellyfish traveled in groups. Ricardo wondered how they communicated with one another.

No more jellyfish appeared during the next fifteen minutes. Benjamin unplugged the light. They took the bucket containing the six jellyfish to the laboratory and returned to the motel. In the morning they would excise and freeze the jellyfish rhopalia containing the eyes to take them back to their laboratories for analysis.

Chapter 13

Ricardo stuffed Kleenex in his ears to dull the enervating rattle of Benjamin's snoring. That he couldn't sleep, however, had nothing to do with Benjamin's snoring or the room's noisy air conditioner. Even after the long day and night collecting jellyfish, Ricardo felt elated and energized. The majesty of *Carybdea* rising from the depth obsessed him. The scene played over and over in his mind. He longed to tell Lillian about Harold and the jellyfish and the mangrove swamp. He went to the window and peeked through the slats of the Venetian blinds. It was a dark, dreary night without stars. A stray dog sniffed an open garbage can across the street. The motel room had a musty odor. He thought he heard cockroaches scampering in the bathroom, but concluded correctly that cockroaches don't make noise, at least none that humans could hear.

Suddenly overcome with anxiety, Ricardo lay down again. He felt claustrophobic, squeezed by the darkness, as if trapped with no escape. The sporadic noise of the window air conditioner was welcome company. Benjamin, sleeping soundly on his back, had finally stopped snoring. Ricardo imagined himself in a coffin with his hands folded across his chest, but didn't like the idea of being dead. He pretended that he was asleep, but that didn't work either. He listened to the tick-tock of his bedside clock. If only he could manipulate time and make the sun rise early to chase away these nocturnal demons. He wished he had brought his Valium to La Parguera.

He thought of Lillian. She was his light in the dark shadows of the night. If only he could talk to her into the early hours of the morning, as he had in the past. She would stroke his arm and say nice things, reassure him, love him. He would hug her.

He always assumed that she would outlive him.

Exhausted, Ricardo nestled his head between two pillows to block Benjamin's snoring, which had started up again. He closed his eyes and floated in a boundless universe of nothingness. His anxiety faded as if carried downstream by a gentle current. He was no longer in a hurry for the morning. In the twilight zone before sweet sleep, Ricardo remembered Lillian's hand in his, her flesh firm and warm, not withered like when she died. He imagined his lips against hers, moist and receptive like when they were young. How good it felt!

A surge of anger flashed through his brain. What gave cancer the right to rip Lillian away from him? What did the jellyfish do to deserve being hijacked from their home and imprisoned in a metal bucket? It was all so unfair.

Finally Ricardo succumbed to sleep. He dreamed of the mysterious jellyfish by the dock. Like messengers rising from the depths, they propelled themselves through the water effortlessly. He heard them saying, "We are alive." It was as if they were heading to a known destination, yet drifting at the same time. They were impossible to grasp and slipped through his fingers when he reached out to touch them. More groups of jellyfish streamed into his dream. They pulsed in synchrony as if linked, yet each was an individual, alone, like him. A few jellyfish were large—adults; others were small—like children. They dissolved and reformed, over and over again, dissolving and reforming, merging and separating.

A diverse fauna, including sponges, corals, sea anemones, starfish, and sea urchins entered his dream. The various species clumped with their own kind, although a few mavericks trespassed into groups of other species. The feathery sea pens resembled plants more than animals. One wondrous sea pen lifted magically from its spot and started writing in the water as if it were a quill dipped in black squid ink with no hand to guide it. The words dissolved, hiding a secret story.

"It's a blur," Ricardo told Benjamin at breakfast the next morning, frustrated that he couldn't relate his dream more specifically. "But maybe the details don't matter," he said. "Dreams are so often that way; memories and yet not, images without explanations. It was mysterious and beautiful."

Benjamin listened patiently.

As they finished their breakfast in silence, Ricardo thought about the *Tripedalia* that swam in groups in the mangrove swamp and about the six *Carybdea* that appeared one after another at the dock. He recalled how the jellyfish merged and separated, dissolved and reformed in his dream, and how invertebrates clumped with their own kind, except for the occasional maverick. Of course he couldn't explain it to Benjamin. He didn't understand it himself, but he did know that it felt right.

Chapter 14

The six *Carybdea* were swimming in circles in their buckets when Ricardo and Benjamin returned to the laboratory after breakfast.

"Sort of pitiful, isn't it," said Ricardo.

"What's pitiful?"

"The jellyfish. Swimming aimlessly, going nowhere."

"That's all they ever do, Ricardo."

"Remember our excitement when the jellyfish suddenly appeared from who knows where last night?" asked Ricardo. "Like angels from the depth."

"Yeah."

"They were regal." Ricardo gazed into the distance. "Why do you think that all six came within a few minutes, one after another, after all those hours of waiting? Not a single one for the whole evening and then they arrived one right after another. Do you think that there are jellyfish waiting for them to return?"

"C'mon. Let's collect and freeze their rhopalia. We've got a plane to catch." Benjamin seemed impatient with Ricardo's incessant anthropomorphizing these globs of jelly.

"It's sad," Ricardo persisted. "We kidnap these animals from their homes without any idea about their lives. Worse yet, we don't care. They've been on this planet a lot longer than we have. What makes you think they're so insignificant? Because they can't speak our language?"

"Stop this nonsense, Ricardo, we don't have much time."

The salty sea smell of the laboratory was like perfume to Ricardo as he excised the rhopalia from the jellyfish. He loved the marine environment.

"I should have been born fifty years earlier when it wasn't necessary to moonlight to do this kind of basic research," he muttered quietly.

After a moment Benjamin said, "Moonlight? I think vacation is more accurate."

Ricardo shot Benjamin a resentful glance. "Vacation again?"

"How come you're the poet and I'm the one here for enjoyment?" Benjamin asked.

Ricardo had to smile. "You got me there," he said. But the fact remained that he hadn't come to La Parguera on holiday. He had been sincere when he wrote on his travel request that he wanted to extend his research to jellyfish eyes. He truly believed that his jellyfish studies might ultimately have some clinical relevance, even though his immediate curiosity was what evolutionary secrets might be hidden in those jellyfish eyes.

As Ricardo dissected in silence, Lillian's gaunt image riddled with cancer entered his mind. What would she have thought of his jellyfish excursion? As much as he loved her, and he did with all his heart, her death had freed a part of him. Now was his opportunity to be a maverick that trespasses into the forbidden space of another species. Hadn't a lifetime of conformity earned him the right to do as he pleased?

Anyway, they wouldn't fire him from the Vision Science Center. Dr. Topping had said that he was a star. His travel request had been accepted and he was following up on his former discoveries in a new way. If they wanted him gone, all they needed was a little patience for him to depart, to answer Nature's call, like everyone does, although hopefully not as painfully as Lillian had.

Benjamin interrupted Ricardo's thoughts. "All done," he said when he finished packing his supplies. "Ready to go?"

"Yeah. Pretty successful trip, wouldn't you say? We've lots of samples to bring back." Ricardo had flipped back into the sober scientist again.

Chapter 15

It was late in the afternoon back in his Washington DC laboratory, and Ricardo was tired after having spent over two hours analyzing Pearl's failed experiments. He should have summed up his appraisal of her progress concisely and suggested how she might change course or consider some new experiments. But he liked Pearl's presence and had not been in a hurry to dismiss her from his office. She shared a triangular-shaped face and high cheekbones with Lillian, though she was more sensuous than he remembered Lillian at that age. Pearl's soft, light brown hair was longer than Lillian's had been, her complexion smoother and her sway more obvious when she walked. Sometimes Ricardo blushed when Pearl, with her coal-black eyes, looked up at him from her half-closed lids like a woman who liked her mentor too much, or was she teasing the old man?

Ricardo saw a flash of pink skirt whiz past his office door, which Pearl had failed to close when she left. It couldn't have come from Pearl because she was wearing a white laboratory coat. Before he could blink, the color disappeared. The footsteps—clickety-clack, clickety-clack—faded into the distance.

The flash of pink and the steady tapping of footsteps on the hard floor interested Ricardo. Putting down his pen, he went to close his office door as an excuse to look down the hallway. She was gone, so he returned to his desk, stared at the rotating blue-green lines of his computer screen-saver and then turned his attention to an unfinished manuscript he was writing. His mind drifted. The flash of pink and the feminine footsteps revived Monique's memory.

Monique: his one infidelity. He'd met her on a balmy July day in his early fifties during his first and only trip to Nice on the Cote d'Azur in the south of France. He'd delivered the prestigious keynote address at the International Biochemistry Congress. The beautiful women on the beach, in the shops and along the streets had dazzled him. As the star of the meeting and in the prime of his career, Ricardo had been bursting with self-satisfaction.

The lecture had gone perfectly and his colleagues were enthusiastic about his research. After his lecture they had taken him to one of the best restaurants in town, where he drank more than his share of Bordeaux. When he returned to the hotel, he was high on the success of the lecture and the wine he'd consumed. His eyes landed on a young lady with a very short skirt standing by the elevator, and he knew he had to go for a brief walk around the block to cool off.

Ricardo ambled towards music floating from a discothèque across the street. A man at the door motioned for him to enter. He obeyed. The tables were occupied with couples flirting and enjoying the atmosphere. He sat at the bar, ordered a glass of red Zinfandel and listened to the woman on stage singing French cabaret songs. The tension in his shoulders and back eased. After a few moments he noticed the woman on the stool next to him. She was tending a half-filled glass of wine. He returned her self-conscious smile. At first she appeared middle-aged, like him, perhaps in her fifties, but then he realized that the dim light was playing tricks on him and she was younger than he was, maybe in her mid-thirties. She had lightly applied blue eye shadow and pink lipstick. Her eyes, blue-gray, were inviting. To avoid the embarrassment of his attraction, he looked at her feet dangling from the stool. Her pink shoes contrasted with the dark floor. His eyes traveled up her firm legs to a pink, form-fitting skirt that stopped just above her knees, and then his eyes roamed still further north to an iridescent pink blouse. Her perfume was intoxicating. The blond hair at the nape of her neck, thin strands of gold, shimmered in the low light.

"I don't speak French," he said.

The left corner of her mouth curled slightly upwards. "Non? Ça ne fait rien."

"Do you speak English?" he asked.

"Oui, a little." She put her index finger close to her thumb to indicate how much. He noticed that she wasn't wearing a wedding ring.

She said she was a visitor from Paris on a 'petite vacance." She told him that she was a nurse. He tapped his foot in rhythm with the music and finished his wine; she sipped hers by his side. When he finished his wine he asked the bartender for another, and then another after that. They laughed at each other's clumsiness at foreign languages and joked light-heartedly about the customers at the tables. On occasion she placed her hand on his arm. At first this made him uncomfortable, but then he let it rest there. She was appealing, charming, but there was a deeper side beneath the surface that drew him in. She cast her eyes downward, like she was trying to camouflage disappointment in a way that made him want to console her, although he had no idea for what.

He told her that he gave the keynote lecture at the Congress in town. She seemed impressed and asked him what he talked about.

"The eye," he said.

She wanted more details, so he told her about the cornea and Fuch's dystrophy. She leaned closer to hear every word. He shared with her his love of science and how he viewed Nature as a paradise filled with beauty and adventure. Science was more than a tool to cure disease, he'd said, it was an art. She was spellbound. Then he told her how he had always wanted to know what animals thought about and told her about his cat Mulligan. She laughed and said she had wondered what was in her dog's mind when she was a little girl.

They listened to the cabaret singer for another half hour, and then he asked her if she wanted to go back to his hotel with him. He knew it was wrong but he couldn't help himself. The wine had freed his tongue and he was in France. It wasn't really him somehow. She blushed and looked uncertain. She allowed him to put his arm around her waist when they walked to his hotel, her high heels going clickety-clack.

The next morning Ricardo awoke in an empty bed. He had overslept and missed several of his colleagues' presentations.

Monique faded into a private memory over the years, but she never disappeared. Who was she? Where was she now?

A knock at his office door jolted Ricardo away from his daydream.

"Come in," he said, feeling like a kid caught with his hand in the cookie jar.

"I'm going home now," said his secretary. "Don't forget that your annual report is due tomorrow."

"Oh, that's right. Thanks for reminding me."

When the door closed Ricardo's thoughts turned once again to Monique. Simultaneously, he saw Lillian's picture on his desk. He had never revealed his escapade to her. Perhaps he should have, perhaps not. It was one of those choices—guilt by admission or remorse by avoidance—that hangs in the balance. He had chosen the latter by continual procrastination. "I'm sorry," he told Lillian's photograph. His apology fell on deaf ears, like his "promise" to honor Lillian's dying wish. While still looking at Lillian's photograph, he visualized Monique's pink lipstick and the sweet curl of her upper lip, her iridescent, pink blouse and brilliant pink skirt and shoes. All that pink. He imagined the clickety-clack of her spiked heels hammering rhythmically on the sidewalk as they made their way to the hotel. Then he remembered the hidden sadness that he had sensed in her, that she hadn't shared with him, and his loneliness when he had awakened to an empty hotel bed.

Chapter 16

Before tackling the annual report, Ricardo ate spaghetti and meatballs for dinner and watched the evening news on television. An outbreak of blindness in Detroit and videos of overcrowded emergency rooms with blind patients groping in fear startled him. All the patients had a high fever and complained of a sore throat a day before they lost their sight. The fever and sore throat disappeared the next day when they became blind. It was not known yet if or when sight would be regained.

Ricardo switched channels for more information and happened on an interview with a physician from the Communicable Disease Center and a Congressional Representative from Connecticut. The physician refrained from making any unsubstantiated claims, stating only that ophthalmological tests had yet to be conducted. The Congressman condemned the medical community for not doing more to improve public health, and mentioned the Vision Science Center. As a self-proclaimed authority on medicine and research, the Congressman said in a shrill voice, "Scientists receive enormous amounts of taxpayer dollars to find treatments and vaccines for these horrible diseases, and after endless promises they shrug their shoulders and say more research is necessary. They are asking to be rewarded for their failures! The situation is reprehensible. We must stop funding academics who use taxpayer money to study bugs and vermin and I don't know what else instead of humans." He cited statistics of how many new outbreaks of disease had been reported in the last year and how much money that had cost the country.

Suddenly the Congressman stopped speaking, swallowed hard, and appearing scared, said, "I think I'm getting a sore throat. I need to go home now. God bless you all."

Ricardo expected to see another editorial in tomorrow's newspaper by Randolph Likens damning basic scientific research. He turned off the television and his mind wandered to jellyfish. It seemed that all he could think of these days was jellyfish. Did they ever go blind and if so, how did blindness affect their behavior or survival?

Realizing he was procrastinating, he powered on his computer and settled down to write his annual report. Just looking at the blank annual review form on his computer screen bored him. "Same old, same old" he uttered to himself. "What a waste of time." He reacted similarly every year, and every year Lillian had told him to "relax and just do it." Although he assumed that his annual reports were little more than skimmed, his pride still pushed him to impress—whom?—Dr. Topping? Probably. It bothered him that he cared. Nonetheless he started filling out the form until the telephone rang and interrupted him.

"Marcus here. Have you got a moment, Ricardo?"

Ricardo was caught off guard. Why would Dr. Topping call him at home? Did it concern the Detroit outbreak? No, that didn't make sense.

"I hope that I'm not disturbing you. Since I haven't received your annual report yet, I assumed you were possibly working on it now."

Marcus Topping, the perennial Director! Did he have Ricardo on the radar screen day and night? Ricardo was furious. However, Dr. Topping said that because of Ricardo's present circumstance a shortened annual report would be acceptable. How frustrating for Ricardo to not know whether to be angry or grateful! Before hanging up, Dr. Topping added, "Just please make sure that you relate your research clearly to medical advances, especially since the Scientific Priorities Committee pointed out last time that you tended to drift from stated targets." Ricardo assured him that he would do his best with the annual report. He hung up and decided to drown himself in beer.

Ricardo never lacked appreciation for the importance of medical advances, but it would have been a lie for him to claim that his research goals were to treat disease. For Ricardo, basic research meant raising new questions, adding depth to scientific knowledge and nudging science in new directions. For Dr. Topping and the politicians, basic research meant searching for missing pieces of medical puzzles in order to provide treatments for disease. In Ricardo's mind, he wanted to compose music, while Dr. Topping asked for notes.

Ricardo worked into the night, submitted his annual report the next day as a dutiful employee and then called his faithful friend, Benjamin.

"I've had it with these annual reports," Ricardo complained. "I want to go back to La Parguera. I'm just about out of frozen rhopalia. Maybe we should return there and collect more samples. What do you think?"

Disappointed that Benjamin didn't respond immediately, he asked again, "Do you want to go back to La Parguera?"

"Maybe. Depends." Benjamin was evasive.

"On what?"

"I don't know. On what we're after, I suppose."

Ricardo was annoyed. "Yeah, but..."

Benjamin didn't let Ricardo finish. "Look, Ricardo, I overheard postdoctoral fellows in the halls saying they wished that they could go on vacation to the Caribbean like I did. When I told a few of my colleagues about our jellyfish research, they smiled and sarcastically wished me "good luck." Jim Sash even said that it was irresponsible for me to fool around with irrelevant work in my position."

"Irrelevant? Jim's always been a short-sighted sourpuss."

"That's not the point and you know it."

Ricardo was taken aback by the harsh quality of Benjamin's voice.

"When I mentioned our jellyfish research at our annual department retreat," Benjamin continued in a gentler voice, "people looked bored. No one asked me questions and, frankly, I felt uncomfortable. Where's this jellyfish work going?" Benjamin paused as if suddenly sorry to be disappointing his friend. "It's a different era, Ricardo. What do people think about your jellyfish research at the Vision Science Center?"

"Well..." Ricardo started slowly, "when I gave a research progress report to some colleagues about jellyfish, they seemed interested and there were a few questions. But maybe they were being polite. How would I know? I admit that Dr. Topping doesn't sound thrilled about jellyfish, but that's Marcus for you."

"Well, I'm not surprised. He's under a lot of pressure to secure funds. Look, I loved going to La Parguera with you, and it was interesting for sure, but it was a side trip for me."

"Come on, Benjamin. Jellyfish vision is an untapped goldmine! You know that."

"My grant needs renewal, I have a pile of unfinished manuscripts on my desk, I promised to give some lectures, I'm teaching a course...anyway, it goes on and on. I'm really, really busy."

"I have no idea where the jellyfish research is heading," admitted Ricardo, going back to Benjamin's earlier question.

"Neither do I," Benjamin said. "And it consumes time, my most precious resource. Also, Mattie says that I should pay more attention to the grandchildren. They're growing up faster than I can keep track. Gloria is going into the second grade already."

"How's the cactus stuff coming along?" Ricardo asked, ignoring Gloria.

"Actually, now that you ask, I've been doing some experiments on cactus. But...I must say..." Benjamin stalled.

"Tell me, or don't you trust me to keep it quiet?"

"Of course I do. I'm just not sure..." Benjamin was being cautious again.

"...that it will turn out like you hoped?" This time it was Ricardo's turn to finish Benjamin's sentence for him.

"Maybe," admitted Benjamin.

"Really?"

"I've made a bunch of different extracts from the cactus paddles and, believe it or not, have injected myself with them. It's crazy, I know, but I need an assay for finding out what gives the peculiar feeling after being stuck by those thorns."

"My god, Benjamin! Aren't you afraid of having some kind of allergic reaction or being poisoned?"

"A little." Benjamin hesitated.

Ricardo didn't interrupt this time.

Benjamin continued. "After yesterday's injection I couldn't sleep all night. My mind was roaming all over the place. I never felt as close to Mattie in my life. I had all kinds of insights about my experiments, about my kids, about everything. I felt like I was someone else and myself at the same time. How can I put it? It was like being *connected* to everyone and everything, even non-living things. I felt physically tethered to people and objects. The chairs and sofa and tables, all the furniture seemed like extensions of my body, like I was structurally part of my surroundings, and then the more I thought about that, the more sense it made."

"How's that make sense?"

"Well, the feeling was a new view of reality, a deeper reality. My furniture, my house, my car, my surroundings *are* all integral parts of my life. I supply a need for them as much as they fulfill my needs. Without me they would have as little importance as I would be lost without them. Do you know what I mean? I'm beginning to sound like you!"

"Not quite, but close."

"It didn't stop when I finally went to sleep either," Benjamin continued. "Remember your jellyfish dream in La Parguera? Well, last night I dreamed that I could talk to the prickly pear cactus. When I woke up Mattie asked me what I was dreaming about since I kept mumbling in my sleep. She laughed when I told her. She said that I should stop messing around with cactus."

"Are you going to stop working on cactus?"

"There's something special about them. I feel it," said Benjamin.

Ricardo knew Benjamin wouldn't drop his cactus project. He asked him how he was going to pursue it.

"The active agent seems small by chromatography and is destroyed by several enzymes that digest proteins, so it's almost certainly a small protein."

"And your only assay is injecting different preparations into yourself?"

"Yeah. Now I want to isolate the pure protein. I wish I could find another way to test for this substance besides injecting myself. Perhaps I could inject a dog or a cat and observe some behavioral change."

"Do you have a name for this magic substance?"

"Cactein for the moment. It seems catchy and combines the facts that it's from a cactus and it's a small protein. I may need to change the name if it turns out to be something else."

Whether it was hearing Benjamin's confidence or that Benjamin had excluded him from the cactus work, Ricardo felt like an ant squashed under a heavy thumb.

"Sounds great, Benjamin. I've got to go. Someone is waiting to speak to me," he lied. "Keep me posted on your progress."

Ricardo didn't get much accomplished the rest of the day. Cactein was like a thorn in his brain. Was it a new chemical that would unravel mysteries of the nervous system or find a medical application? Was Cactein present in other cacti or plants or animals? How did it differ from mescaline—which is known to be in some cacti—or from other narcotics, like LSD or marijuana? Was it in jellyfish? Benjamin had a story to tell, a new and original story, while he had nothing but idle dreams and fragments of data on jellyfish. Benjamin stood at the epicenter of action while Ricardo was on the outside looking in. It did not feel good to be eclipsed by his friend. He needed to return to La Parguera as soon as possible.

Ricardo applied again for travel funds, justifying the second trip on the need for additional rhopalia to complete his experiments, which he claimed were "promising."

"How promising?" Dr. Topping asked.

Ricardo exaggerated his inconclusive data. "I think I've located one of the two genes in jellyfish that may be related to those that are associated with Fuch's dystrophy." It was true that he had found a possible jellyfish gene that was similar to the mouse gene. Then he added, "I'm still optimistic about hunting down a jellyfish counterpart to the growth hormone for corneal endothelial cells, but that's going much slower." It certainly was. Ricardo had made no progress on that. "I need more samples. I can't draw any meaningful conclusions at this point."

Once again, Ricardo received permission to go to La Parguera. While Ricardo was eager to pursue his studies on jellyfish, he was also sad to go back to La Parguera without Benjamin. Something felt not quite right about the whole thing.

Chapter 17

Harold was concentrating on his work at the computer when Ricardo entered the laboratory in La Parguera. A half-eaten chocolate bar was on Harold's desk, as usual. The dissecting microscopes, the half-filled chemical bottles on the shelves and the jars containing marine specimens had lost their luster. The novelty was gone.

"Ricardo? You startled me. Good to see you. Where's Benjamin?"

"He couldn't make it. He had too much to do."

"Too bad," said Harold. "I was looking forward to seeing him again."

"I'll only be here for a couple of days."

"I'm busy with deadlines for our annual reports and all that crap and so I can't go out on the boat with you this time."

"No problem. I plan on collecting at our usual spot in the mangrove swamp. I know where it is."

"Just getting more eyes?"

"Yes, but maybe I'll try a few other things as well. I'm not sure."

"What other things?"

That was the difficult question to answer. Collecting more rhopalia was the easy part, but it wasn't enough. He needed to find a story—a jellyfish story—that would show Dr. Topping, the Scientific Priorities Committee, his peers, and most importantly himself, that his creative days weren't over, that he was still a force to reckon with. And then there was Benjamin and his goddamn cactus. As much as Ricardo wanted to deny it, he was envious. Rivalry was transcending his friendship. Ricardo wanted to equal Benjamin, or outdo him, and jellyfish seemed his only option. In addition, there was his pride. He'd preached the importance of taking chances in science, the importance of destination-free research and studying species that others ignored—platypus in the past, and now jellyfish. This seemed like his last chance to prove himself correct.

All he had was an intuition that jellyfish held important secrets, but his interest in jellyfish perception was abstract and undefined. If a young investigator came to him with such diffuse ideas for a research project he would tell him to crystallize—sharpen—the questions. Destination-free research wasn't undisciplined research.

"Is there a boat I could check out? I'm anxious to get started," Ricardo said, ignoring Harold's curiosity about what he was going to do this time with the jellyfish.

"Yup. Good luck with whatever you're going to do."

"Thanks." He needed luck.

Ricardo spotted an old oscilloscope that he hadn't noticed before in the corner of the laboratory. He placed it on the bench top and brushed off the dust with his hand. It looked archaic with its rusty dials and old wires. He remembered using an oscilloscope when still a student and wondered how he might make use of it.

Ricardo gathered the dip net, a bottle of fresh water and a bucket, and headed for the outboard motor boat, whistling as he walked to the dock amid a warm breeze.

After a few hours in the mangrove swamp, Ricardo returned to the laboratory with a bucket full of jellyfish. He distributed them into four bowls of sea water, and then transferred a jellyfish from the bowl to a Petri dish under the dissecting microscope. What a pleasure to work in the laboratory unencumbered by the nagging obligations he had at the Vision Science Center. Thoughts on Benjamin and his cactus melted into the background. Only the present moment existed, and it was his alone. He marveled at the magnified view of the rhopalium in the microscope with the two complex eyes at right angles to one another and the two specialized clusters of photoreceptor cells on each side of the eyes, exactly as diagrammed in the book on invertebrate vision that night he first learned that jellyfish had eyes. Also, the statocyst—the organ that oriented the jellyfish telling it up from down—was at the end of the rhopalium just as it was supposed to be.

"Magnificent," Ricardo mumbled to himself. Hundreds of millions of years of evolution had produced a biological sensory apparatus—the jellyfish rhopalium—as remarkable, if not more so, than anything Ricardo could think of that man created. How was it possible that the jellyfish rhopalium had barely been investigated? Few even knew of its existence, and even fewer cared about it. Ricardo cared. He cared a great deal.

He leaned back in his chair, rubbed his eyes and looked at the discarded paper towels scattered on the floor, the used glass pipettes, the scale with a few spilled grains of salt on the weighing tray, the black ballpoint pen on the coffee-stained notebook filled with diagrams, all trappings of messy science in action. Ricardo felt at home in this unpretentious, tiny corner of the world where he could admire Nature's awesome miracles. But, he still needed a novel idea, a new story to tell, *his* story as interesting as Cactein. He could not hide behind Nature's veneer forever; he needed to act. He would return in the evening to collect the rhopalia from his day's catch to take home for analysis, and then he would try to chart a path for further investigations, a path that he could develop into his story.

Chapter 18

Ricardo returned to the laboratory that evening refreshed after a shower and a quick dinner. "Hello, little fellows," he said, greeting the jellyfish that pulsated in the bowls on the table. He sat on the stool next to the table and closed his eyes. Everything felt lonelier at night, and more personal.

"I miss you," he sighed, speaking softly to Lillian's ghost.

"Me too," she answered.

How wonderful that he could still be with her in his mind.

"So much," he continued. "What did you do today? Protect an abused child?" Ricardo imagined an anorexic teenage girl, paper-thin with eyes as empty caverns. Lillian had helped many such kids.

"I'm afraid she'll die," Lillian answered.

Ricardo opened his eyes and Lillian disappeared, but he retained her image in his mind. Did all animals with image-forming eyes retain traces of what they saw? Did jellyfish? He imagined that tracing visual memory back to jellyfish would make a more remarkable story than Cactein. But how could he identify the visual memory of a jellyfish? No one even knew what a jellyfish saw, much less remembered.

Ricardo imagined Benjamin sitting on the stool across the table. "What do jellyfish see?" Ricardo asked. Speaking to Benjamin helped him think.

"You. The laboratory. Each other."

"Really? How do you know? Do they remember images?"

"They don't remember, Ricardo. They're jellyfish. I don't have time for this. I have important work to do," Benjamin said, before disappearing from Ricardo's mind.

But, Ricardo conjectured, just because Benjamin was dismissive of jellyfish remembering, it didn't mean that he was correct.

Ricardo turned on the radio for company and heard magnificent voices singing *Don Giovanni*. He hummed along with the music as he netted a jellyfish from the bowl and placed it on a Petri dish under the dissecting microscope in order to excise the rhopalia. He was happy that jellyfish didn't bleed. Ricardo collected rhopalia from most of the jellyfish and froze them in order to take the samples back to his laboratory.

"Okay, small fries," he said to the few jellyfish that had been spared after two hours of work. "What am I going to do with you?" He put a finger in a bowl that contained three jellyfish. "Beautiful," he whispered, meaning both Mozart's masterpiece and the grace of the jellyfish. He wondered whether the jellyfish sensed the rhythm when he swayed his finger in time with the music in the same way Helen Keller absorbed music through vibrations when she placed her hand on a violin being played. In his little-known book, *The Formation of Vegetable Mould through the Action of Worms and Observations on their Habits,* Darwin concluded that potted earthworms placed on a piano responded to the vibrations of the notes when the keys were struck.

Ricardo looked at an adjacent bowl containing four jellyfish; two were huddled together and he imagined their tentacles entwined. He remembered when Lillian had said that two adjacent jellyfish in the Baltimore aquarium were lovers. Maybe she was right, thought Ricardo. The distant pair of jellyfish in the bowl swam towards the lovers. Were they joining the party or mounting an attack, or neither? How could he have any idea of the social dynamics going on in the bowl?

Ricardo imagined he saw Lillian in the bowl with the jellyfish, waving her arms sensuously as if they were tentacles. "Come join me," she beckoned him. He wished he could. How strange the feeling to be inhabiting two worlds simultaneously: his and that of the jellyfish.

Salisbury whispered in Ricardo's memory. "You're an artist and a scientist, Ricardo, like me."

Then he heard Lillian's voice. "Don't let the artist trump the scientist," she said. "Be careful."

Ricardo glanced at the oscilloscope and had an idea. He plugged the oscilloscope into an electrical outlet, deftly removed the largest jellyfish from the bowl next to him and placed it on a Petri dish under the dissecting microscope. He inserted the end of a thin wire extending from the oscilloscope into one of the jellyfish eyes; an electronic line jumped on the screen and wobbled as the impaled jellyfish lay helplessly on the dish.

"Good. Something is still working on this old machine," he said.

Next, Ricardo delicately placed the jellyfish back into the bowl, careful not to disengage the end of the wire in its eye. The line on the screen extended and formed equidistant peaks as if graphing something. But graphing what? The jellyfish didn't seem harmed, but Ricardo worried that it might be in pain. The distances between the peaks became irregular and blinked when the jellyfish pulsated in the bowl.

Ricardo had no inkling of what was going on. The rational scientist in him cautioned that the antiquated oscilloscope was unreliable, and/or the wire, though thin, may have penetrated more than just the eye, complicating any interpretation he might make of the data. The optimistic, imaginative artist in Ricardo considered that the dynamic oscilloscope lines might represent the jellyfish eye responding differently to different views of the laboratory through the glass bowl.

He stared at the bright oscilloscope screen, debating whether to listen to the skeptical scientist or the artistic optimist inside himself. He remembered that he had often congratulated postdoctoral fellows when they couldn't understand their data and didn't know what to do next, and told them that they were finally in a position to discover something new. If only that were true, he thought now, suddenly filled with compassion for his students, and feeling foolish.

Ricardo pulled the wire out of the jellyfish and unplugged the oscilloscope. The jellyfish continued to swim in the bowl as if nothing had happened. It was time to go back to the motel and sleep for a few hours.

The next day Ricardo returned to the Vision Science Center with another batch of frozen rhopalia to analyze. More importantly, however, he sensed elusive ingredients for a story that he might write—a jellyfish story—but what exactly was that story? He still needed to find *his* Cactein.

Chapter 19

"Paul, it's been an eternity since I've done any electro-physiology and I'm sure the technique has changed enormously since my graduate student days," Ricardo said on the telephone the day after he returned to his laboratory in Washington. Paul Sing, a colleague in the Vision Science Center, was an expert on electrophysiological recordings from the retinas of rodents. "I need your help."

"Sure. What's up?"

"I've been moonlighting a bit. Can we get together for lunch?"

"Moonlighting? Now I'm curious. How about meeting me at the cafeteria at noon?"

Ricardo arrived at the cafeteria ten minutes early. When Paul came, they grabbed sandwiches and sat down at a table in the corner.

"So tell me about this moonlighting. Making gin?"

"No. This is more important."

"Really? More important than gin? Then its got to be big time."

"Actually, I'm not sure exactly what it is yet, but I hope it's big time. It's about, well, let's see, about the evolution of vision right now, but ultimately I hope that it's also about the evolution of visual memory, and of...I don't know, whatever." Ricardo wished he had a better grasp of what he was after.

"Hold on there, Ricardo. Start at the beginning. What animal are you talking about?"

"Promise you won't laugh?"

"Promise."

"Jellyfish."

"I promised, so I won't laugh, but did I hear you correctly? You said jellyfish?"

"Yes." And then Ricardo told Paul that jellyfish have complex eyes with a lens and a retina.

"You got permission to go to Puerto Rico to study jellyfish eyes?" said Paul incredulously.

"Few people have studied jellyfish eyes, as amazing as that sounds. I proposed to look for jellyfish versions of the corneal endothelial cell hormone I discovered in mice, as well as versions of the genes I found that are associated with Fuch's dystrophy. Those are legitimate questions.

"So, what do you want from me?"

Ricardo recounted his observations that jellyfish swam in groups and that light attracted them at night and that he had tried to make recordings from the jellyfish eye with an old oscilloscope. "I need help in interpreting the oscilloscope data."

Paul squinted as if he was searching for what to say. "An oscilloscope? I haven't seen one of those in years. How would I know what's going on?"

Ricardo pressed him further. "You don't understand, Paul, I want to know what a jellyfish sees and whether it remembers the information for future use. It's far-fetched, I know. I'm looking for an entry point to study the evolution of visual memory and thought." There, he told himself, it's getting clearer.

"Whoa, Ricardo. Have you been drinking?"

Drinking? Paul's question triggered a different question. What if he took some of Benjamin's miracle Cactein? Would that affect his ability to understand jellyfish? Benjamin did say Cactein unlocked some ability to connect with external beings. With jellyfish, he wondered? Crazy, but still...

Ricardo didn't notice Paul looking at him strangely.

"Ricardo? Hello?"

"Oh, sorry. I haven't sorted out my ideas yet." That was true.

"Are you sure you know what you're doing, Ricardo? I can't imagine anyone interested in jellyfish these days. It's dangerous territory. Remember how Sam Sharpe was pressured to leave the Vision Science Center when the Scientific Priorities Committee gave him a very poor review for studying, what? I remember it was nothing medical."

"Penguins. He was doing fascinating research."

"If you say so, Ricardo."

Ricardo thought that vision in amphibious birds was particularly interesting. He was frustrated that the hearts of other scientists may have been in the same place as his, but that they all submitted to the pressures of the times.

"I'm curious, Paul. I want to know what it's like to *be* a jellyfish." Ricardo avoided saying that he was also looking for his own version of Cactein.

"You're really hooked, aren't you?"

Ricardo nodded.

"Look, I'm nowhere near retirement and don't want to be squeezed out. But, I wonder..."

"Wonder what?"

"I've heard about a new computer developed by NASA. I think it converts digital data into images and graphs. I know Frank Pizzaro who works there. You might want to talk to him."

Ricardo begged him to call his friend at NASA, which Paul did, then and there on his cell phone. Ricardo went to NASA the next day.

"It's small but powerful," Frank said. "The software was written by the Defense Department for deciphering codes. It can generate three-dimensional images from even the most bizarre data. We're still tweaking it."

"Sounds interesting." Ricardo said, belying his excitement.

"Paul told me you're studying jellyfish?"

"That's right.

Frank looked skeptical. "How do you want to use our computer?"

"I'm not sure. I guess I would need some electrodes that can join the computer to the jellyfish as a starter. Is that possible?"

"No problem. The electrodes are little computers themselves and are made for recording from nerve cells. They are very thin and water-proof, and once you give the computer the proper settings, the electrodes will communicate wirelessly to the computer. It's very sensitive."

"Wow. Great," said Ricardo. "I'll repeat what I did with an oscilloscope but using your computer. Make sense?"

"I'm not sure. Jellyfish? They're hardly animals."

Ricardo chalked up Frank's condescending comment to ignorance about biology. "I can't tell you how I'll interpret or use information I don't have yet," he said. "But I'd love to try out your computer."

"Sounds a bit sketchy to me, but what the heck. Please don't keep it very long. And don't tell anyone. It's not supposed to circulate yet."

"What if I get some data that I want to publish?"

"With jellyfish?"

The next day Ricardo called Benjamin and told him about the oscilloscope data. He was aching to tell him about the NASA computer, but he'd promised Frank to keep that quiet.

"I think jellyfish eyes are responding to different views around them," said Ricardo, echoing what he imagined Benjamin saying that night in La Parguera.

"Hmmm," said Benjamin. "It almost makes me want to go back to La Parguera with you and see for myself."

Ricardo wasn't sure he wanted that to happen anymore. "Can I ask a huge favor of you?" he asked with apprehension.

"Sure." There was that warm voice of his old friend.

"I'm curious—preoccupied—with these jellyfish."

"I get that."

"I remember you said that Cactein gave you new insights, made you feel *connected* with people and even objects. I want to try to connect with jellyfish, whatever that means. I know that I'm grasping for straws but I need help. If I could try your magic cactus potion at La Parguera, maybe I could... *experience*...being a jellyfish." Ricardo hesitated. "Does that sound crazy?"

Ricardo's hands were trembling. He didn't worry about sounding far out since Benjamin knew him well, but asking for Cactein was another matter: that was trespassing into Benjamin's sacred space.

"You want some Cactein?"

"If you don't mind. Just a little. I'm not even positive I would try it."

"You think Cactein might allow you to enter the world of jellyfish?"

"I guess that's what I mean. It can't hurt, can it?"

"I suppose not. I'm not sure what you would experience, but actually it would be an interesting experiment."

"Really? I think so too," said Ricardo.

"Okay. Why not?" agreed Benjamin. "But please, write down your feelings and thoughts when you use it. I'll send you some of my preparation. Keep it frozen. And don't tell anyone about Cactein! I need to publish first. You understand, don't you?"

Ricardo did. It seemed that he was collecting secrets.

Chapter 20

The day after Ricardo had borrowed the NASA computer from Frank, and eager to return to La Parguera, he applied once again for travel funds. He justified the trip by stating, as before, that he needed more samples to finish the ongoing, approved project on jellyfish eyes. Dr. Topping happened to be out of town attending a conference, and so the overworked acting Director rubber-stamped the travel request. He had no reason to question the previous approvals that the highly regarded Ricardo had received from Dr. Topping.

Ricardo entered Harold's laboratory in La Parguera with the NASA computer under his arm. The old-fashioned laboratory looked brighter than it had the last time he had visited, and Ricardo felt optimistic.

"Here I am again," he said to Harold, who was correcting students' exams when Ricardo entered the office.

"Hi, Ricardo. You look upbeat. Benjamin's not with you?"

"No. He's very busy. He said to say hello."

"Too bad he couldn't make it. He's doing some important stuff …what's it called…birdshot retinopthy?"

"Retinopathy." Ricardo corrected. "Yes, he could help a lot of people if he makes headway on treating the disease."

"Yup. Smart guy. I'm sorry that I can't help you collecting jellyfish this time, but Robin told me she's free. Remember her? She'd love to make a few dollars if you want her help. She's had experience collecting."

Robin's cheerful personality made Ricardo forget his age as they collected jellyfish, but her sharp vision that repeatedly spotted tiny translucent jellyfish swimming in the distance reminded him that he was no spring chicken. Ricardo doubted that she was oblivious to his glances when he pretended to scratch the bugs off his neck or check his watch or admire the picturesque waterways lined with mangrove trees.

With Robin's capable help, they soon had enough jellyfish to refresh his supply of rhopalia and still have some left over for his experiments with the NASA computer. After two hours he wanted to return to the laboratory. She looked disappointed because each hour of collecting meant more money in her pocket. Realizing this, he paid her considerably more than she expected, as much to see her smile as to be generous.

"Just let me know if you need more help," she said.

Soon after they returned, the sky darkened, followed by torrential rain. Whitecaps decorated the ominous, blackened water.

After waiting out the squall in the laboratory, Ricardo made his way back to the motel for a short rest. Annoyed by the lost afternoon when he awoke near dinnertime, he showered, had a hamburger at Harold's favorite greasy diner, and went to the laboratory. A full moon in a clear sky lifted his spirits. It was time to try out the NASA computer.

With the evening in front of him, Ricardo settled down to work. He powered up the NASA computer and fiddled with the settings so the electrodes would communicate wirelessly to the computer. He placed a jellyfish in a Petri dish under the microscope, carefully impaled one of its eyes with the thin electrode. He took care to slip the point of the electrode around the back of the eye so it would not block the line of vision, and made every effort to not go deeply into the retina in order to not damage it, or at least do minimal damage. He had no idea how fragile the jellyfish eye was and what it could withstand. Once he was satisfied that the electrode was firmly implanted and the eye still appeared healthy, he transferred the impaled jellyfish into a water-filled bowl. It immediately started sinking. "Oops, what've I done?" he said softly and wrinkled his brow, but sighed with relief when the jellyfish started to move before it reached the bottom. How beautiful it was with its gentle pulses! After a few seconds the computer screen lit up with bright, multicolored lines that danced before his eyes. He reached into the bowl and gently tapped the electrode to make sure that it was still solidly implanted in the back of the eye in order to eliminate the possibility that the lines on the computer screen were the result of a loose connection between the electrode and the retina.

The impaled jellyfish moved slowly around the bowl. Lines and dots appeared on the computer screen. There were no images on the screen. Somewhere in these data lines hid *his* Cactein, *his* discovery yet to make, although he had no inkling what it might be. He ambled into Harold's office to steal a square of chocolate which he assumed would be on the desk, as usual. Harold loved chocolate.

Suddenly a thought flashed through his mind: perhaps a jellyfish needs a type of brain to interpret the eye signals that appear as lines and dots on the computer screen, just as he, Ricardo, needs a brain to interpret the satisfying taste of chocolate. A jellyfish brain? He remembered bringing up that possibility to Dr. Topping partly in jest and without really believing it. The only organized nervous system in jellyfish that Ricardo knew about was the nerve ring surrounding the midline, and that was assumed to control movement. But what else might the nerve ring do? He didn't know of any studies on the nerve ring from the viewpoint of perception. He was determined to consider every possibility, no matter how remote.

Ricardo removed the jellyfish from the bowl and placed it under the dissecting microscope, being careful to not disturb the electrode in its eye. He inserted a second electrode into the middle of the jellyfish where the nerve ring was located. A black horizontal line with projecting spikes appeared at the bottom of the screen the moment the electrode pierced the nerve ring, and this was accompanied by a dull buzz accented with clicks and bleeps from the computer.

Ricardo scratched his head. "In you go, little fellow," he said as he placed the jellyfish back into the bowl. "Teach me something new."

"Whoa!" Ricardo exclaimed when a blurred image of the laboratory shelves close to the jellyfish bowl appeared above the horizontal line on the computer screen. As the jellyfish circled the bowl a series of distorted images as if seen through a curved lens appeared on the screen. First he recognized the pH meter on the table, then the centrifuge next to the pH meter. After that he saw an image of the open door to Harold's office. These changing images looked like a video of what the jellyfish should see from inside the bowl! Ricardo was ecstatic. The truly remarkable finding was that the images didn't appear on the computer screen until he recorded simultaneously from both the eye and the nerve ring. It seemed that the nerve ring *was* necessary to translate the signals from the eye into recognizable visual images. A 'nerve ring brain'?

To verify this astounding possibility, Ricardo removed the electrode from the eye, left the electrode in the nerve ring and put the jellyfish back in the water. The laboratory images disappeared. Ricardo's mind was ablaze. Yes! The visual images of the laboratory were present only when the computer received impulses from the eye and the nerve ring together.

"This must be a first in the history of science," he said out loud, unable to contain his excitement. Perhaps he was reading too much into the data and trespassing the boundaries of scientific discipline. But the possibility that the jellyfish nerve ring interpreted visual information to generate an image—that the jellyfish nerve ring might be acting like a brain—took his breath away. He swelled with pride and ambition. Benjamin may have Cactein, but Ricardo now had jellyfish eyes that saw images via a *brain* embedded in their nerve ring. That would put jellyfish—and Ricardo—on the map.

As this remarkable story was crystallizing in his mind, Ricardo asked himself how vision affected jellyfish and whether they remembered what they saw? How could he test for whether jellyfish retained a visual memory? He needed to *be* a jellyfish to know what it remembered.

Ricardo turned his attention to the spiked horizontal line below the images. Fortunately, Frank had given Ricardo a handful of electrodes, each a tiny computer that interacted wirelessly with the computer. Therefore, he placed a fresh jellyfish under the dissecting microscope, inserted a new electrode into its nerve ring, and put the jellyfish into the bowl with the doubly impaled jellyfish. The computer now would receive information from three electrodes: the two that impaled the eye and the nerve ring of the first jellyfish, and the third that impaled the nerve ring of the other jellyfish. He fiddled with the computer software to split the screen so that he could view separately the impulses generated from each jellyfish. At first, each side of the split screen showed different patterns of spikes, and apparently emitted different sounds, although the sounds were garbled since they were both coming simultaneously through the single speaker. When the two jellyfish passed next to each other, however, the line patterns and sounds synchronized; when the jellyfish separated, both the spike patterns and the sounds randomized. The jellyfish seemed to be communicating in some way when they were next to each other.

Ricardo noticed one more perplexing phenomenon. When the two jellyfish were next to one another, the one with electrodes in both the eye and the nerve ring generated an oblong, amorphous image with bulges that replaced the laboratory images, and a couple of times the amorphous image switched to a series of more complex, abstract images. When the jellyfish separated, the abstract images disappeared and the laboratory images appeared on the side of the screen that received recordings from the doubly impaled jellyfish.

Ricardo stepped back from the computer screen, perplexed, and took a sip of warm ginger ale from a can that he'd opened some time ago. Why didn't the jellyfish see each other if they were able to see objects outside the bowl? Was the environment like an impressionistic painting for the jellyfish that only appeared recognizable from a distance? Perhaps that was an evolutionary adaptation that would give them time to escape from predators. And, what were the amorphous images on the screen when the jellyfish were close to each other?

As Ricardo puzzled over his findings, he heard Lillian's reassuring voice in his mind: "You're smart. Something will click, you'll see." She'd been right in their youth; he hoped she would be right again.

It was then that Ricardo remembered Cactein.

Chapter 21

When he left for Puerto Rico, Ricardo knew that he was going to try Benjamin's cactus cocktail; it was just a matter of when. The euphoria brought on by his extraordinary observations and his frustration at his inability to interpret them converged at this perfect moment to inject himself with Cactein. He retrieved the sample from the refrigerator, filled a syringe and injected the extract into his thigh. He waited. Nothing. After about ten minutes, his eyes became scratchy and he felt drowsy, neither the result he'd expected nor wanted. As he willed himself out of sleepiness he swatted a tiny bug off his arm. "Sorry," he apologized to the stunned insect.

Ricardo looked at the two jellyfish in the bowl and decided to call them Mutt and Jeff like the outdated comic book characters. Mutt's impaled eye faced the pH meter on the bench next to its bowl, and a blurred image of the pH meter was displayed on the computer screen. A moment later an image of the balance replaced that of the pH meter. This was consistent with Mutt seeing the objects in the laboratory. Mutt suddenly changed directions and swam towards Jeff. As soon as Mutt faced Jeff, an oblong shape with bulges replaced the laboratory images on the screen. The oblong image had a velvety texture, similar to moss, and many small pores covered the surface. The pores were so pronounced that Ricardo couldn't understand why he hadn't noticed them before.

As Ricardo puzzled over why Mutt saw the oblong shape instead of Jeff, his eyes drifted to the marine specimens in formaldehyde-filled bottles on the shelves. There were starfish, some with few and some with many arms, snails with and without shells, round and flat worms, a lobster, a few small fish, and many other species. Ricardo caught sight of a bottle containing a sponge that resembled the gray-brown, porous image on the screen. He went to the shelf for a closer look. The screen image and the sponge in the bottle looked similar and had the same velvety texture, although the color of the bottled sponge was more washed out than the gray-brown image on screen. How could Mutt have seen such detail from so far away? Also, Mutt's impaled eye was not even facing the sponge on the shelf. It was staring at Jeff.

Ricardo started pacing back and forth, thinking. Just when he thought he would never make sense of his results, he noticed, taped to the wall, a crayon picture of a tree with multiple branches drawn by Harold's four-year-old nephew. Ricardo's jaw dropped.

He glanced again at the bottled sponge on the shelf and then at Mutt and Jeff and exclaimed, "When Mutt looks at Jeff he sees a sponge, Jeff's evolutionary ancestor! Mutt sees the evolutionary tree!"

Instantly, Ricardo was transformed from a bewildered scientist with a dwindling career into an invigorated one ready to write an extraordinary story. He had discovered that the "lowly" jellyfish processed visual images by using a diffuse "brain"—a brain!—within the nerve ring. But that wasn't even the most extraordinary part. The jellyfish saw an ancestor—a sponge—of its own evolution when looking at another jellyfish. He interpreted that to mean that the jellyfish stored a visual memory of past events, including even evolution.

Ricardo was momentarily awestruck by these remarkable findings and then, unexpectedly, he thought of one of Papi's abstract portraits. He hadn't recognized Carlos in the portrait when he first saw it as a boy. The pinched, stick-like green neck, the bright orange hair atop an oval flesh-colored head, the sloping shoulders with extended planes for arms, and clubby hands projecting twisted tendrils as fingers looked nothing like Carlos. However, after living with the picture for several months he recognized that buried within the improper anatomy, the painting revealed David's disjointed character rather than his physical features. "Good for you," Papi had said. "Mysteries dissolve when you see the underlying truth." Ricardo's epiphany of jellyfish visualizing past evolution resonated with his boyhood insight and gave him confidence that he had revealed an underlying truth—an astounding truth—of jellyfish vision and even memory.

However, the changing images that occasionally interrupted the oblong image generated when Mutt looked at Jeff still bothered Ricardo. He compared the images that had flashed by on the screen with the diverse species of the shelves. The resemblances were striking. He recognized the hemi-chordate, *Amphioxus*, and perhaps a tunicate sea squirt larva among the images that had flashed on the computer screen; both these species were known stepping-stones for the evolution of vertebrates from invertebrates. But that caused a conundrum. Hemi-chordates and tunicates evolved *after* jellyfish, as did most of the species represented by the rapidly changing images. Momentarily discouraged, Ricardo was ready to discard the idea that Mutt saw an ancestor of Jeff's evolution and to accept that these animal-like images on the computer screen were meaningless designs generated by the computer. Then he remembered Harold telling him about the predatory nature of jellyfish, and that tiny ingested crustaceans and fish could often be seen in their stomachs. When Ricardo looked closely, he could see such undigested morsels in Jeff's stomach, as well as in the stomachs of some of the jellyfish in the other bowls. Maybe he could still rescue his theory. Maybe jellyfish recorded sequential flashes—like videos, not just static images—of evolutionary pathways. The more advanced the species that the jellyfish would look at, the greater number of images of evolutionary ancestors would appear on the computer screen. If that were the case, when Mutt looked at some parts of Jeff, the computer screen would show only a sponge-like species, which represented Jeff's evolutionary ancestor; but when Mutt's eye focused on Jeff's stomach, the computer screen would flash ancestors of the undigested contents—that of the crustaceans and small fish that Mutt saw.

Ricardo understood that it was absurd from what is currently known about science to think that jellyfish retained a visual memory of its own evolution, but at least that was a part of the *past* history of the species that one might envision recorded in the genes. If all species inherited DNA sequences of their ancestors, which they did, maybe it was possible for species also to store images of their ancestors. But how could jellyfish have a visual memory of the evolutionary ancestors of species that evolved *after* it? That would mean that jellyfish recorded *future* events with respect to its own evolution.

Ricardo feared once again that his theory was in trouble and that he might have to abandon it. However, to rescue his hypothesis this time, he rationalized that since jellyfish were among the first complex animals to evolve, they had ample opportunity as a species to witness the evolution of marine species that evolved after they did. That he couldn't conceptualize immediately how they might do this or what survival advantage the jellyfish might gain by recording images of their ancestors shouldn't require him to abandon his hypothesis. Where would science be if hypotheses were discarded because they were not fully understood when they were first conceptualized? Didn't science edge towards truth by modifying ideas as more data were acquired? Hypotheses didn't come prepackaged.

Ricardo became increasingly convinced that jellyfish recorded "videos" of the evolutionary history of species in their line of vision. They had evolved a type of visual memory that was more dynamic and complex than humans possessed. A more ancient species didn't mean a less sophisticated one, as he'd told Lillian many years ago. Quite the opposite: more evolutionary time gave a species longer to develop sophisticated ways to engage with their environment.

"The past and the present are viewed simultaneously by jellyfish," Ricardo muttered, astounded at his own speculations. His insight was so beautiful that it had to be true. He had a computer filled with concrete images obtained through experimentation that supported his hypothesis of jellyfish sensing evolution. The data were not fabricated. It was up to him to write the story.

Finally, Ricardo turned his attention to the strange sounds generated by the jellyfish. He remembered Lillian telling him that he should listen more and talk less. There was much to learn by listening, and in this instance listening to jellyfish. And so Ricardo concentrated on the the discordant clicks and bleeps coming from the computer. After a few moments the noises melded together and began to sound harmonious and natural. He felt among friends as he had in his dream of jellyfish on his first trip to La Parguera. His toes and fingertips began to pulse in sync with the jellyfish in the bowls. He savored this chimerical moment in which he imagined himself part man and part jellyfish, the viewer and the viewed. He had violated the natural rule to live within his own niche and ignored the invisible 'No Trespassing' sign posted at the border of the jellyfish universe.

He had to document his observations while they were fresh in his mind, and he wrote the following summary:

"La Parguera, Puerto Rico, July 18, 2047: Tonight with the help of advanced computer technology I entered the jellyfish mind, so to speak, and I discovered that jellyfish use their nerve ring to integrate electronic signals from their eyes to perceive the surroundings, suggesting that the nerve ring is a kind of brain. And, even more remarkable, this "brain" seems to perceive images, albeit somewhat abstract, of species comprising the evolutionary history of any marine organism that the jellyfish eye sees, even a species that evolved after the jellyfish evolved. These images change from one to another in a way that is consistent with the evolutionary pathway of the species that the jellyfish is looking at, suggesting that jellyfish see videos of evolution!! How those visual memories are recorded remains an unwritten chapter in this extraordinary story."

Ricardo leaned back in his chair feeling both calm and excited simultaneously, wanting to meditate and shout at the same time.

Was this the all-encompassing emotion that others felt immediately after they had made a great discovery?

Ricardo closed his notebook and started to ponder practical applications for his discoveries, which he anticipated would be necessary to justify his research in the present political climate. His findings might lead to dividing long-term memory into genetic and non-genetic components. He speculated that evolutionary pathways recorded by jellyfish might act as a guide to select reasonable animal models—those closest to humans—for medical research, especially if other, more recently evolved species were also able to visualize evolution. Thus, his discoveries would open a new branch of research. Understanding in detail how jellyfish recorded visual information might provide new ways to prevent or treat amnesia or, better yet, dementia and Alzheimer's disease. It might also lead to innovations in computer technology.

"Imagination is the only limiting factor for practical application of basic knowledge," he muttered to himself. His experiments were a bonanza that could be applied in many ways.

Ricardo looked at his watch. It was already five o'clock in the morning, almost sunrise. He cradled his head in his crossed arms on the table and closed his eyes for a moment.

"Dr. Sztein...Dr. Sztein,"

"What? Who's there? Where am I?"

"It's Robin. Wake up. You must have fallen asleep."

"What time is it?"

"It's nine o'clock. I've got to go to class. Professor Freeman should be in soon."

Ricardo removed the electrodes from the jellyfish, which were pulsating peacefully in the bowls, and then Harold entered the laboratory.

"You're here already? You look tired. Did you work late last night?"

"Yeah, I'd say so," said Ricardo. "I dissected a lot of rhopalia to take back with me. They should keep me busy for awhile." He wondered whether Harold could hear his heart pounding. "I also got some interesting data of nervous activity from these jellyfish and ended up falling asleep in the lab. Robin woke me up."

"Really. What did you find out?"

"I'm not sure what it all means yet. I have to think about it. I..." Ricardo stopped in mid-sentence, remembering Lillian's warnings about speaking too much.

"You what?" asked Harold.

"I had a productive trip." Ricardo felt unsatisfied with this answer, yet he was pleased with his self-control.

Harold wished him luck with his experiments and went into his office. Ricardo placed the NASA computer and electrodes in the padded case, took his canister of frozen rhopalia and went back to the motel to check out. His plane was scheduled to leave for Washington that afternoon.

Chapter 22

Crowds milled around the San Juan airport. The rhopalia were frozen in an insulated canister that fit snugly in Ricardo's carry-on bag as he stood in the security line. Since he had both his U.S. government passport and his identification badge as a scientist at the Vision Science Center, he didn't expect any difficulty in transporting his frozen biological samples; he hadn't had any problems bringing frozen specimens home before. This time, however, the inspector was examining the bags of the passengers more rigorously, almost as if he were angry. When Ricardo's carry-on went through the x-ray machine, the inspector looked puzzled.

"Open the bag, please," said the official.

Ricardo complied.

"What's in that container?"

"Just a few scientific specimens—nothing living—that I'm taking back to my government laboratory in the United States." Ricardo pulled out his Vision Science Center identification card. "I'm a scientist and am collaborating with Professor Freeman at the Marine Station of the University of Puerto Rico in La Parguera."

"Oh, yeah? Specimens?"

"Believe it or not, they're jellyfish eyes." That would certainly calm the man down. How threatening could jellyfish eyes be?

"You've got to be kidding," responded the inspector with a sarcastic grin.

Ricardo tightened his lips. "Jellyfish have eyes." He paused, realizing that the official couldn't possibly believe that jellyfish had eyes—who would? To add credibility Ricardo added, "Almost no one knows that."

"What the heck would a jellyfish see? Next you'll tell me jellyfish have half a brain. Open the container; let me see what's there," said the inspector.

"The specimens will thaw out and be ruined," Ricardo said, thinking that half a brain was more than the inspector had.

"Open the container or leave it here," demanded the official. With each exchange his voice increased a decibel. "You can't take it on the airplane until I see what's in it."

Ricardo barely even heard the inspector since his thoughts suddenly drifted to the inexplicable sounds that he heard in the computer from the jellyfish. He figured that they must be a code of some kind. Why did the random clicks and bleeps from Mutt and Jeff blend so pleasantly when the jellyfish were close to one another?

"Very strange," he said quietly to the air, and then he muttered to himself, "If a jellyfish has a brain, what's going on in it?"

"What?" asked the inspector, looking confused. "I told you to open the container." He was almost shouting now.

"If you insist." Ricardo unscrewed the lid and removed the small tube with the frozen rhopalia, which immediately started thawing.

"Why is the stuff in the tube so black?"

"The black tissue is the pigment that's in all eyes, even ours. That's why your pupils look black." Ricardo the teacher was speaking. "These jellyfish eyes are ruined now. I can't possibly use them for my experiments. Just keep them." Ricardo wasn't angry anymore; he had a new mission. "I'll need my canister back though."

Ricardo tossed the ruined eyes in the tray that had just gone through the x-ray machine, replaced the empty canister in his bag and walked away. The inspector, appearing bewildered, watched helplessly as Ricardo left to return to La Parguera. Ricardo didn't care what the inspector thought. He didn't care that he wouldn't appear the next day in his laboratory as was scheduled. Dr. Topping could care less if he returned a day or two later, and probably wouldn't even know. The Vision Science Center wasn't Ricardo's problem at the moment.

Jellyfish were on his mind. He wanted to know why the spike patterns synchronized when Mutt and Jeff were side by side. What was the meaning of their "singing" to each other? Did they really have a brain, or perhaps half a brain as the inspector suggested sarcastically? How ironic that the angry official had given him the freedom to return once again to La Parguera.

Chapter 23

Ricardo returned to the motel. He put his bag in his room and left a voice message for his secretary that he would be detained for at least another day. It was eight o'clock in the evening when he went to the laboratory. Harold wasn't there. Partially corrected student examinations and, as usual, a half-eaten chocolate bar lay on his desk.

The quiet atmosphere of the laboratory had that musty smell of salt air that he loved. Salt from evaporated seawater crusted the windows. Ricardo was turning into a nocturnal owl and he liked it. It helped with his insomnia during the long, lonely nights.

Fortunately, Harold had not yet discarded the few jellyfish in the bowls. Despite having been repeatedly punctured, Mutt and Jeff still looked healthy.

"You're resilient buggers," he said. "No wonder you guys have survived on this planet so long."

Ricardo marveled how Harold's laboratory in far-off La Parguera, just a foreign name to him not long ago, now felt like home. Perhaps it was the city's Latin flavor that reminded him of his native Buenos Aires. Dr. Topping and professional obligations didn't exist in La Parguera. The sense of freedom was intoxicating.

Ricardo's return to La Parguera that afternoon felt like a bold and heroic act. He wished he could have told Lillian that this was one time his impulsive nature had its benefits. He laughed out loud when he imagined the befuddled inspector not knowing what to make of the rhopalia thawing before his eyes.

"Back to work," he warned the jellyfish, determined to figure out what all the sounds meant. But how to do that? He would start by confirming his previous results.

"Oh, hi. I thought you had gone back to Washington," said Robin, peeking into the laboratory through the open door.

"Robin! What are you doing here so late?" Ricardo said, surprised and happy to have company.

"I was just returning a book I borrowed from an office down the hall." She entered the laboratory. "I saw the light on so..."

"I decided to extend my stay for another day," Ricardo said, trying to sound casual.

"What are you working on?" Robin asked. She edged towards Mutt and Jeff.

"Just some experiments I'm doing. I..."

Robin interrupted him. "Are you studying jellyfish reproduction?"

"Reproduction? Why do you say that?"

She pointed to Mutt. "Because he's a he. See the thin white streaks along the bell? He must have spent his sperm because his gonads are hardly visible." Then she pointed to Jeff. "And she's a she. See the faint orange ovaries and pale orange embryos inside?"

Ricardo was stunned and embarrassed. How could he have not noticed that?

"Good observation, Robin. I didn't even think about that." He didn't say more, but his mind was racing. Male and female? "Music" when they were next to each other? Synchronized patterns of spikes? What did it all mean? Sex! Could the "music" be a courtship serenade and, if so, what would happen if he placed two males or two females in the bowl instead of a male and a female?

"Are you going to work much longer?" Robin asked.

Ricardo, preoccupied, hunched over the small pool of jellyfish in another bowl, looking for a healthy male to use for his experiments.

"Hello? Robin to earth. Are you going to be here late?"

"Oh, sorry. I'm not sure." Ricardo wanted to be left alone to get on with his experiments.

"Let me know if you want help to collect more jellyfish tomorrow," she added.

"Thanks. I may need to since the dumb inspector at the airport ruined the rhopalia I'd collected."

Robin waved good-bye as she headed out the door.

Ricardo placed the NASA computer on the bench top and looked with renewed interest at Mutt and Jen—no longer Jeff! He laughed at the preposterous idea that Mutt serenaded Jen when he looked at her. He remembered Lillian working out at the gym wearing a baggy sweatshirt, horn-rimmed glasses, too-long shorts that came to her knees and worn-out sneakers without socks. She had that special something, smiling eyes that coyly suggested riches beneath the surface. Ricardo knew well the magnetic pull between man and woman. But what did anyone know of jellyfish attraction?

What good luck that Robin had come by.

He needed to repeat his experiment with Mutt and Jen to confirm the synchronization of sounds when they were close to each other, and then he would make similar recordings from Mutt and a male jellyfish. He re-inserted the electrodes into Mutt and Jen more or less where they had been and was relieved to be able to repeat the same results as before: the laboratory images on the computer screen turned abstract, the random spike patterns synchronized and the disjointed sounds harmonized when the jellyfish swam by each other.

"Incredible. Great," he said aloud. Repetition of experimental results is crucial and never guaranteed.

Next, he replaced Jen with a male jellyfish. When the two jellyfish swam apart, the laboratory images and random spikes appeared on the computer screen, as expected, and he heard randomized clicks and bleeps. But this time when the two male jellyfish approached one another the patterns of spikes generated from each jellyfish jumped about wildly and were accompanied by screeches rather than harmony.

He wondered whether Mutt's different reaction to a male or female was a fluke. He needed to test the effect of additional jellyfish on Mutt. Therefore, he placed sequentially two different males in the bowl with Mutt, and then two different females. Mutt generated low-level discordant bleeps when confronted with the first male, but exceptionally loud, unpleasant screeching noises in response to the second, larger male. In contrast, Mutt generated soothing sounds when the first female swam by, but remained silent when next to the second female. Puzzling. Why would Mutt react differently to a neighboring jellyfish depending on its gender and something else as well, whatever that was? Its personality? What would Benjamin, who always interpreted data with caution, say about these findings?

Thinking of Benjamin reminded Ricardo that he had at least one dose of Cactein left. "Why not?" he said softly to himself, and then he injected the extract into his thigh.

Ten minutes later Ricardo felt serene and closely connected to his environment as he had the first time he'd injected himself with Cactein. He turned off the lights and imagined the various computer sounds as a jellyfish language. How he wanted to join their society and know what they were saying to each other.

Pulsating jellyfish danced in his mind as fellow living beings rather than experimental subjects. His mind's eye saw Robin's face on a jellyfish. He imagined flirtatious exchanges between two jellyfish as a love duet in an opera, and Mutt and Jen's tentacles entangled in a tender embrace. What a story he had to tell!

Ricardo turned the light back on in the laboratory and fixated on the small orange dots—embryos—that filled Jen's cavity. She

would have released her babies into the mangrove swamp of La
Parguera if he hadn't scooped her up to conduct his experiments. He
thought of Lillian and all her miscarriages and felt sad.

Ricardo nodded off, brimming with questions. How do jellyfish
experience emotions? How do they differ from human emotions? How
do they communicate with one another? He was certain that they did.
What makes a jellyfish like or dislike another jellyfish? What does
"like" or "dislike" even mean to a jellyfish?

8:30 am. Sunlight streamed through the window. Ricardo
rubbed his eyes and stretched, stiff from sleeping on a wooden chair
for a second time in as many nights. He made himself a cup of coffee
using the crusty coffee maker in the laboratory and left a good-bye
note on Harold's desk: "I came back to do a few more experiments.
Sorry I missed you. Please say good-bye to Robin for me. Thanks for
everything."

Ricardo checked out of the motel feeling foolish for having paid
for a room that he didn't use. This time he had no trouble going
through security since he didn't have any rhopalia with him. He
didn't need them. His job now was to publish the results of his
extraordinary experiments. Everything else was on ice.

Chapter 24

After a quick hello to his secretary, Ricardo entered his office. He had generated a rough outline for his article on the airplane and was eager to start writing.

Ricardo's heart sank when he opened his inbox to a long list of emails: a required refresher course with lengthy instructions of what to do and whom to contact in case of suspected terrorism; a reminder to attend the obligatory yearly ethics training; the time and place for the meeting of the Vision Science Center promotion committee; a workshop on how to evaluate laboratory personnel; a high-priority request for a synopsis of his research during the last year for Dr. Topping to incorporate into his report to Congress; instructions on how to write a paragraph of his research contributions during the last year for the development office; inquiries into whether he would review three grants from private foundations and two manuscripts for scientific journals; requests for antibodies and DNA clones that had been made in his laboratory.

He logged out of his email and stared into space, wondering what would happen if he just ignored these emails. He thought of the mangrove swamp, of the jellyfish pulsating in the brackish water, and of Harold, who never looked harried and boasted that he had his priorities in order.

Pearl came by and looked into Ricardo's office. "Welcome back. Have you got a second?"

Ricardo was not in a mentoring mood, but he always gave his students a high priority and asked what was on her mind. She entered the office carrying an X-ray film, pointed to a black smudge on it and said that she had thought—been positive—that the protein it represented would disappear when she fed the corneal cells an oxidizing agent.

"But it's still there," she said, looking disappointed and confused.

Pearl's tendency to insist that her experimental predictions would be realized frustrated him.

"Why were you so sure that the oxidizing agent would get rid of the protein, Pearl?" he asked with a tinge of annoyance. As soon as the words left his mouth, he regretted his tone. Wasn't *he*, too, stretching the interpretation of his jellyfish data?

"Sorry, Pearl. Why don't you raise the dose of the oxidant and repeat the experiment?" He was uncertain if it was the best advice, but he figured that it couldn't hurt. She often neglected to take the time to confirm her experimental results. He arranged to go over her project in detail the following week.

After responding to a few emails, Ricardo called Frank Pizzaro at NASA. He wasn't going to let himself be sidetracked from his jellyfish for long.

"Frank, your computer is fantastic. I have all kinds of data from jellyfish stored in it, but I need your help to get power point slides and hard copies of the data. I don't know how to do that with this program and I don't have the right printer."

"How about this afternoon after three?"

Frank was impressed with Ricardo's results later that day and didn't think that they could be explained by experimental artifact. He thought that the clicking and bleeping sounds that Ricardo told him about—Ricardo hadn't activated the program to store sounds so he couldn't play them back—were "strange."

It seemed to Ricardo that "strange" constituted anything a scientist couldn't explain, like jellyfish congregating at one spot in the mangrove swamp or a cellular protein not disappearing as expected under certain conditions. Everything was supposed to fit within the fragile structure of present knowledge; never mind that so many experimental results and observations that were "strange" initially became commonplace with more knowledge.

At the end of their session together, Frank said, "I don't know what it all means, but overall these data look interesting. I'm impressed."

Impressed. That's what Ricardo wanted to hear. He ignored that Frank also said that he didn't know what it all meant. Ricardo refrained from sharing his idea yet that jellyfish record evolution.

"Thanks," said Ricardo. He put the reams of hard copies they had printed and the small flash drive containing the data in his briefcase and went back to his laboratory, eager to call Benjamin.

"Calm down, Ricardo. I can't follow you. The jellyfish recognize each other and communicate? They see videos of the evolutionary history of the animals they look at? That sounds ridiculous."

Ricardo tried his best to be calm and speak slowly. Lillian had cautioned him many times to let others come to their own conclusions, to not be overpowering.

"Here's the scoop, Benjamin. Frank, the guy who lent me the computer, said that he was impressed with the electronic data. And, by the way, don't tell anyone about the NASA computer. I wasn't supposed to tell anyone about it, but how could I tell you about my experiments if I didn't? I don't think there's any question that jellyfish see images of what's in front of their eyes when they swim. Why have eyes with lenses if you can't see?"

"The lenses could be used to magnify light," said Benjamin. "In any case, I can believe that jellyfish see images. I'm not so sure about the jellyfish interacting or being attracted to each other, though. And the bit about jellyfish seeing evolution; sounds like fantasy."

"Well, maybe, but..."

Benjamin wouldn't let Ricardo finish. "Maybe each jellyfish generates some kind of electric field around itself that affects the images of the jellyfish next to it and different jellyfish generate fields of different strengths, especially under captivity, or even depending on gender. Who knows what's going on?"

"Fine. But couldn't electric fields be the language with which they communicate?" Ricardo recognized that Benjamin had valid points and took note to be cautious when he wrote his manuscript, but he was disappointed by Benjamin's negativity and lack of imagination.

"By the way, I used Cactein when I was in La Parguera. It's quite something."

"Really." Benjamin perked up. "How did it affect you?"

"Just as you'd said. I felt connected with everything around me and especially the jellyfish. It was like I got into the mind of the jellyfish. I actually felt like I *was* a jellyfish. I wasn't stoned or anything like that. It's just that suddenly all my data—the designs on the screen and the synchronizations of the spike patterns—seemed to make sense. I was convinced that there's a lot of interaction going on between these creatures. Cactein allowed me to close the distance between them and me."

"Great! That's what I think Cactein does. It stimulates some yet undiscovered part of our brain that promotes a type of telepathy that may allow us to understand without words what's really there. It's kind of a reception enhancing substance. I think it may have medical potential in psychiatry." Benjamin paused.

"I suppose so," Ricardo said.

"By the way," Benjamin continued, "did you ever add Cactein to the seawater in which the jellyfish swam? Or inject them with the stuff? That would be even better. If they have some kind of brain, as you think, whatever that means in the case of jellyfish, maybe Cactein would affect them too."

Ricardo became silent. "No. I never gave the jellyfish Cactein. I guess I was exploring my ideas about the jellyfish."

"You say you were exploring *your ideas* about jellyfish. I thought you were exploring *jellyfish*," said Benjamin, suddenly sounding aggressive.

Ricardo was taken aback and wondered whether his jellyfish research threatened Benjamin as Cactein had threatened him.

Benjamin continued before Ricardo had time to respond, "Where do you plan to submit your article for publication?"

"I don't know yet; probably *Science* or *Nature*."

Benjamin didn't say anything.

"What do you think, Benjamin?"

More silence.

"*Nature* or *Science*? I don't know," Benjamin finally responded. "What about Cactein? You can't write that up before I do. Also, you told me that you weren't supposed to publish your use of the NASA computer until Frank did."

That was true. He had to talk to Frank about that.

"Don't worry, Benjamin. My article will be only about the data I collected from the jellyfish. Anyway, I hope you'll read it before I submit it. I need all the help I can get."

"Of course," answered Benjamin. "It really does sound interesting."

Chapter 25

Ricardo worked hard for a month on drafting his jellyfish article. He was frustrated that he had promised not to submit the manuscirpt for publication until Benjamin had published Cactein and NASA had formally announced their new computer. Promises were promises, and Ricardo waited. The months dragged on. During the interval Ricardo mentored Pearl, whose research was finally progressing, and he read extensively about brains, including those of invertebrates, and about animal behavior in general. Most of what he read about invertebrates had been published at least twenty years earlier since that kind of basic research had been out of fashion for some time. The more Ricardo learned, the more he became convinced that his experiments would revolutionize ideas about memory and that many other invertebrates were much more than "reactive machines," as Harold had called jellyfish.

Dr. Topping never asked Ricardo about his jellyfish experiments and Ricardo knew better than to try to impress him with the results. It was best to keep a low profile. He had justified his travel requests by proposing to extend his previous research on corneal growth factors and Fuch's dystrophy-associated genes to jellyfish, but he had departed from those stated goals. Also, the political climate had become even more frigid with respect to taxpayer-supported research without direct medical involvment. Likens's news broadcasts had increased from once to twice a week on prime time television. Highly conservative political candidates achieved landslide election victories to Congress and State legislatures throughout the country, and these conservative politicians promised to make certain that "every penny of taxpayer money directly benefit the taxpayer and health." Every research program at the Vision Science Center was connected to at least one common disease. Even rare diseases were not well funded because the cost-to-benefit ratio was too small. Ricardo didn't agree with these politcial trends, but decided to remain quiet until the publication of his article, which he hoped might jolt people back to appreciating basic research.

Benjamin finally published his article on Cactein and NASA theirs on the computer. The idea that Cactein could tap a new brain function that modulated the ability to communicate stirred excitement in the scientific community. The importance of Cactein for understanding brain function and Benjamin's proposal of how Cactein might be used to treat psychiatric illnesses, especially depression, gave him immediate acclaim, and he was elected to the American Academy of Sciences that year.

Ricardo called Benjamin the moment he heard about his election to the prestigious academy. "That's fantastic, Benjamin! I'm really happy for you. You deserve this." He was sincere.

As genuinely happy as Ricardo was for his friend, Benjamin's election to the elite status of the American Academy changed their relationaship. They were no longer professional equals. The balance of power had shifted and Ricardo felt the undertow of the turning tide. Benjamin became friendlier than ever, almost patronizing. As much as Ricardo disliked the subtle tension that popped up now and then when they had been on equal footing, it was preferable to the smooth veneer that developed with Benjamin's elevated professional standing. When Benjamin joked about becoming a member of the "old farts' society," Ricardo laughed but felt a painful wedge between them. There was no way he could retaliate with a "joke" of his own. He became more guarded and conscious of his closest friend having new power to benefit or, potentially, to damage him. Ricardo feared that even a casual disparaging comment about his jellyfish research by Benjamin to a member of the academy—even if Benjamin meant to be funny—might diminish his professional standing. Having his best friend in the limelight and closely connected with the elite scientific establishment was a double-edged blade. While Benjamin's backing was potentially helpful, his glamour raised the personal stakes of Ricardo's jellyfish article, which now loomed as his last chance to reach the lofty height of his friend. The competition nourished his ambition.

And then there was the lingering question of Cactein. Benjamin's publication had eliminated any hesitation for Ricardo to discuss Cactein in his article, but he feared that disclosing its use might shift the focus away from his work on jellyfish to Benjamin. He was also worried that his use of Cactein might damage the credibility of his findings, though Benjamin's article clearly stated that there was no evidence that Cactein caused any hallucinations or delusions, and that it did not operate through any of the known brain receptors used by hallucinogens or other mind-altering drugs such as mescaline or LSD.

"The jellyfish data support my interpretations," Ricardo said when pressed by Benjamin about why he omitted Cactein in the draft of his article. "Isn't that enough?"

"The part about the laboratory images coming from the jellyfish eye is very good," Benjamin said. "But, Ricardo, I worry about how you interpreted the sounds and jellyfish behavior in general. It seems too anthropomorphic. Why didn't you mention Cactein? You did use it. If you discussed what you observed in terms of Cactein, it would make more sense."

"In terms of Cactein? Are you kidding? More sense? Why's that?"

"It would extend my hypothesis that Cactein taps into a new compartment of the brain that facilitates people connecting to each other and their surroundings. Your experiments extend that communication from people to animals. That these animals can be jellyfish is extraordinary. Imagine feeling—believing—that you're in the mind of a jellyfish! That's wild. I bet that these new brain functions affected by Cactein are at the root of a host of mental disturbances. Do you realize the implications? I'd be happy to communicate it to the *Proceedings of the American Academy of Sciences*."

Ricardo did his best to throw cold water on the fury that welled within him at the thought of being Benjamin's pawn. This was *his* turn to shine—*his* idea—and he knew that he had something important, even if it wasn't yet directly connected to alleviating disease.

"This article is about *jellyfish* perception," Ricardo said, trying to re-establish his footing, "just plain jellyfish, those blobs no one really cares about, until when my article is published, I hope."

"You've got to mention Cactein somewhere in the manuscript. It's not honest otherwise," said Benjamin coolly.

Ricardo knew that Benjamin was right, thanked him for his opinion and hung up.

Why didn't Benjamin understand how he felt?

Chapter 26

Knowing that he had to deal with Cactein in some fashion, Ricardo mentioned it in the 'Acknowledgements' at the end of the manuscript with the following sentence: "I am grateful to Dr. Benjamin Wollberg for participation in the early phases of the research, for constructive criticisms of the manuscript, and for the gift of Cactein that was helpful in assuring strict alertness during a few observations that lasted throughout the night." Ricardo figured, with reservation, that this was an honest declaration of his use of Cactein. He also thanked Paul Sing for "advice" and Frank Pizzaro for "the invaluable NASA computer."

Benjamin exploded when he read the dismissal of Cactein in the final draft that Ricardo planned on submitting for publication. "Strict alertness during a few observations at night? You've got to be kidding! What do you think Cactein is, a cup of coffee? Cactein sharpens insights. It's revolutionary. You should make a point of that in the manuscript."

Ricardo tightened his jaw and squinted, a habitual facial expression when he was controlling his anger. Hadn't Benjamin got the message that he wanted to stress jellyfish—*his* story—not Cactein?

Benjamin backed off. "Look, Ricardo, I think you have a lovely article. It's original, bold. What can I say? It's provocative in a positive sense. But, really, think about it. Cactein would enhance your article and tie it to a new concept of human brain function without taking any attention away from the jellyfish. Don't you see that?"

Of course Ricardo saw that, which was the problem. Cactein would significantly enhance Benjamin and his research, especially given Benjamin's new visibility. But he couldn't tell Benjamin that he was jealous of him, that he wanted equal recognition. How could he admit that? It was the same dilemma he had when he couldn't tell Papi years ago that he wanted to win a Nobel Prize. Some secrets just can't be exposed.

"My article isn't supposed to be 'lovely', as you say, or about Cactein," Ricardo said. "It's about jellyfish and the evolution of memory, including new concepts of memory. I need to stress that."

"Who else have you shown this article to?"

"Actually no one but you," Ricardo admitted.

"Well, give it to Frank Pizzaro or Pearl, although she might be too intimidated to say what she really thinks. See what someone else thinks."

Benjamin was right. He gave the article to Frank Pizzaro and Paul Sing. A week later Paul got back to Ricardo and two days after that Frank called. They each had different reservations, which was what Ricardo had feared would happen.

Paul, who had a bent for the humanities, thought parts of the article were scientifically interesting but in general it was too "novel-like."

"Novel-like?" Ricardo was baffled.

"I know that sounds strange. The writing is exquisite, unusual for a scientist, almost too good, as odd as that sounds, and it's very broad. It makes me think that you were more concerned with the prose than the science. The title is an example: *Jellyfish: Shedding Light on the Dark Matter of Evolution, Emotion and Memory*. The word 'jellyfish' will attract biologists, ecologists, and even laymen with interests in marine animals, but 'shedding light' makes it unclear whether it's an experimental, theoretical or philosophical article, and equating jellyfish with 'dark matter' confuses biology with astronomy or perhaps even spirituality. 'Evolution, emotion and memory covers just about everything! What specifically is the article about?"

Ricardo listened patiently though he thought these were absurd criticisms. "What about Cactein?" he asked finally.

"Cactein? Oh, yeah. You mentioned that in the Acknowledgements. That's Wollberg's cactus compound, right? It was featured recently in the New Findings column in *Nature*, wasn't it?"

"Yes."

"Really fascinating stuff. You could stress that more, but I don't know much about Cactein."

Ricardo thanked Paul for his input.

Frank had a different opinion. "I liked *some* of it, but..."

"But what?" Ricardo asked.

"I liked the section where the jellyfish see images of their surroundings. Who would have guessed? Jellyfish! Your data convinced me that it was true. Isn't that a great computer? You could have emphasized its novelty now that it's published."

Ricardo ignored the fact that Frank, like Benjamin, saw the world in his own terms. After all, he, Ricardo was no different. And he agreed that the data showing that jellyfish see images were rock solid. Benjamin thought so too.

"But," Frank continued, "the parts about jellyfish recognizing one another and interacting...well, I think those ideas are a stretch."

"It is pretty amazing though, isn't it?" Ricardo said, feeling pride rather than thinking he should remove those ideas from the manuscript. "What about the jellyfish seeing evolution?" he asked.

"Are you really planning to keep it in the article?"

"Sure. That's..." Ricardo, once again, remembered Lillian's cautions for him to listen more. He had asked for Frank's opinion, and now he should listen to it. He didn't have to change the manuscript if he didn't want to. He had gathered the data honestly through experimentation with no preconceived expectations and was surprised himself by the results. He expected his conservative peers to balk at the notions that jellyfish interacted with each other and visualized evolution. Those were new concepts. They would reject anything that elevated jellyfish above a glob of protoplasm and water.

"That's what?" asked Frank.

"Helpful," Ricardo answered. "Thanks for reading the manuscript. I'll think about the comments and try to address them."

Ricardo didn't know what to do. Paul said it sounded too much like a novel, Frank wanted to highlight his computer and scrap the parts about jellyfish interacting and visualizing evolution, and Benjamin wanted to advertise Cactein. He decided to show it to Pearl after all. She was young but smart. He hoped that since she wasn't a seasoned scientist she wouldn't be threatened by political realities and she wouldn't focus on tooting her own horn.

"Oh, yes, I'd love to read your manuscript," Pearl said the next day. "I'm flattered. I'll read it tonight."

Ricardo smiled. "Tonight's fine. Thank you, Pearl."

The next day Pearl said that she loved, absolutely loved the article. "It's so well written and amazing," she said. "Why do you think that the jellyfish congregate only at one spot in the swamp? And they're attracted to each other. How great is that!"

"What about the evolution part, Pearl? What do you think about jellyfish seeing evolution?"

"It's a very imaginative interpretation of the data. I don't know. It's certainly new, but I admit, it's hard to understand how it works. Do you really think it's true?"

"I think so, yes. And Cactein. You know, the cactus extract that my friend Dr. Wollberg discovered that I used a couple of times. Were you concerned about that?"

"Was Cactein in the article? You used it?"

"Just a tiny bit. I mentioned it in the Acknowledgements."

"I must have missed it. I don't know anything about Cactein. Is there a problem with it?"

"No. Benjamin claims it just sharpens the senses to what's there."

"Oh. In any case, I think your article is very interesting and should give people a lot to think about."

"Thanks, Pearl."

That afternoon Ricardo overheard Pearl saying that his article was "wildly imaginative" and she hoped that one day she would be able to do "fun stuff" like that.

Ricardo modified his manuscript by emphasizing the speculative nature of his interpretations that jellyfish interact with one another and visualize evolution. However, he maintained that these concepts were new, potentially important and should be studied further. He then asked Benjamin if he would take one more look at the article, since his was the only opinion that Ricardo really respected.

"I'm just trying to interpret my data in a creative way," Ricardo told Benjamin, who still thought that Ricardo should limit his article to jellyfish seeing images. "For centuries no one believed that the earth goes around the sun just because it looked like the sun went around the earth. Last century, scientists were shocked when they discovered that individual genes comprised disconnected DNA sequences. A gene made up of bits and pieces contradicted everything they thought then, but it turned out to be the case." Ricardo was struggling to draw the thin line between being stubborn and being persistent.

"Come on, Ricardo, it's hard enough to get anyone to even pay attention to jellyfish today. Don't you think it's better to play it safe? Why give anyone the ammunition to hurt you or to further disparage basic research?" Benjamin was speaking as a friend, not a scientific reviewer.

Ricardo sighed. "You're probably right, Benjamin. I know the problems today." He hesitated. But despite everything, Ricardo believed that jellyfish were much more complex than anyone ever imagined, that his data *did* suggest that jellyfish interacted with one another, and that it was possible that they stored memories in ways that were completely foreign to scientists. And why couldn't jellyfish have memories of evolution? Wasn't DNA a repository of past evolution, and wasn't it possible that these memories could be expressed as "memory genes"? If he was correct, he wanted full credit, and the only way to achieve that was to publish it first. At his age, opportunities were running out.

"Look, Benjamin, maybe I don't have it quite right, but there's something important going on with these jellyfish. I'm convinced that jellyfish have a brain of sorts. Of course we don't understand them yet. How could we? We hardly know anything about any species that live in niches that are uninhabitable by us. I used the latest computer technology available and I had no preconceptions. I'm just making an interesting story with the data I've obtained. I haven't made up anything. If a few people don't believe my story, so be it. But I can't imagine that there wouldn't be a lot of scientists who are interested in it, and they should be. All science is made up of stories created from observations and data, and all these stories are modified in time with new information. Science isn't just a collection of so-called facts. Science is a work in progress. I can't tell you what the jellyfish story will be in the future. But I can say that my jellyfish story begins a new chapter, and I predict that the story will be a page turner."

Ricardo was resolved. He couldn't have said it more directly. He may have had his quirks, but he wasn't stupid or naïve. He was an honest scientist studying Nature, and he'd been doing it for a long time.

Benjamin looked with soft eyes at his friend. "I know, Ricardo," he said. "And I'm with you." He hadn't forgotten how much Ricardo had impressed him with his imagination and enthusiasm—his humanity—when they first met many years ago, and Ricardo was still the man he was then. He had that genius for seeing past the details.

"It *is* a fascinating article," said Benjamin. "And I agree that you've toned down the speculations. Let's see what happens."

As much as Ricardo wanted his jellyfish work published in a prestigious scientific journal, he didn't ask Benjamin to communicate it to the *Proceedings of the American Academy of Sciences*. He shied away from leaning on Benjamin's success for his own advancement. Pride. Vanity. Envy. Maybe all three.

The editors of both *Science* and *Nature* returned the manuscript within a few days of submission claiming that it was of insufficient general interest. The editors of the highly regarded specialized journals *Cell* and *Neuron* thought the work premature for publication. *Brain Research*, a relatively new journal, stated that it was more suited for a less specialized journal or for a journal devoted to marine biology. One reviewer wrote, "Does the author truly believe that jellyfish have brains? It would be difficult to come to that conclusion without appropriate controls. And what would such controls be?" All the reviewers complained that the article had no medical significance. As for jellyfish visualizing evolution: "quite ridiculous" seemed to be the consensus.

The one criticism that Ricardo found substantive was the lack of experimental controls. However, the reviewer himself seemed unsure what would constitute a proper control for these experiments. One could test the effect of a drug by comparing experimental results obtained with the drug and without it. But what does one compare to determine whether a jellyfish is attracted to another, or whether a jellyfish is visualizing evolution? In addition, controls could be misleading. For example, many stimuli can activate an unfertilized egg in the absence of spermatozoa, but that doesn't mean that a spermatozoon isn't the natural activator of embryonic development.

Disappointed but not defeated, Ricardo decided to submit his manuscript to *Observation and Discovery*, a widely circulated, popular journal for laymen that was often read by scientists. It was quickly accepted for publication.

The ambiguity of the title, elegant prose and imaginative ideas in Ricardo's article attracted diverse readers. Word of the article spread like wildfire in a windstorm among the nonscientific community. However, it seemed to Ricardo that his peers ignored the article. The publication never came up in conversations and he received no emails of acknowledgement or requests for further information as he usually did after he'd published an article. Ricardo rationalized that his colleagues, who prided themselves on being overworked with no time to spare, hadn't seen his jellyfish publication. But his greater fear was that they had read the article and dismissed it. Whatever the truth, being ignored was painful.

Chapter 27

The months following Ricardo's jellyfish publication passed with neither storms of protest nor waves of interest. His beloved jellyfish hadn't rocked the world.

"Let sleeping dogs lie," Benjamin advised Ricardo when he was in Washington for the annual meeting of the Academy.

They were having dinner at Le Vieux Logis, an atmospheric French restaurant that had been in Bethesda forever, when Benjamin surprised Ricardo. "You know, Ricardo, I was kind of hard on you before you published your jellyfish work. I'm sorry I was so skeptical. I feel badly about it."

"Really?" Did he mean this, or was Benjamin, who was sailing on professional success, just trying to give him a boost?

"Really," said Benjamin. "I'll tell you something else. I was envious of your courage. I mean, bucking the establishment, allowing your imagination to roam, expressing yourself as a true artist as well as a scientist. I've always respected that in you."

Ricardo thought of his long-dead mentor, Vince Salisbury. He missed him. "It didn't get me very far. Maybe I was just born at the wrong time."

"Just wait. You never know. Remember your father's premature realism hypothesis?

"What do you mean?"

"Maybe your ideas are correct, but just premature. Sometimes ideas are ahead of their time. Premature. We didn't become humans by the wave of a magic wand. We evolved from somewhere. Remembering and thinking and feeling must have started long ago. Your evidence, and it is evidence of sorts, that jellyfish contain the seeds of higher brain activity in some form...is ...I don't know...*bold*. You've opened the door. Nothing is clear right away. Ideas evolve just like life evolves. I admire you and your work, Ricardo. I really do. You've got guts and imagination."

Ricardo was speechless. His eyes moistened. Benjamin was a loyal friend. He loved him. If only he could tell him that.

Instead, Ricardo said, "Well, you did the same thing, with your cactus and Cactein. Congratulations to you."

"I was lucky."

Ricardo didn't respond.

"So, are you going to pursue jellyfish?" Benjamin continued, as he cut another morsel from his duck entree. "We still don't know how they would respond to Cactein."

"True. Do you want to collaborate on that?"

"In principle, yes, naturally. But...well...I'm very busy. I'm writing two grant proposals, have ongoing research, and two clinical trials with pharmaceutical companies to see what effect Cactein has on depression and bipolar disease. Also, the grandkids are taking up a lot of time, and Mattie says...."

"I get the message," interrupted Ricardo. "Maybe I should retire when Pearl leaves. She's doing great. Her work might be useful for treating wounded corneas. Who knows? After she reported her findings at the regional eye conference, she received three job offers from industry and two from medical schools."

"What's she going to do?"

"She's mulling it over. She's funded to stay another year in my laboratory, which she might do. Marcus was excited about her results when I met with him to discuss the budget. He asked me to write a paragraph on her work for him to present to Congress."

"Corneal problems are a lot more sellable than jellyfish!"

"I know. But, you won't believe this."

"What?"

"When I was in Topping's office, guess what I saw on his desk?"

"The Bible."

Ricardo laughed. "Not quite. A copy of *Observation and Discovery*. It was open to my article, and he had even underlined some parts."

"Are you sure?"

"No doubt. So I mentioned it to him."

"Yeah. What did he say?"

"That he had read my article...twice... and..."

"Twice? And what? A little faster, please."

"And...why the hurry?" Ricardo liked teasing Benjamin after all those years of friendship.

"And," Ricardo stalled again to take a sip of water. "He liked it. He said it was imaginative, brilliantly so, and that I was a trendsetter. He seemed to be sincere. He told me that he collected worms as a kid and always wondered whether they thought about anything. He even knew about Darwin's book on worms. Life is full of surprises."

"That's fantastic, Ricardo."

"That's what drives me crazy about Marcus," Ricardo continued.

"What's that?"

"His petty need for power infuriates me, but then when we're together, he's friendly and intelligent and I like him. It's schizophrenic!"

Benjamin shook his head. "Complicated, eh?"

"There's more."

"Go on."

"After we chatted for a few minutes, he said that he wished he could fund larks like my jellyfish. Larks! Can you believe it! I looked up 'larks' in the dictionary. One of the definitions was 'silly games'. Another was 'mischievous play'. Silly! Mischievous play! He said that as Director he had social responsibilities. So there you are."

Benjamin let Ricardo vent.

"In any case, I'm not even sure what I would do next with jellyfish." Ricardo paused. "Thanks for listening, Benjamin. I appreciate it."

"Talk of listening, want to hear the latest gossip?"

"Always."

"Your first mentor, Richard Winelly, remember? Mister squeaky clean, married with four kids. He's having an affair with Linda McElroy.

"Who is Linda McElroy?"

"You don't know? She's the young woman who works on Gilbert's disease. She just got into the Academy."

"Really," he uttered without much enthusiasm, more to cover his sense of insignificance for being repeatedly excluded from the inner circle than for caring about whom Winelly slept with or Linda what's-her-name's career.

"The dinner's on me," Benjamin volunteered when the waiter brought the check.

"Let's do it fifty-fifty," insisted Ricardo, and he whipped out his credit card.

They split the check. Benjamin went back to his hotel and Ricardo went home wondering how Cactein would affect jellyfish and how old Linda McElroy was.

She was 42 years old.

Chapter 28

Benjamin emailed Ricardo as soon as he returned home from the Academy meeting and asked Ricardo to call him when he had some time to talk. It was important.

"So, what's this all about, Benjamin?"

"It's Randolph Likens, the rabble-rouser with the television show, Your Money/Your Health."

"What an asshole." Even Likens's name drove Ricardo crazy. "He's determined to abolish basic research, but he's not the first opportunist to go on a witch-hunt. So, what's new about him?"

"My colleagues at the Academy are pretty nervous. People are angry beyond reason about the economy, and 'angry people' translates into votes. Likens is gaining traction with the politicians. He's dangerous."

Benjamin didn't make it a habit to speak negatively, so Ricardo listened carefully.

"In other words, Ricardo, don't dismiss Likens too quickly."

Ricardo, well aware of the prevailing anti-scientific attitude, couldn't believe that many people in the United States didn't even believe in evolution.

"It's scary, Ricardo. Have you been following Henry Wiggler's campaign for re-election?"

"He's your Representative in Minnesota, isn't he?"

"Correct. Listen to this."

Benjamin told Ricardo how Wiggler had berated basic research in a campaign speech. "The audience cheered when Wiggler accused basic scientists of misusing federal funds. His campaign slogan is 'War on Fraud'. When he was finished everyone started chanting in unison: 'War on Fraud, War on Fraud'. It was frightening."

"War on fraud?"

"I'm worried, Ricardo. Didn't I warn you about traveling to La Parguera on laboratory funds? Collecting jellyfish in Puerto Rico could be made to sound like a vacation at government expense. You're not exactly a household name. None of us are. But you're well known in the field of vision, and you're an established government scientist. You could be an ideal target for Likens."

Ricardo remained silent. Was it possible that he really was in trouble?

"And listen to this, Ricardo. Wiggler said that he supported Likens in his effort to curb irrelevant research."

"What's *irrelevant* research?" Ricardo asked, tightening his grip on the telephone receiver.

"I think you get the sense of it."

"Is cactus research irrelevant?"

"Come on, Ricardo. You know we're doing clinical trials to see if Cactein can be used as a treatment for depression. How much more relevant can that be? Besides, I never used government money to collect cacti or anything like that."

Before Ricardo could respond, Benjamin softened. "Look, I'm on your side. I think we might be gravitating from funding to even greater difficulties. I'm not a prophet, but you might begin to think of a response if Likens starts harassing you."

Of course he could rebut Likens. What was the world coming to when a credible scientist was afraid to seek answers to important biological questions?

"Ricardo? Are you listening? Say something."

"What do you mean, 'greater difficulties'?" Ricardo said, becoming worried that he knew the answer, but looking for reassurance that 'greater difficulties' wouldn't be that bad.

"I don't know, Ricardo. Bad publicity, maybe even legal problems. It's like we're at the water's edge on a shallow beach and high tide is rushing in."

Ricardo's hands trembled. In truth, he had no idea how to prepare for the possibility that Likens might target him. That couldn't happen, could it? He hadn't done anything wrong, had he?

Chapter 29

Ricardo hoped that Benjamin was overreacting to the threat of Randolph Likens. Then one day while he was in the restroom stall, Ricardo overheard two postdoctoral fellows talking.

"Hey, Adam, did you see the editorial in the *Washington Post* today about basic science?"

"Who's got time to read all that stuff?"

"It was about government funding for research."

"Oh, yeah?"

"Some guy called Likens said that there should be more oversight of basic scientists. Apparently he's on a rampage about wasting government funds on irrelevant research. He targeted two biochemists at the University of Utah who went skiing using their grant money, claiming that they were planning experiments."

"They were pretty dumb to try a stunt like that in this economy."

"You're right. But, you know Ricardo Sztein down the hall?"

"Of course."

"His postdoc, Pearl, told me that he went to Puerto Rico on some research project on jellyfish, and he concluded that they see evolution, or something like that. It sounded weird. He published it in some lay journal I've never heard of. *Observation and Discovery*, I think. Anyway, Sztein came to mind when I read the editorial by Likens in the *Post*."

"Strange. But so what? I'd go to sunny Puerto Rico too if I were in his position. I admit he seems strange and a bit reclusive. I seldom see him at seminars. I guess he's getting old. Pearl is doing pretty interesting stuff though on the cornea. Maybe he'll retire soon."

Strange? Reclusive? Old? Retire soon? When Ricardo returned to his office, he read the *Washington Post* article online. It was even more damning than Adam had said. The last paragraph praised Wiggler and his 'War on Fraud' and predicted that the Utah scientists were just the beginning. Likens accused basic scientists of "rampant dishonesty," and he called what they did with taxpayer money "outright stealing." The last sentence of the editorial jolted Ricardo: "It's time to prosecute scientists for outrageous expenditures of taxpayers' dollars on obscure, irrelevant scientific projects."

Ricardo called Benjamin right away.

"I know," Benjamin said. "I read that editorial in the *Star Tribune* today."

"Do you still think Likens will target me?" Ricardo asked in a thin voice. He had finally understood the serious nature of Benjamin's concern.

"Maybe you should discuss it with Dr. Topping. After all, he approved your trips to La Parguera."

"Maybe. But, I don't want to give the impression that I feel guilty." Ricardo didn't believe he'd done anything wrong, yet he had to admit that he had stretched the justification for his last trip to La Parguera.

"You know I'm one hundred percent in favor of basic research," said Benjamin. "Your jellyfish stuff is original and potentially important. But I'm not the person you need to convince. You've got to be careful, Ricardo. The ivory tower has crumbled."

Two months later Ricardo found a thin envelope from the U.S. Department of Justice in the mailbox when he came home from work. The blood drained from his face and his knees weakened. With a heavy sigh he opened the envelope. A subpoena ordered him to appear the following month at the courthouse in Baltimore for a Grand Jury hearing on the misuse of taxpayers' money. The nightmare had come true.

Ricardo was too rattled to speak to anyone right away. The next morning he looked up Grand Jury proceedings on the Internet. Due to their rising numbers, Grand Jury trials—most on tax evasion charges—had been simplified. It didn't require a great deal any more to conclude that there was enough cause for a criminal trial. The prosecutor was often an Assistant United States Attorney as in the past, but that Attorney could now designate another lawyer in his place to avoid delays. Witnesses were used sparingly since those who were indicted reserved them for the criminal trial, should it be necessary. The questioning generally took no more than one or, occasionally, two days. Some said that Grand Jury trials had eroded into kangaroo courts.

Ricardo called Benjamin.

"My god, Ricardo, that's horrible news. Despite my fears, I never believed that you would actually be targeted. I just thought that you should be on guard for vultures like Likens. I'm sure that you'll be cleared. You're a serious scientist with so many accomplishments. And your jellyfish basic research is...what can I say...mind blowing, in a good sense. I'll vouch for you. You can count on me."

"Thanks."

"I mean it," Benjamin said. "You know that. Do you have a lawyer?"

"I know one. David Lass. He was helpful to Lillian and me some time ago. I'll consult him."

"Good. Keep me posted, okay? Good luck, old friend."

Although David Lass was about to retire, he agreed to help Ricardo since Grand Jury trials had become notoriously short. Ricardo requested a leave of absence from the Vision Science Center to prepare for the trial.

"Of course," said Dr. Topping. "I'm sorry you have all this trouble. I look forward to your speedy return.

"I hope so," Ricardo said meekly. Then, remembering Benjamin's advice to test Dr. Topping's loyalty, Ricardo asked if he would be willing to stress that his trips to Puerto Rico were approved on the basis of their scientific validity.

Dr. Topping clenched his jaw and narrowed his eyes. "I had no problem with your initial trip. That was clearly an extension of your corneal research, even though it involved jellyfish. I approved the second trip, perhaps too quickly, because you said the work was progressing well and that you needed more jellyfish samples to complete the job. However, to be honest, I was skeptical.

Ricardo wondered why Dr. Topping felt he needed to specify when he's being honest.

"As for the third trip," he continued, "I was out of town when you made the request. It was approved by my assistant. When I returned it was too late to do anything about it. I certainly didn't expect your research to venture into such unsubstantiated speculations."

Dr. Topping's tone was cold and disturbing, and it left Ricardo uncertain as to the extent to which the Vision Science Center would support him.

For the next few weeks Ricardo prepared for the upcoming trial—or "inquisition" as he called it—with David Lass. David instructed Ricardo to link his motives to medical issues as much as possible, rather than to argue for the importance of basic research. Ricardo said he would try his best. He had sleepless nights and lost seven pounds.

When the day of the Grand Jury trial arrived, Ricardo went to Baltimore with David, consumed by anxiety and suppressed rage, petrified one minute, confident the next. The prosecuting attorney was a man in his thirties at most who had been appointed by the Assistant United States Attorney. Ricardo didn't know if it was a good or bad sign when he overheard the prosecuting attorney say to a colleague, "I don't expect this to take very long."

When the hearing began the young prosecutor showed a stern face. "We understand, Dr. Sztein, that you traveled to La Parguera in Puerto Rico three times to collect jellyfish eyes: once in June two years ago, once in May of last year, and then again in July of this year. Is that correct?"

"Yes, sir."

"Beautiful resort, La Parguera. To study jellyfish eyes, correct?"

"Yes again."

"Fascinating, that jellyfish have eyes."

Ricardo nodded. He noticed that several members of the jury appeared interested in the fact that jellyfish had eyes. So far, so good, he thought.

"And the Vision Science Center paid for the trips?"

"Correct," Ricardo answered in a low voice, remembering Benjamin's concern about his having used government funds for the trip.

"To advance your studies on Fuch's dystrophy of the cornea?" The prosecutor had done his homework.

Ricardo wiped sweat off his forehead with the back of his hand and explained matter-of-factly that he was looking for evolutionary precursors in jellyfish to the Fuch's dystrophy-associated genes that he had identified in mice.

"Did you find these precursors?"

"It's not easy to identify genes conclusively," Ricardo said evasively.

"I'm sure. Did you continue to look for these genes in the subsequent trips to La Parguera?"

"Yes, but even more interesting questions surfaced." Ricardo was now sweating profusely. He considered giving details, but David had told him not to say anything more than direct answers to the questions.

The questioning continued. "These more interesting studies were about jellyfish perception and memory?"

Ricardo scratched the scar left by Mulligan on his hand, a nervous tic. "New questions always arise in basic science. Yes. I made exciting observations suggesting that jellyfish have a type of brain and memory." He stalled for a moment. "Unexpected observations often lead to progress."

The prosecutor frowned. "Progress? What progress did you make from your trips to La Parguera?"

"It will take more research to follow up on my observations, but they open new vistas for research. However, now I'm busy on my corneal research with mice, which has medical implications for treating corneal injuries," he said, trying to influence the jury that he was interested principally in medical research.

"So the jellyfish research didn't go anywhere. Is that correct?"

Ricardo shook his head slowly from side to side and looked at the jury. "New opportunities are progress, sir. It takes time, often years."

The prosecuting attorney walked across the room gazing at the floor, rubbed his chin and changed the topic. "Why did you choose to go to La Parguera? Couldn't have you have obtained the jellyfish eyes at the Baltimore aquarium? That would have been much closer and less expensive."

"The Baltimore aquarium? I don't believe they had the species of jellyfish with complex eyes—those are eyes with lenses and corneas—that I needed. Not all jellyfish have complex eyes, sir. They're almost exclusively restricted to cubomedusans, and some of these are found in the mangrove swamp of La Parguera. A different jellyfish species with a dangerous toxin and complex eyes exists in the Great Barrier Reef in Australia, but that would have been much more expensive to pursue. And, Harold Freeman, an expert on jellyfish on the faculty at the La Parguera Marine Station, kindly offered to help me collect cubomedusan jellyfish in the mangrove swamp."

"Is Harold Freeman a professor at the University of Puerto Rico?"

"Yes, sir. He's not published much so he's not well known, but he has lived in Puerto Rico a long time."

"Not published much. I see. A long-time resident in La Parguera."

Ricardo sighed, exasperated that he couldn't answer any question in a way that the prosecutor didn't twist to make it sound unreliable. He glanced at David, who moved both hands, palms down, to tell Ricardo to relax.

"Yes, sir," said Ricardo in a calm voice. "Harold Freeman is originally from Nebraska. He married a Puerto Rican woman and remained in La Parguera."

"Did you travel to La Parguera by yourself?"

"My colleague, Dr. Benjamin Wollberg from the University of Minnesota Medical School and a member of the American Academy of Sciences accompanied me on the first trip." Ricardo hoped that Benjamin's prestige would help his case.

"Did his medical school fund his trip? Or did the American Academy of Sciences?"

Ricardo hesitated. "No. He paid for it personally. Dr. Wollberg's research is less connected with jellyfish than mine."

"And the jellyfish eyes that you collected: you analyzed them in your laboratory at the Vision Science Center with federal research funds. Is that correct?"

"Yes, sir. All the research in my laboratory is funded by the government."

"You must have found *something* interesting since you returned to La Parguera twice to obtain more rhopalia."

Ricardo was impressed that his inquisitor knew about rhopalia, but he was at a loss to explain the nature of his research to someone who had no clue of how research is actually conducted and expected quick results.

"Dr. Sztein?"

"Yes, sorry. I have found one jellyfish gene that shows a partial relationship to one of the two mouse genes that I showed are associated with Fuch's dystrophy."

The prosecuting attorney turned away and said in a low voice, "*One* gene, *partially* related." Then he faced Ricardo again and asked, "Is Dr. Wollberg still involved in your jellyfish research in any way?"

"He's very busy with many postdoctoral fellows and he travels a lot giving lectures and doing things for the Academy."

"I see," said the inquisitor. "He's tied up with his responsibilities and commitments."

"Yes, sir."

"Just curious, Dr. Sztein, how similar is a jellyfish eye to a human eye?"

"It looks remarkably similar and seems to share many biochemical properties for vision, but of course it does have differences. For example, both humans and jellyfish have transparent lenses, but the main proteins in the lenses, which are called crystallins, are different in humans and jellyfish."

Ricardo suddenly regretted he'd mentioned the differences in crystallins between human and jellyfish lenses. David had warned him about saying anything more than necessary.

The prosecutor picked up on Ricardo's error. "So would you say that you're stretching the connection between jellyfish and humans?"

"No, sir. Many species have different crystallins in their lenses, whereas most of their other eye proteins are conserved and their eyes are quite similar."

"Conserved?"

"The same, not changed significantly during evolution."

"I see. But..."

"May I continue, please?" said Ricardo, and then without waiting for the answer tried to make up for his error of mentioning lens crystallins and attempted to connect his jellyfish research to humans and medicine. "It's very interesting that crystallins differ in many species, including jellyfish. The comparative analysis might teach us something about the range of properties that are required for the functions of crystallins. That would be helpful in treating or, better yet, preventing human cataracts."

"Perhaps. But at what cost?"

Ricardo shrugged. "Hard to estimate costs until you know more. That's the nature of basic research, sir."

"Let's get back to your experiments in Puerto Rico. Is it correct that you poked jellyfish eyes and nerves with electrodes to figure out if jellyfish remember and recognize each other? It sounds a bit far-fetched to me," said the prosecutor in a more aggressive tone.

"Far-fetched! Certainly not!" retorted Ricardo. "I was exploring fundamental questions of biology. Jellyfish are at the base of the evolution of higher animals, including humans, although admittedly they may be an ancient branch of the evolutionary tree."

Once again Ricardo wanted to kick himself for saying more than necessary. How could non-scientists appreciate the complexity of evolution when many of them, incredibly, didn't even believe in evolution?

Ricardo continued in a calmer voice. "I'm confident that jellyfish will bring new insights to many unanswered questions relevant to medicine. All major advances in biology have stood on the shoulders of so-called 'simple' systems. None are really simple, of course. For example, bacteria have opened the door to understanding gene regulation in animals, including humans. We have a tendency to minimize the relevance of organisms that we don't know much about. We shouldn't confine our research to the same few species or ask the same questions over and over again. How would we learn anything new if that's all we did?"

Ricardo felt pleased with this response. He had said what he believed.

"Well, what exactly did you learn that was new, Dr. Sztein? I'm still trying to understand that."

"In a nutshell, my research indicates that jellyfish are far more complicated than ever imagined, and that they see images, interact and, possibly, visualize evolution. Visualizing evolution—well—that would be revolutionary, an entirely novel, genetically encoded visual memory. Imagine! The possibility must be explored further."

"It sounds a bit like shooting bullets in the fog, doesn't it? Can you give an example, or at least speculate, on something useful, medically or otherwise, that might come from your jellyfish research? We're not scientists."

Ricardo wanted to ask the prosecutor how he expected the jury to judge his science if they weren't scientists. Instead, trying to remain cool, he said, "Basic research is gaining fundamental knowledge that physicians and other scientists can use clinically or apply in whatever way they see fit. No one person can do it all." Ricardo knew that his answer sounded trite and not specific enough to satisfy the prosecutor, but it was the truth after all, or at least how he saw it.

The prosecutor waited for more, so Ricardo reluctantly went on. "Who knows, understanding exactly how a jellyfish eye works may give insights for treating blinding eye diseases. Or, the ability of jellyfish to see evolution, if true, might reveal animal relationships that allow us to choose more relevant animal models to investigate human diseases than we do now."

Ricardo sat up straight and looked directly at the prosecutor, trying to appear more in control than he felt. What else could he say? That he had a specific plan for applying his jellyfish research medically? He didn't. Therefore, he looked directly at the jury and said in an authoritative voice, "Jellyfish are living in a different conceptual universe than humans. We need to explore that biological universe just like astronomers explore the galaxies." That had to suffice. How could anyone not understand that? He looked at David for support. David smiled back faintly, but broke eye contact quickly.

The prosecutor scratched his head.

Ricardo, submerged under a wave of insecurity, thought of Lillian and Benjamin, the two pillars in his life warning him to be careful. He was despondent that no one seemed to see the obvious importance of his jellyfish research.

The prosecutor scribbled a few notes and then changed the subject. "Let's get back to money, Dr. Sztein, which is why we're here. How much did all your jellyfish research cost the Vision Science Center?"

"Not much, relatively speaking. Considering everything—research and travel—I'd say $30,000 to $50,000, give or take a bit. That's a very small portion of my laboratory budget."

The prosecutor nodded and changed the subject once again. "Why did you choose to publish your jellyfish research in *Observation and Discovery*? Your other articles were published in more scholarly scientific journals."

Suppressing his frustration about this point, Ricardo explained that some journals didn't think enough readers were interested in jellyfish. "That's a shame for science," he said. Then he added, "Sometimes it's necessary to make a bold leap to jump a huge chasm of ignorance and journals don't like to take that risk."

"And Cactein, Dr. Sztein? Could that have influenced your conclusions?"

Cactein again. Why did he even use it?

"Dr. Wollberg, the discoverer of this remarkable compound, concluded that it is not hallucinogenic. Anyway, the computer data are the source of my conclusions, and that's independent of Cactein."

Ricardo had to endure several more hours of grilling. The prosecuting attorney repeatedly brought up laboratory expenses. He also questioned Ricardo about the reasons for choosing to study jellyfish in the first place and whether he planned on continuing jellyfish research. Ricardo said he did not, but the prosecutor didn't seem convinced.

Ricardo was glum as he and David drove home.

"What do you think, David? Did I do all right?"

"Many of your answers were on the mark. It's hard to tell what the jury will conclude."

Ricardo didn't respond.

"It's a tough situation, Ricardo. It's best not to second-guess a jury."

"I'm worried. What happens if I'm indicted?"

"You know that. There would be a court trial. This would have never happened a few years ago. But today…" David stopped.

"What about today?"

"It's ugly for academia and the ivory tower of the past. If only the economy would rebound. Anyone found guilty for misuse of government funds gets a mandatory sentence of ten years. It's ridiculous, I know. I certainly hope the Grand Jury doesn't find cause for a criminal trial."

Ricardo rubbed the small of his back that ached more than usual. They drove the rest of the way in relative silence.

The next day the Grand Jury indicted Ricardo for misuse of government funds.

PART III

Chapter 30

Ricardo paced back and forth in his living room for some time stewing about the Grand Jury verdict and then called Benjamin, who virtually shouted on the phone. "I can't believe that you are going to trial! I never thought that it would come to this. Likens! Obnoxious! Dr. Topping will come to your rescue. He can be irritating, but I've heard him praise your work many times."

"I don't know, Benjamin. It looks bleak. Following up your suggestion before the Grand Jury trial, I asked Marcus if he would support me since my trips to La Parguera were approved."

"What did he say?"

"It was more how he said it. Cold as ice. He told me that he approved the first trip since I had said that the purpose was to extend, although loosely, my previous work on the mouse corneal hormone and genes associated with Fuch's dystrophy."

"Fair enough."

"Then when I had told him the work was progressing but I needed more jellyfish samples, he said that he approved the second trip, but reluctantly.

"And what about the third trip?"

"He said that he wouldn't have approved it if he had been in town. He wants to cover his ass, not mine. He may change his mind, but I'm not optimistic."

"Messy."

"An ambitious and ruthless journalist I can comprehend," Ricardo said. "There're always people like Likens. But how could a Grand Jury of laymen cast judgment on my research and conclude that I'm fiscally irresponsible? After all the years that I've run my laboratory on budget."

Discouraged and angry, Ricardo called David Lass as soon as he said good-bye to Benjamin.

"Well, David, we'd better start thinking about what to do next. My trial starts in three months. We need a new approach. Basic science by itself doesn't seem to carry much weight these days."

"There's a mean streak out there for sure, and a desire to find people to blame for the state of the economy," said David.

"What can we do?"

"I can't do anything, Ricardo."

"What do you mean?" Ricardo was stunned. He felt the rug being pulled out from under him.

David told him how much more time a criminal trial would take than the Grand Jury trial, and how he had promised his wife that he was going to retire. He couldn't take on a new, complicated case, not now.

"Can't I twist your arm? I don't know who else to turn to."

"I just can't do it, Ricardo, but I can recommend another lawyer."

"Go ahead."

"My daughter Sophia has been employed by Backus, Smith and Runner for a few years and is up for Partner pretty soon. She's smart and loves interesting, ambiguous cases. She's got the instincts of a maverick. I'm sure that your case would interest her. I bet she would really throw herself into it. Why don't you talk to her? You have nothing to lose."

David was right: what did he have to lose by meeting her?

Sophia Lass greeted Ricardo with a cheerful, "Hello!" when he arrived at her office two days later.

Sophia was transparently natural, genuine. She was roundish, diaphanously so, and diminutive, no taller than Ricardo's nose. She wore a blue-green cotton dress hemmed just below the knees; her sturdy feet stood in flat, black leather sandals. Mother of pearl-rimmed spectacles framed her eager green eyes. Her arms swayed fluidly from relaxed shoulders.

Ricardo liked her looks, but smiled internally at the ridiculous notion that she reminded him of a jellyfish. He told her about his dilemma, and she sympathized with his plight: an idealistic scientist unfairly attacked in the autumn of an admirable career.

When Ricardo said, "Why don't people understand that knowledge comes first and relevance later, not the other way around?" she rebounded without hesitating, "Because they're ignorant. It will be our job to educate them."

Ricardo liked that answer.

She continued. "I'll study your article on jellyfish, but I'm not a scientist. You'll have to tell me in plain language, not jargon, why you think your jellyfish work has medical relevance. That's the problem, isn't it? Medical relevance? We need to find the medical connection between your research on jellyfish and the ailing taxpayer."

"Of course my work is relevant." Ricardo didn't notice Sophia cringe when he said that.

Sophia noticed him looking at the rows of law books covering a broad array of legal issues in her bookcase. She said that she liked diversity and challenging cases.

"Well, mine is challenging," he said. "So where do I go from here, Ms Lass?"

"I think your case is interesting and important. I have some time right now if..."

"...if I hire you?" finished Ricardo.

Sophia lowered her eyes. "I'd do everything I could. You're talking about academic freedom versus so-called social responsibility. You need a philosopher as much as a lawyer. These are subjective issues, not legal ones. I'm amazed that you're in this pickle. Perhaps I could understand if the Vision Science Center threatened to limit your laboratory budget or something like that. It seems more like an internal matter than a criminal case. It feels to me like you're a scapegoat for our miserable times. Unemployment is approaching twenty percent. And people are worried to death about all the sickness popping up. I know I am. It *is* scary! I don't know, Dr. Sztein...may I call you Ricardo?"

"Please do, Sophia." He liked her fire. "Do you think my case is hopeless?"

"It's a tough one all right," she said. "But nothing is impossible." She smiled gently. "You've got a lot going for you. I confess that I checked you out on the Internet before our appointment and was impressed. You've published hundreds of articles, won awards—the LeBlanc Prize, the Melon Medal. You're clearly a well-known, respected scientist. I can't believe that there's such a fuss over this."

"I agree," Ricardo said. "I didn't do anything wrong."

"Also..." She paused.

"Also what?"

"Also you seem like a nice guy, honest. Personal impressions are important in jury cases, especially when the law is fuzzy."

"Thanks."

Sophia continued, "But nice is not enough. I keep thinking of Stan." She pointed to the photograph on her desk. "My husband. He's a geologist for a big oil and gas company. He loves rocks as much as you love jellyfish and the nicest guy you ever want to meet, but he'd be fired in a heartbeat if he went off to some mountain to satisfy his curiosity about something or other at his employer's expense, even if he believed that the company might eventually profit from his trip."

"My situation is different. The Vision Science Center gave me permission to travel to Puerto Rico to do my research. They approved my trips. I didn't just go off on my own. I have all the paperwork in my files," Ricardo countered.

"That's good. Do you think we could get your Director to back you up?"

"Marcus Topping? Good luck! When I talked to him about that, he made it clear that he wouldn't stick his neck out far. He told me that my research in La Parguera didn't follow the course I had said it would. That's a lame excuse. Everyone knows that new questions always come up in any basic research project. If my Grand Jury trial taught me anything it was that it's almost impossible to make a layman understand the nature of basic research. In any case, I think that Dr. Topping is more concerned about protecting himself than protecting me."

She nodded.

Ricardo looked around the office, his mind playing ping-pong with his conflicts. Time was short and he wanted to get started on his defense, which he could do if he hired her now. But she was young. Lillian—always practical—would have advised him to try and find a more seasoned lawyer. However, he liked Sophia, liked her realistic but positive outlook. She seemed smart, and she seemed eager to have the job.

Settle down, he told himself. He was an honest scientist with a solid track record who'd done nothing wrong. If he trusted his intuition it didn't mean that he was being irresponsibly impulsive.

"How much do you charge, Sophia?"

"My company has a minimum charge of $350 an hour. It would be a lot more if I were a partner."

Ricardo thought that he had enough savings to afford that. Of course he didn't know how many hours his case would require. But at his age and with no one to inherit his estate, what difference did it make? A more senior lawyer would cost more and not be necessarily better.

He extended his hand and said with more confidence than he felt, "Sophia, let's beat the system together!"

She beamed; they shook hands.

"You did what?" said Benjamin on the phone the next day.

"You heard me. I hired Sophia Lass as my lawyer."

"A thirty-something woman still wet behind the ears? What were you thinking?"

Chapter 31

Ricardo and Sophia prepared their defense during the three months before the trial. She studied his research and laboratory budget. "You should've paid for the La Parguera trips yourself," she told him on several occasions, echoing Benjamin. He realized that now. She expressed concern about the equipment he'd purchased and wondered whether they were for his regular work or for his jellyfish experiments.

"Both," he said. "I've got to keep up with the latest technology."

"You're very imaginative," she said when he wove different aspects of his research into fascinating stories, but she reminded him that it was critical to address the *relevance* of his work and to find credible witnesses to support that.

And so it went from day to day. He remained optimistic, she cautious. He taught her science, she stressed the need to find links between his jellyfish research and medicine. There was no single scientific or legal argument that could convict or acquit him. The subjective line between judgment and law was blurred.

The morning the trial began Ricardo and Sophia sat side-by-side at a rectangular table between the elevated bench of the judge in front and the gallery of spectators behind. The jury sat in two rows on the right side of the front of the courtroom, below a window.

The federal prosecutor for the Justice Department, Mr. Carl Jenkins, and his assistant sat at a table next to Ricardo and Sophia's. In his mid-fifties and a shade over six feet tall, the prosecutor had penetrating blue eyes, a round face, ruddy complexion and dyed brown hair. A muscular build supported his pressed, pin-striped, navy blue suit. He wore a baby blue shirt with a white collar and a sky blue bowtie. He had a brilliant, gold-embedded sapphire ring on his left pinky.

Ricardo leaned to Sophia, who was busy assembling her notes. He whispered, "He's a study in blue, like a Picasso painting."

Everything seemed polished about the prosecutor except for a tic causing the right corner of his mouth to move in synchrony with a twitch in his right eye, a consequence of mild hemi-facial spasm. He sat behind a pile of documents, a notepad, two ballpoint pens and a laptop computer, and was very busy consulting in hushed tones with his assistant.

Ricardo surveyed the spectators. Loyal Benjamin, who insisted on coming to support his friend throughout the trial, sat in the second row. He smiled and clasped his hands together at chest height to wish Ricardo good luck.

Ricardo recognized Randolph Likens in the back row of the spectators. Likens was thinner than he looked on television, his face more drawn, his demeanor less threatening. A closed laptop rested on his knees. He looked almost bored as he waited for the trial to commence.

There were at least a dozen other journalists chatting among themselves in the back of the courtroom. It had become possible and fashionable for reporters to attend trials involving fiscal matters. Nonetheless, Ricardo was baffled that *his* trial had attracted so much attention.

A sense of anticipation permeated the courtroom. Butterflies fluttered in Ricardo's stomach. He twisted around in his seat and glanced at Benjamin again for reassurance, as a child clings to his blanket for security. Oh, Benjamin, Benjamin, Benjamin, so many years together. Benjamin was Ricardo's honorary, and only, family.

The judge entered the chambers. "All rise," said the bailiff. When the judge was seated, the stenographer exercised her fingers, preparing to transform words into recorded history, fragments into narratives.

The opening statements began. The prosecutor started off by saying, "Dr. Sztein holds a high position of responsibility and heads a prestigious, well-funded government laboratory in the Vision Science Center, which has a clear mandate to seek treatments for eye diseases. For many years," continued the prosecutor, "Dr. Sztein has lived up to that responsibility. Therefore, let me be clear: Dr. Sztein is being tried only for his jellyfish research in which he ignored both his stated research proposal and the mission objectives of the Vision Science Center." He then said in a professional, serious voice, "The court will show that Dr. Sztein squandered taxpayer dollars to pursue personal rather than public interests."

The prosecutor went on to describe in painstaking detail Ricardo's jellyfish adventure: that he had made three trips to La Parguera to study jellyfish at government expense; that the trips had been approved because he had falsely claimed that his research would be confined to an extension of his previous, medically relevant work; that his research had wandered off to jellyfish behavior without clear direction or goals; that he had concluded, as preposterous as it sounds, that jellyfish interact, have brains and see evolution; and, finally, since the professional scientific journals rejected his article he resorted to publishing his research in a lay journal designed more for entertainment than serious science.

After delivering this summary, the prosecutor allowed a few moments of silence to let the jury digest what he'd said. He then continued by belaboring his earlier accusation of fiscal irresponsibility: "It is the State's opinion that, even if the dollar amounts involved were not enormous, Dr. Sztein is guilty of squandering taxpayers' money on his jellyfish research and betraying his obligation to support the medically relevant mission objectives of his Center. Our citizens depend on the government to *serve* them, not to *exploit* them."

The prosecutor took a deep breath, shook his head disapprovingly and added slowly and with venom, "Frankly, I find it reprehensible when so many are struggling financially, for a government scientist mandated to search for ways to treat dreadful diseases to have the gall to satisfy his own whims, to vacation by the seaside and play with *jellyfish*. For those unfortunate souls who expired from diseases that may have been treated successfully if research scientists like Dr. Sztein had stuck to their job...well, it's like they have been *murdered* by neglect."

There was a collective gasp from the audience.

Finally, with flair befitting an evangelist, the prosecutor ended by saying, "J-*e-l-l-y-f-i-s-h*," pronouncing each letter equally, "are *not* human beings."

Murmurs rippled throughout the courtroom and many spectators nodded in agreement.

Ricardo glanced at Benjamin who shook his head in disbelief.

Sophia's opening comments comprised an eloquent appeal for common sense and justice. She called Ricardo a devoted scientist and an artist. "The boundaries between art and science can be fuzzy," she said. "They both involve creativity." Sophia referred to Ricardo's long and impressive list of publications in prestigious scientific journals and emphasized the recognitions he'd received for medical research, especially the widely acclaimed LeBlanc Prize and Melon Medal. She argued that to convict Dr. Sztein was to punish creativity and limit scientific progress. "How would *that* benefit the country?" she asked. "Would *that* be justice?"

She next surprised Ricardo by considering Galileo's fate as an example of what can happen in a close-minded society repressing creativity. Sophia's eyes glistened as she told the jury how that great scientist first saw earth-like craters on the moon, discovered small satellites orbiting Jupiter and rings around Saturn, and figured out the movements of celestial bodies. "Where would we be today if such advanced thinkers and risk takers did not see further than the mainstream of their times?" She ended boldly: "Galileo's courage to explore the heavens changed mankind. Certainly no one today would support his prosecution by the Church."

Ricardo was embarrassed but flattered to be compared to Galileo.

There was an uncomfortable silence when she finished. Her footsteps sounded mechanical against the wooden floor when she walked back to her seat.

"Galileo?" Ricardo whispered in her ear. "Isn't that extreme?"

"Shh, not so loud!"

"Yes, but...."

"People need to be reminded of past mistakes. No one will buy simple logic. They need something to rebel *against*, in this case history."

He scrunched his brow pondering her point, but he was worried. Ricardo fixed his gaze on the tabletop to avoid attracting attention, but he couldn't help sneaking a peek at the members of the jury. They remained poker-faced, except for one middle-aged woman in the second row who had a softer, more sensitive expression. She had a distinctive white streak dividing her black hair into two halves. Ricardo hoped that she might be on his side.

"Black and white," he muttered under his breath looking at her hair and wondering why everything must be black or white. What happened to gray?

Although the trial had just begun, Ricardo was overcome by fatigue.

Chapter 32

The first two witnesses for the prosecution were Congressmen whose knowledge of science was limited to sound bites useful for re-election campaigns. Richard Thomas was a junior Senator from Oklahoma and Sandra Biggs was a seasoned Representative from Utah.

"Here we go," mumbled Sophia, when the politicians began their testimony.

Thomas and Biggs testified as predictably as a machine clicks on when the start button is pressed. Both witnesses gave statistics for the number of people suffering from various forms of cancer, the high percentage of fatal heart attacks and the lack of treatments available for Alzheimer's disease, for muscular dystrophy, for multiple sclerosis—the list was extensive. Thomas showed pictures of a ten-year-old boy in a wheelchair, bald from chemotherapy. He had died of cancer the week before. Biggs showed a video of an older woman with ALS lying in a hospital bed surrounded by doctors in spotless white coats. The doomed patient was trying to respond to her tearful husband by blinking her eyes, the only motor function she had left. Both the Senator and the Representative stressed that not only have these horrible diseases plagued people for centuries, new diseases were sprouting up at high frequency and creating havoc. "This level of medical ignorance is unacceptable in the mid-twenty-first century," said Senator Thomas, almost shouting, his eyes wide. Representative Biggs riveted the jury by listing medical catastrophes within the last year: the blindness epidemic in Detroit; the mysterious cases of paralysis afflicting thousands in Indonesia; the dysentery affecting approximately a quarter of the population in the Caribbean Islands; one hundred times the usual number of pancreatic cancers in France; the devastating respiratory flu threatening financial collapse in Sweden because thirty percent of the population remained trapped at home, either sick or too afraid to leave the house. The problem was not restricted to the United States. It was international and the United States had a responsibility to lead.

Biggs concluded by emphasizing that it was imperative to fund research that would ultimately reduce the strain of medical bills on taxpayers. "Scientists have a moral responsibility. Government-funded research with no clear medical direction or tangible benefit to society—jellyfish research, for example—is a travesty." She paused for effect. "Is *that* justice?" she concluded, mocking Sophia's introductory remarks.

"No's" were sprinkled throughout the audience.

"Quiet!" said the judge.

One fat man on the jury set his jaw and shook his head, leaving no doubt as to his agreement with the Representative.

When Sophia asked in her cross-examination of Representative Biggs for examples of medical advances that had resulted from basic research in the last twenty-five years, the prosecutor pounded the table and said, "Objection, your Honor. The witness is not a scientist or a physician, and the question does not relate to her testimony."

"Agreed," said the judge.

When Sophia asked for the source of their statistics, both witnesses claimed that it was "common knowledge."

"I've read countless letters from stricken patients and their families," said Senator Thomas.

"It's heartbreaking," said Representative Biggs. "I'll never lose the image of six-year-old Pamela, who should have had her life in front of her, as she gasped her last breath in her mother's arms, her eyes bulging, her face paler than eggshell, unable to breathe due to a lake of mucus in her lungs. When you see these patients—victims—you understand. My god! This must not go on! The millions of taxpayer dollars given to research must help the taxpayers!"

The spectators, glued to their seats, nodded in agreement.

The testimonies were featured in national news broadcasts on television that evening. The next day the headlines in the NY Times read: "Millions for Research, Heartbreak for the Sick."

Chapter 33

The audience at Ricardo's trial the next day overflowed as a consequence of the newspaper headlines and television coverage. Eager reporters lined the back of the courtroom. Randolph Likens was among them, his trusty laptop in hand. Marcus Topping, the Director of the Vision Science Center himself, was about to testify. The tension was palpable. The angry spectators wanted blood, a beheading, a scapegoat. For the government, the trial was a chance for public redemption for the poor economy. A guilty verdict would assure the electorate, "We're on your side. We understand. We too have had enough. Your money must be used to help *you*."

Dr. Topping ignored Ricardo as he passed him on the way to the witness stand. Why wouldn't Marcus look at him? Was he shielding an attack, a planned sabotage? Typically Dr. Topping walked with a loose stride; now his gait was stiff with short steps, and he wore polished black shoes instead of his usual athletic canvas shoes.

"He looks severe," Ricardo whispered to Sophia, who would have had no way to discern these differences from Dr. Topping's normal appearance and behavior.

After taking the oath, Dr. Topping sat down and glanced self-consciously at Ricardo. He passed his hand along the side of his head making sure his impeccably combed hair was in place, and adjusted his wire-framed glasses on the bridge of his nose. He placed one hand on the railing of the witness box and then quickly put it on his lap, twitching his fingers. Ricardo was impressed by how quickly Marcus's insensitivity could be replaced by an apparent vulnerability, more worried about being judged than judging. Ricardo found himself furious at Dr. Topping one minute and sorry for him the next. His job wasn't easy.

Ricardo looked at the juror with the contrasting silver streak in her coal-black hair. What was it that drew him to her?

The prosecutor walked slowly to the witness stand and began his questioning. "When did you become Director of the Vision Science Center, Dr. Topping?"

"Approximately twelve years ago."

"Could you please tell the court your credentials?"

"Certainly. I performed biomedical research for ten years after my medical fellowship in ophthalmology, published sixty-two articles on glaucoma and was a Professor at Yale Medical School before being appointed Director at the Vision Science Center."

"Very impressive, sir. How long has Dr. Sztein worked for the Vision Science Center?"

"Dr. Sztein was recruited as a Laboratory Chief some forty years ago, long before I came on as Director. He has remained in that position ever since. He has published many research articles, reviews and book chapters. I don't know how many publications he has. Hundreds."

"Do you have a cordial relationship with Dr. Sztein?"

"I think that we're on very good terms." Dr. Topping winked at Ricardo, who groaned inwardly at the inappropriate familiarity. "We have lunch together when we can, although we're both very busy. He's conscientious and helpful, at least when he's in town."

"He travels a lot?"

"I would say so. I'm told he often went to Australia when he was doing research on platypus. That was before I was Director, of course."

"Objection," cried Sophia. "Where Dr. Sztein traveled some fifty years ago is irrelevant."

"Objection sustained," said the judge, who instructed the prosecutor to confine his questioning to the period under consideration.

The prosecutor pointed out that he was establishing a pattern of behavior consistent with the defendant's character, but the judge stood his ground and said that the trial was restricted to Ricardo's misuse of government funds for his jellyfish research, not his character.

The prosecutor's words, "pattern of behavior," slipped into Ricardo's mind like a spider disappearing in a crack between rocks. Was his previous research on the esoteric platypus part of a pattern of behavior? No one objected to that over forty years ago. But that was then, the golden years of curiosity; now was the demise of curiosity-driven scientific creativity—and in Ricardo's opinion, the blinding of personal vision. The judge may have temporarily slowed the prosecutor's attempt to attack Ricardo's character, but would that stop it from influencing the jury?

Dr. Topping continued. "Recently Ricardo has traveled to Puerto Rico for his jellyfish work, as you know. He attends meetings all over the world and took a fair number of vacations before his wife Lillian died."

Lillian? What did she have to do with anything? Why would Dr. Topping bring up vacations and Lillian? Anyway, there weren't many vacations, not nearly as many as Lillian wanted.

"Has the Vision Science Center paid for these trips as well as the research?" asked the prosecutor.

"Of course not his personal vacations. Otherwise, yes, unless the organization that invited him paid, which was generally the case."

"And his laboratory budget: is it high?"

"It used to be several million a year. The Vision Science Center supported many postdoctoral fellows in his laboratory throughout the years, a full time technician and a facility where they mutate genes in rat and mice to study eye development, cataract formation and various corneal diseases."

Ricardo felt a flash of pride.

Dr. Topping continued: "Lately, however, his budget has shrunk to six hundred thousand a year due to restricted funds. Also, he's slowing down."

The prosecutor returned to his table, looked at his notes and whispered something to his assistant, who seemed to agree. He then walked back to the witness box.

Dr. Topping sneaked a glance at his watch, making sure that everyone noticed. He was a busy man, the Director, ambitious.

So was Ricardo, still ambitious.

The prosecutor stood tall. "The taxpayers are angry about the economy and government waste. Do you believe that Dr. Sztein is aware of his social responsibility to the taxpayers who pay his way?"

"Of course I am," Ricardo whispered to Sophia.

"He's aware, naturally. But I believe he can be—how to say it—more passionate than compassionate sometimes."

Ricardo's heart skipped a beat. Be compassionate, Lillian had said. Help others. You're a scientist. Her ghost wouldn't die.

"How is Dr. Sztein more passionate than compassionate, Dr. Topping?" The prosecutor asked slyly.

"He gets more carried away with jellyfish vision than with human blindness."

"I see," said the prosecutor, looking at the jury.

Benjamin squirmed in his seat.

Dr. Topping continued. "I know that jellyfish have eyes, and so do scallops and snails; Dr. Sztein taught me that—and it *is* interesting. But is that *compassion*? Do those creatures go blind? Do they suffer? Even if they did and we could treat them, what good would that do for humans? We're not veterinarians." Hints of laughter sprinkled throughout the audience. "There's only so much money these days. It's no secret that there has been a surge in diseases in the last few years. Why is that? We *must* prioritize." Dr. Topping paused for a moment and then added with conviction, "We each have a social responsibility." He looked down at his shiny shoes and then said calmly, almost to himself, "I wonder if Dr. Sztein really believes that Congress cares more about what jellyfish see than why people go blind?"

Ricardo leaned towards Sophia. "How dare he say I'm not compassionate? I'll tell you who lacks compassion: him!"

"Ricardo, quiet!" Sophia whispered, straining to keep her voice low. The prosecutor's assistant glanced at Sophia.

Ricardo continued, "*He's* the blind guy. He can't see what's good for the Vision Science Center or for the advancement of science for that matter."

The judge glared at Ricardo.

"Sorry, your Honor," said Sophia.

"Damn," grunted Ricardo louder than he'd intended. He couldn't hold it back any longer.

"For God's sake, Ricardo," Sophia pleaded.

The prosecutor continued. "So you have trouble defending the *relevance* of Dr. Sztein's research, Dr. Topping?"

"Well, the truth is, somewhat. I think that he does too. For example, when I asked him what he was going to tell the Scientific Priorities Committee that reviews his laboratory every five years, he said he was going to bring up his idea of studying jellyfish eyes. His principal justification was that almost no one—and that includes scientists—even knows that jellyfish have eyes, and that it was important to learn as many of Nature's secrets about vision as possible if we wanted to be trailblazers in the field. He was right that few know about jellyfish eyes. I didn't know that, but..." Dr. Topping paused in midsentence.

"But what, Dr. Topping?"

"But when I asked him what was the medical relevance of his jellyfish project he answered, 'that's for the physicians to tell me' or something like that. Frankly, I was upset, but I kept it to myself."

"*Did* he tell the reviewing panel about his jellyfish ideas?" asked the prosecutor.

"He might have mentioned jellyfish at the end of his presentation. I don't remember."

Ricardo leaned towards Sophia and whispered, "He can't remember, although it upset him so much?"

"Hush, Ricardo," Sophia cautioned.

"Are you saying that Dr. Sztein down-played his plans to study jellyfish from the reviewing committee? That he tried to hide his intentions for future research?" asked the prosecutor.

"Objection!" Sophia's face was red. "The prosecutor is drawing conclusions that the witness didn't make and is leading the jury in a false direction."

"Sustained," said the judge.

The prosecutor looked at the jury as if he was a confidante to them. He then asked Dr. Topping, "Is there anything else you would like to add about Dr. Sztein before we conclude?"

"N-o...not really. Well...there is one thing I might mention, but maybe it's a bit peripheral."

Ricardo sat up in his chair, curious what Marcus was about to say now. Sophia picked up her pen in preparation to record what bombshell she expected Dr. Topping to deliver.

"Yes. Go on." urged the prosecutor.

The judge interjected, "Dr. Topping, you don't *need* to say anything more. You have already answered the prosecutor's questions."

Anticipation gripped the room.

"I understand, your Honor," said Dr. Topping.

The prosecutor moved closer to the witness stand, closing the gap, as if he was preparing to receive a confidential disclosure.

Randolph Likens cocked his head so as not to miss a word.

"I'll be concise," said Dr. Topping. "In the last round of grant submissions to the Vision Science Center I've heard that a significant handful of junior scientists referred to Dr. Sztein's article and proposed to follow up on some of his ideas. That's bizarre since Dr. Sztein's jellyfish publication was in a lay magazine. I doubt we will fund those grants, but the funding panel was surprised and concerned—alarmed—because the proposals came from the promising young scientists who are the wave of the future."

This was good news to Ricardo. Apparently his jellyfish article had invigorated basic research, especially for up and coming scientists.

"It appears to me that Dr. Sztein has unwittingly undermined the mission of the Vision Science Center. He 'steals', as it were, the best and brightest away from treating human disease. It's worrisome. This isn't the twentieth century anymore. It's 2051. People need medical treatments. Too many years have elapsed since the recombinant DNA revolution of the last century and the promise of miraculous genetic therapies, without clear successes." There was a note of sincerity in Dr. Topping's voice.

Was Dr. Topping seriously accusing him of undermining the Vision Science Center by 'stealing' young scientists, that he was being held responsible for what junior scientists he never met put in their grant requests? Ricardo thought that this was absurd.

"That will be all, Dr. Topping. Thank you."

Reporters typed feverishly on their laptops. Spectators exchanged glances of community solidarity. Ricardo wiped off trickles of sweat decorating his forehead with crumpled Kleenex.

Marcus glanced at Ricardo with a look of sadness on his face when Sophia got up for her cross-examination.

"Let's start with your last statement, shall we, Dr. Topping," Sophia said sweetly. "Do you have any reason to think that Dr. Sztein tried to influence anyone to write grant applications connected with his ideas?"

"No."

"Have you read these grant applications?"

"My colleagues on the funding panels have told me about them."

"So, Dr. Sztein is hardly 'stealing' anyone away from anything, wouldn't you say. Doesn't stealing require intent?"

"I was speaking metaphorically, of course. We have a mission—a social responsibility—to perform research directly relevant to human disease." Dr. Topping looked annoyed.

"Speaking metaphorically. Yes. Thank you for clarifying that, Dr. Topping. I understand." This time it was her turn to look at the jury. "Let's return to jellyfish," she continued. "You said that you *thought* Dr. Sztein *might* have mentioned jellyfish at the end of his presentation. It's ironic that you cannot remember. Can you remember what Dr. Sztein did talk about?"

"Certainly. He reported his research on the growth of corneal endothelial cells, and then a bit about the lens and cataract. He also speculated about the genetics of Fuch's dystrophy. His studies always concerned the front of the eye—the lens and cornea—rather than the retina, where the crucial photoreceptor cells for vision are located."

"You mean he explored the window of the eye that bends the light in order to focus images on the retina so we can make sense of what we see? I thought that any disorder that makes the cornea or lens—that window—opaque leads to blindness, and that's one of the major causes of blindness worldwide. Correct me if I'm wrong, Dr. Topping. I'm not a scientist."

Ricardo was pleased that he had taught her well.

"You are correct," Dr. Topping conceded.

"Sounds quite *relevant* to medicine to me," she added. "No light on the photoreceptors, no vision. Right?"

Sophia was smart, just as her father had said.

"I didn't say that Dr. Sztein's research *never* had *any* medical relevance. He's a good scientist. We supported him for years. I thought this trial was specifically about his misuse of federal funds for his *jellyfish* work."

"I agree, Dr. Topping. Dr. Sztein must be a very good scientist who does medically *relevant* research or the Vision Science Center wouldn't have supported him for so long, or he wouldn't have garnered numerous honors, like the prestigious LeBlanc Prize and Melon Medal. These honors do bring distinction to the Vision Science Center, don't they?"

"Yes indeed. We're very proud of him."

"Very proud. Yes. We all are proud of Dr. Sztein's many accomplishments."

Sophia paused a moment and then added as if an afterthought, "Just one more question, Dr. Topping. Could you estimate the percentage of research projects that are targeted to answer specific questions about a disease that actually lead to treatments?"

This question impressed Ricardo. He had never thought of asking the question quite like that. There's power in numbers.

Dr. Topping cleared his throat.

"That's very hard to answer. Researchers build a collective network of information. Every relevant project adds to that network in one way or another. Medical treatments evolve from this structure."

"Interesting. Medical advances come from a collective network of information. I suppose that such information often must come from unexpected sources. Is that correct?"

Some jury members nodded. Others just looked on without expression.

"That's correct," said Dr. Topping.

"Please clarify your point, Ms Lass, or stop this line of questioning," interceded the judge.

"I'm trying to reconcile how 'a collective network of information', to quote Dr. Topping, is assembled without gathering nodes of basic information that aren't immediately relevant but ultimately prove crucial for medical application, your Honor. In other words, how is collecting a network of information different from basic research?"

Dr. Topping fidgeted in his seat. "We're not against basic research. We're all for it. Dr. Sztein's first excursion to La Parguera was worth the risk and I approved it. But then he went astray from his original proposal. I don't need to repeat it all—jellyfish vision, jellyfish interactions, and so on. He drifted away from his stated goals. Certainly none of the other scientists at the Vision Science Center have picked up on it."

"But you told us earlier that a number of the promising young scientists *have* picked up on Dr. Sztein's ideas in their grant proposals."

Dr. Topping didn't react.

"Thank you, Dr. Topping, that will be all."

This time Ricardo didn't care that Marcus walked out without looking at him. He was troubled, however, when he noticed that Sophia's hand was shaking when she took a sip of water.

Chapter 34

After the trial adjourned for the weekend Ricardo and Sophia went together for a pizza dinner. Ricardo thought that Sophia's cross-examination of Dr. Topping had scored points for them, although Sophia complained of "bad vibes," but couldn't explain exactly what she meant. However, they were both cautiously optimistic that the coming week might tip the jury in their favor. Two of Ricardo's students were going to testify on his behalf. The first was Ann Silvan, who had been his best postdoctoral student fifteen years earlier. Exceedingly bright, she now held an endowed professorship at Dartmouth. The other witness was Pearl. After Ricardo's students, Benjamin was scheduled to testify. Ricardo expected Benjamin's prestige and loyalty to be enormously helpful for his case.

The judge called the court to order on Monday morning at nine sharp. Dr. Silvan went to the witness box, placed her hand on the Bible and swore "to tell the truth, the whole truth and nothing but the truth, so help me God." She wore a modest black wool skirt, gray blouse and Haida silver bracelet that she had bought in Vancouver when she was a postdoctoral fellow in Ricardo's laboratory. If Ricardo had had a daughter, he would have wanted her to be like Ann.

Ann projected authority and confidence as she sat in the witness box. She was one of the leading figures in eye research with a specialty in retinitis pigmentosa, or RP, as it was known. Sophia started by having Ann recount her excellent credentials and professional accomplishments, which were impressive: full professor at 39, almost 100 publications in the most prestigious journals for eye research, and keynote speaker at numerous international conferences.

"Do you think, Dr. Silvan, that your experience in Dr. Sztein's laboratory was an important influence for your future success in *medical* research?" asked Sophia.

"Very much so."

"Could you please summarize for the court what it was like in Dr. Sztein's laboratory?"

"Objection," said the prosecutor. "This trial concerns Dr. Sztein's research on jellyfish, not the research he did previously."

The judge paused for a moment and then overruled the objection. "Technically, you are correct, Mr. Jenkins, and I did sustain Ms Lass's objection when you were trying to establish the defendant's character through his patterns of behavior. The present question, however, is not about character but about the defendant's influence on postdoctoral students, which has been raised as a relevant issue. Please answer the question, Dr. Silvan."

Ricardo was happy with the judge's call. Maybe he was on his side after all.

Ann went on to talk about her postdoctoral years. She insisted on calling him Ricardo rather than Dr. Sztein. "He's just that way," she said. "Very warm and personable." She reported that his laboratory had bustled with research activity and enthusiasm virtually around the clock when she was there, that it was a very stimulating scientific center, that he was deeply engaged in all the projects and that he made sure that all his postdoctoral fellows published articles to advance their careers. She published four articles as a postdoctoral fellow with him, all on gene expression during early development of the embryonic mouse eye.

"And this training prepared you well for your career in *medical* research?"

"Absolutely. Especially for gene therapy, which I'm working on now." She looked in Ricardo's direction and half-smiled at him.

When Ann was giving her testimony, Ricardo doodled designs resembling double helices on a piece of scrap paper, relieved to have her support. The woman with a white streak in her hair had her eyes closed, and the jury foreman was staring out the window. Several spectators were whispering to each other. And Likens was gone! Where was he? Had he heard any of Ann's testimony? Was he coming back? When? Apparently, that Ann liked Ricardo, that he was a serious scientist and a good mentor, was boring and not worth noting. If positive testimony didn't exonerate Ricardo, what would?

"Thank you, Dr. Silvan, that's all the questions I have." Sophia went back to the table and touched Ricardo on the shoulder as she sat down.

The prosecutor sauntered to the witness stand to cross-examine Ann. "You like Dr. Sztein a great deal, don't you, Dr. Silvan?" he asked in a thin voice.

"Yes, very much so. He's a wonderful person and mentor."

"It seems so, doesn't it?" said the prosecutor, still using that thin, quiet voice so that a few spectators cupped their ears with their hands to hear.

Ann fidgeted. The jury perked up. Likens reentered the courtroom.

Then the prosecutor continued in a fuller voice that commanded attention. "But the defendant's nice *character* is irrelevant, isn't it Dr. Silvan?" He glanced quickly at the judge. "We're here to determine whether he fraudulently used federal funds earmarked for medical research to study jellyfish." He paused. "And jellyfish are *not* relevant to human disease."

Sophia objected, stating that the prosecutor had no basis for concluding whether jellyfish were or were not relevant to disease.

"Sustained," said the judge.

"All right," said the prosecutor, who then turned his back to the judge and told the jury in a soft voice, "I guess I don't know a jellyfish from a human being."

Just when Sophia raised her hand to object to the prosecutor's arrogant remark, the judge intervened. "Please limit off-the-cuff comments, Mr. Jenkins."

Ricardo was furious. Why didn't the judge insist that the jury disregard the prosecutor's inappropriate comment and threaten him with contempt of court?

The prosecutor continued harping on the same theme, returning to his thin, prissy voice. "Dr. Silvan, you made it clear that Dr. Sztein is a nice person and that you had a good rapport with him. But *nice* really has nothing to do with this case, does it? A wonderful person can misuse funds, wouldn't you say?"

Ann stiffened, but didn't reply. The veins in Benjamin's forehead protruded, his ears were scarlet, and his jaw clenched.

The prosecutor changed the subject. "You said that there were a number of different research projects in Ricardo's laboratory when you were a student. Is that correct, Dr. Silvan?"

"Yes, sir," she said.

"With all these diverse projects, were any directly relevant to disease, like glaucoma or cataract or other eye disorder?

"Everyone worked on his or her own ideas. Ricardo was supportive and always said that diversity is a strength." She then added, "I believe that too, strongly."

"No specific goal? Just trying this and that because it was...*interesting?*"

"Ricardo always assured us that someone would use new knowledge for medical advances. He said that we couldn't do everything. The important thing was to do what we did well."

"I guess that's right. No one can do everything. But I suppose everyone can do *something* helpful to those individuals paying the bills."

"Objection!" Sophia blurted out, "Mr. Jenkins's opinion on the medical relevance of the projects in Dr. Sztein's laboratory many years ago has no value."

"Sustained," said the judge. "The jury must disregard the prosecutor's suppositions."

The prosecutor glanced at the jury and shrugged his shoulders. "One more question, Dr. Silvan. Why did you change your research to retinitis pigmentosa—RP as you call it—when you started your own laboratory?"

"All beginning independent investigators need to develop their own area. And RP is a serious eye disease that needed attention. It still does." She started to explain about mutations and how she was making headway on genetic therapy when the prosecutor interrupted her.

"Isn't that complexity you describe so eloquently reason enough to direct taxpayer dollars to solve these vital medical issues rather than to explore biology randomly? There are social responsibilities, wouldn't you agree, Dr. Silvan?"

"Yes, I suppose, but if we don't discover new concepts, we'll dry up, so to speak."

Ricardo nodded in agreement.

"But to get back to what I was saying, we're making headway," Ann continued. "We're on the brink of treating RP with genetic therapy. I can't wait for the day that I can tell my patients that they won't lose their eyesight. These are such exciting possibilities."

"Indeed they are. Possibilities. Thank you, Dr. Silvan," said the prosecutor with a warm, tender voice, as if he were speaking to a close friend. "And good luck with your important experiments on treating blinding disease."

Ann's shoulders slumped and the confident look on her face was gone when she walked away from the witness stand. She acknowledged Ricardo with an apologetic smile when she passed him.

Pearl was summoned as the next witness. She walked briskly to the witness box, her freshly rinsed hair gently bouncing with each step. She looked stunning in her peach colored blouse, black skirt and lucky ladybug pin. Ricardo was impressed by how she captured attention.

Sophia started asking Pearl the questions that they had rehearsed. Pearl answered positively and without hesitation. Yes, she had been a postdoctoral fellow in Ricardo's laboratory for almost four years. She had come immediately after obtaining her PhD degree from Rutgers University. Ricardo was very much involved in her cornea research project. Of course it had a great deal of medical relevance, and she was acquiring the expertise to continue an independent career in medical research, as Dr. Silvan had done. No, his jellyfish research did not interfere with his attention to her work. Jellyfish were strictly Dr. Sztein's domain, although he had asked once for her comments on the manuscript. That flattered her. His jellyfish manuscript was amazing and intellectually stimulating. She was in awe of his imagination.

Sophia kept Pearl in the witness box for half an hour. It was clear that Pearl liked her mentor a lot.

After Sophia concluded, the prosecutor walked slowly to the witness stand. He started his cross-examination by confirming in a capsule what she had said in response to Sophia's questions, and then he began to dig deeper.

"Could you please tell the jury why you chose to do your postdoctoral work with Dr. Sztein?"

Because Ricardo was a fine scientist working in the prestigious Vision Science Center, she said.

"Why the Vision Science Center? Why eyes, Ms Witstein?"

"Because my father had gone blind," she said.

What! She had never said anything to Ricardo about her father losing his sight. Sophia looked as shocked as Ricardo. Did the prosecutor know that Pearl's father was blind? If so, how?

"I'm sorry to hear that, Ms. Witstein," said the prosecutor in a sickly sweet voice. "How did he become blind?"

"Macula degeneration. He went blind when I was in college."

"Didn't you want to do postdoctoral work in a laboratory devoted to that disease, or to blindness in general?"

"I applied to laboratories at several medical schools, but they were full. However, Dr. Sztein had an open position that I applied for. He had a strong reputation and I figured I could learn a lot from him. In fact, my research in his laboratory is on Fuch's dystrophy, a disease of the cornea."

"Are you satisfied with Dr. Sztein as a mentor?"

"Absolutely," said Pearl with genuine enthusiasm. "He's really nice."

"Yes, we know that he's *nice*. Tell me, Ms Witstein..."

From Pearl's beet-red blush and the way she rubbed her left arm with her right hand, a habit she displayed when embarrassed, it was clear that she knew she had put her foot in her mouth. But she recovered quickly. "Call me Pearl, sir. Everyone does."

"Okay, Pearl. What was I saying?" Pearl had that effect on people, even the prosecutor. "Oh yes, how did Dr. Sztein react to your father's blindness?"

Pearl glanced at Ricardo and then quickly shifted her eyes back to the prosecutor.

"I didn't tell him."

"Really? Why's that, Pearl?"

That's exactly what Ricardo wanted to know. Why didn't she tell him? While most people would have been angry or hurt, Ricardo wasn't most people. He was angry with himself for not having been more available to Pearl, for keeping too much of a distance.

"I didn't think it was relevant," Pearl said in response to the prosecutor's question.

"*Relevant?*" said the prosecutor. "You didn't think that blindness was *relevant* for the research in Dr. Sztein's laboratory?"

"Objection," Sophia interrupted without missing a beat.

"Sustained," said the judge. "Please do not lead the witness, Mr. Jenkins."

"I didn't say that he wasn't interested in medically relevant research," said Pearl. "No, sir, I said I didn't think that my problem, or my father's problem more precisely, was relevant, or necessary to speak about in his laboratory."

The prosecutor looked at the jury in disbelief. "Be that as it may, Pearl, it's interesting that you didn't tell Dr. Sztein that your father's blindness motivated you to do research on eyes in his laboratory."

Before Sophia had time to object again, the prosecutor continued. "Tell me, Ms. Witstein—I mean Pearl—what do you think about Dr. Sztein's frequent trips to La Parguera to work on jellyfish?"

"It's none of my business, sir."

"But you work in his laboratory and need his guidance. Does he have enough time for you?" asked the prosecutor again. "It seems he's very, how to put it, independent."

"Objection! Objection!" shouted Sophia.

"One objection is enough, Ms Lass," said the judge.

The audience tittered.

"Objection sustained," said the judge. "How much time Dr. Sztein has for his postdoctoral fellows is not on trial."

"Certainly, your Honor," the prosecutor acknowledged with a false smile. He then drawled in one of his many voices, "It seems that you want to say something more, Pearl. Am I right?"

Pearl squirmed.

"I'm finished with my questions, Pearl, but if you want to add anything that might be helpful, anything at all, please...." he urged, placing his hand with the sapphire ring lightly on the railing of the witness box.

She avoided looking at him, and after a moment asked, "What did you mean when you mentioned Dr. Sztein's 'independence', sir?"

"Just going off on his own, not accountable as it were," answered the prosecutor. He smiled at her.

"Well, he's lucky to be able to do that," she said. "He seems to love it."

Pearl paused on the word love. "Many scientists enjoy their work, the intellectual stimulation, the challenge," she added. "With Ricardo, it seems more than enjoyment. He loves it. You know—love—it's much more than enjoyment. It's *emotional*. He's downright poetic when he talks about jellyfish, and it did go through my mind that..." She hesitated.

"Yes, Pearl. Go on."

Pearl appeared flustered. "Oh, I don't mean anything bad. No, no. I like Dr. Sztein. I envy him."

"Envy what, Pearl?"

"His *independence*, sir," she answered, regaining composure.

"Yes, of course. His independence. Thank you, Pearl. I have no further questions."

The prosecutor passed close to the jury without looking at them when he walked back to his seat.

"Independence, indeed! From whom? From what? It's hopeless," Ricardo whispered, more to himself than to Sophia.

Sophia turned to Ricardo with the creases around her green eyes accenting her sympathetic face.

"Don't despair yet," she said.

"Are you sure?"

Chapter 35

The headlines on the front page of the *Washington Post*—"**Nice is not Enough**"—startled Ricardo when he left his house to go to the trial the next day. Randolph Likens had written the article. Big surprise! Hopefully this day would go well for him. Benjamin was going to testify.

The weather was nasty and the rain pelted the window by the panel of jurists in the courtroom. The chitchat of the spectators faded out when Benjamin was called to the witness box. After taking the oath, Benjamin caught Ricardo's attention across the room and greeted him by moving his lips with a silent, "Hi." Ricardo responded with a nod. The elbow patches on Benjamin's corduroy jacket and the coffee stain on his khaki pants portrayed him as the stereotypical eccentric, absent-minded professor—which couldn't have been further from the truth. He cleared his throat and adjusted the knot of his dark brown tie.

Ricardo assumed that the backing of a member of the American Academy of Sciences would add clout to his case. However, he was aware that any slip that Benjamin might make—a skeptical remark about a jellyfish brain or a loose comment about Ricardo's trip to La Parguera—could be damaging to his case.

But Benjamin was a pro, thought Ricardo, a pro and a friend.

Benjamin had advised Sophia to be brief, so she had only a short list of questions for him. He preferred to not dull the jury with repetition, and he wanted the questions open enough so that he could refute some of prosecutor's past comments if he had the chance.

First, Sophia highlighted Benjamin's credentials, emphasizing his hundreds of published papers on medicine and numerous honors culminating with election to the American Academy of Sciences. Then she turned to Benjamin's cactus project, as they had agreed she would do.

"Dr. Wollberg, Dr. Sztein has used your cactus research as an example of how a research project can start off without a clear destination and then develop medical relevance as it progresses. Could you elaborate on that, sir?"

"Objection," said the prosecutor. "Dr. Wollberg was fiddling with cactus when he was in the Israeli army. He did not do this work at the expense of the U.S. government. And in any case, it would be sheer luck if Cactein turns out to be medically relevant."

"Luck, yes," Sophia muttered under her breath. "Doesn't all research depend on luck to some extent?"

The judge acknowledged that luck was not grounds for objecting.

Sounding indignant, Benjamin said, "I am confident that the ongoing clinical trial will reveal *how* Cactein is relevant for medicine, not *if* it is relevant." Then, in a more neutral voice, he said, "But let me comment about basic research in general. You never know what's lurking in dark corners, those hidden spots that Dr. Sztein has a genius to sniff out. Finding those lucrative corners is as much a mark of a good scientist as the research itself. I've learned a lot from him about that."

Benjamin paused, looked at the floor, and then faced Sophia. "Allow me to make additional comments about Dr Sztein's view of basic research, which I think is relevant."

"By all means, Dr. Wollberg."

"Dr. Sztein is not naïve. He knew that he had to make a connection between jellyfish vision and his research on corneal disorders to have his travel request accepted. So he played the game, as we all do. But he also believes—knows in my opinion—that basic research is like a beast that can't be tamed. Medical relevance can no more be guaranteed than can the outcome of an experiment. Ricardo's research is honest in that respect. Let me be specific. He justified his initial trip to La Parguera as an extension of his previous work on corneal disorders, which it was. However, his experimental results with the jellyfish drove him in new directions. He honestly believed, after his many years of experience, that was where the payoff would be. This is hardly the behavior of a man trying to defraud anyone. He allowed his jellyfish experiments—his wild beast—to guide him, rather than stubbornly stretch medical relevance beyond the truth. It seems unfair to prosecute a scientist for his integrity and imagination. Isn't that what academic freedom, which has been at the core of so many advances, is all about?"

Good old Benjamin, Ricardo thought. He gets it. But will a jury of non-scientists get it too?

"Thank you for that helpfull clarification, Dr. Wollberg. One final question. Have you ever seen Dr. Sztein take drugs?"

"Only for colds. He hates them. He likes to have a clear head."

Sophia smiled, but the prosecutor did not.

The rain had stopped. The sun broke through the clouds and illuminated the courtroom.

"I have no further questions, Dr. Wollberg."

The judge called for a thirty-minute recess before the prosecutor's cross-examination.

When the court reconvened the prosecutor went to work on Benjamin. "Your friendship with Dr. Sztein is heartwarming, Dr. Wollberg. It must have been very painful to you when his wife died?"

"Yes, Lillian was his best friend. I felt so sorry for him."

Ricardo blanched when he heard Lillian's name. He missed her so, yet he was happy that she was not witnessing this farce.

"Is that why you accompanied Dr. Sztein to La Parguera on his first trip? Because you felt he needed a friend for support?" asked the prosecutor.

"NO! I was impressed that jellyfish had eyes and I thought it was fascinating," said Benjamin.

"But, you *stopped* working on jellyfish with Dr. Sztein after that trip. You only went to La Parguera once. I heard from a colleague of yours that you had difficulty justifying the jellyfish research at one of your university retreats."

"Objection," piped up Sophia. "That's unsubstantiated hearsay."

"Sustained," said the judge.

The prosecutor's eye twitched. "Sorry, your Honor. I apologize for bringing up confidential information."

He didn't need to anymore. He'd made his point.

"I didn't accompany Ricardo to La Parguera on his second trip because I was inundated with deadlines and didn't have time," Benjamin volunteered.

"Busy on Cactein research?"

"Yes, as well as lectures, conferences, students—the usual."

"Cactein is a cactus extract?" asked the prosecutor, as if he didn't know the answer.

"Yes."

"It's marvelous that you have a clinical trial underway to test whether Cactein can be used to treat depression."

"Thank you."

The prosecutor continued. "It's well recognized that research on obscure species can be extremely valuable. So, it's not jellyfish being prosecuted here. It's the nature of the work and the *motivation*." The prosecutor paused. "I'm curious why you accompanied Dr. Sztein on his first trip to La Parguera. What was your motivation?"

"I didn't know jellyfish had eyes and I thought that was fascinating, as I'd said before. I was curious."

"Is that all? Curious?"

"Essentially, yes. You never know what discoveries will be made when exploring something brand new."

"So jellyfish were just curiosity for you, not serious research, right?"

"The trip to La Parguera and jellyfish were serious science for Dr. Sztein."

"Is that why the Vision Science Center paid for his trip to La Parguera, while you paid out of your own pocket: because it was serious for him but not for you?"

"We have different objectives. I am not on trial here."

"Very well," said the prosecutor. "Would you say that Dr. Sztein concluded that jellyfish have brains and can visualize evolution in order to catapult his popularity and captivate young scientists rather than advance science, thereby undermining the mission of the Vision Science Center?"

"Objection," said Sophia. "What was in Dr. Sztein's mind is irrelevant. Dr. Wollberg is not a psychiatrist."

"Objection sustained. Confine your questions to facts," the judge told the prosecutor.

Benjamin corrected the prosecutor. "Sir, Ricardo concluded only that jellyfish see images. His data on that are convincing. He did *not* conclude that jellyfish have minds and visualize evolution. He only *speculated* on those possibilities on the basis of his data. And, frankly, he made an interesting argument."

"Indeed. Speculated. But Dr. Topping mentioned earlier, under oath, that promising young scientists are applying for grants on invertebrates with no foreseeable relevance for medicine, and they are quoting Dr. Sztein's research as their model. Stealing the best and the brightest is what Dr. Topping called it."

Sophia objected once more, saying that Dr. Wollberg was on the witness stand, not Dr. Topping.

"Sustained," agreed the judge.

The prosecutor smiled ever so slightly. "I'd like to bring up Cactein once again, Dr. Wollberg."

Benjamin nodded. "Okay."

Sophia objected still again. "I don't see how Cactein is relevant to the defendant's choice of research projects."

"I'm trying to establish the defendant's reliability, your Honor," said the prosecutor.

"Objection overruled. The defendant's reliability is relevant to the case."

The prosecutor continued. "Cactein is a mind-altering drug. Is it a narcotic?"

"As I published," Benjamin said, "Cactein does not bind known receptors for narcotics. I do not believe that it is a narcotic in any conventional sense. I have tested it personally by self-injection. I never heard voices or saw colors or felt any known symptom of narcotics."

"So exactly what did Cactein do to you?" asked the prosecutor.

Benjamin sat upright. "First, it increased my ability to observe details. What I saw was real. I could verify everything that I saw under its influence upon close inspection the next day. I didn't interpret smudges as spiders or colors as rainbows or have any other hallucination. I don't believe that Dr. Sztein saw non-existent things either. He confirmed that the pores that he saw in the sponge-like image on the computer screen generated by the jellyfish looked similar to the pores of the fixed sponge in the bottle. Cactein may have helped Ricardo see what was actually there. That's it. Secondly, Cactein seems to activate some previously unrecognized potential for individuals to bond with one another and even with their surroundings. That's why Cactein is in the midst of a clinical trial. Dr. Stein's experiments suggest that Cactein may even promote bonding between people and jellyfish. We evolved from ancestors after all, so it makes sense that there might be an evolutionary pathway for emotions or thought or, I don't know, something new to us. It's amazingly interesting. I think that Cactein taps new pockets of evolutionary importance in our brains. If anything, Dr. Sztein's jellyfish studies are a powerful example of unexpected discoveries with enormous potential that come from basic research."

"Pockets of evolutionary importance?" said the prosecutor. "Well, you're the scientist, Dr. Wollberg...but people bonding to jellyfish? At government expense? Never mind, just thinking aloud." The prosecutor stole a glance at the jury.

"Just one more time for the record, Dr. Wollberg: Do you swear under oath that Cactein would not induce a type of psychotic state in Dr. Sztein that made him break with reality?"

"Yes I do, for two reasons. The first, as I just said, is that Cactein is not a conventional narcotic. But the second reason is even more compelling, and it's somewhat embarrassing."

Everyone in the jury took note. Ricardo leaned towards Sophia, whispered something into her ear, and turned around to see if Likens was there. He was.

Then Benjamin released his bombshell. "It turns out that the Cactein extract I gave Ricardo had little if any activity."

Ricardo was stunned. A series of "oh's" and "ah's" rippled through the spectators. The judged raised his eyebrows in amazement.

Sophia's face lit up. She turned to Ricardo and said, "That's fantastic!"

After a moment, Benjamin continued. "I didn't realize that until I tested a sample of the extract I gave Ricardo after his article came out." Benjamin stalled. "It was much, much weaker than I had thought, perhaps even inactive. I've tested many different Cactein extracts and none ever lost activity over time when they were frozen so I had no reason to think that this extract was not active. By chance, Ricardo received a very weak extract. Period."

"And you never told Dr. Sztein?" asked the prosecutor, taken aback.

"I should have," Benjamin said, "but I only discovered this recently. Long after his article was published. I was embarrassed. Also, Ricardo had only referred to Cactein in the Acknowledgments at the end of his article. I had wanted him to emphasize Cactein more. Now I'm happy he didn't."

Benjamin looked at Ricardo and muttered under his breath, "Sorry."

"So, Dr. Sztein was under the impression that Cactein affected him more than it could have?" the prosecutor asked.

"Perhaps. However, like I said, Cactein didn't really figure in his article, and he always insisted that his observations and conclusions were based entirely on his data, not his frame of mind. And now I'm sure that Cactein did not have a biological mind-altering affect on whatever Dr. Sztein saw and felt, except perhaps psychologically. Ricardo saw what was there. He was not drugged in any way."

Ricardo was perplexed and angry, although relieved. How could Benjamin not tell him? How weak was the Cactein? Or, was Benjamin just trying to help him in this trial? The prosecutor did not challenge Benjamin any further about Cactein. He couldn't afford to lose any more ground.

"I have no further questions, Dr. Wollberg."

Benjamin looked sheepishly at Ricardo when he passed him walking back to his seat.

Chapter 36

Sophia advised Ricardo not to testify on his own behalf. She said that he would be like a bleeding seal for a shark.

"The prosecutor is cunning, Ricardo. It's different when you're the target in the witness box. You don't know what it's like. Trust me."

"You don't trust me, Sophia?"

"Not for this."

"I *want* to testify," he said. "I've done nothing wrong. The jury needs to hear my side of the story. I won't get carried away. You'll see. I'll be steady as a rock."

"I don't think it's a good idea," she said again.

Ricardo was adamant.

"Okay, Ricardo. But if you're going to testify on your own behalf there's a few things you've got to understand." Sophia's tone was harsh.

"What's that?"

"You've got to stress how much your research has benefitted medicine and, therefore, the taxpayers, and how your jellyfish research is a direct continuation of your past research. The prosecutor is trying to separate your other research from your jellyfish research. You have to link them."

"But I don't think any of my research has actually benefitted taxpayers yet."

"That's crap and you know it. Can't you forget yourself and your jellyfish for once?" Her eyes flashed green, her body resolute.

"This trial is about how you've used government funds, not about you as a scientist or about jellyfish. No one cares how interesting your jellyfish research is or how smart you are. Tell them how your research always was and continues to be fiscally responsible, that your goal is to alleviate human suffering and to find new ways to treat disease. Tell them that finding jellyfish ancestors of the Fuch's dystrophy-associated genes, which you discovered in mice, will yield clues as to the cause of the disease and ultimately to find treatments. That's why you did the work. Tell them that the difference between jellyfish and human crystallins may give hints for preventing cataracts. I don't know, Ricardo. You're the creative scientist, not me. Don't go on about the jellyfish mind and seeing evolution. Those are stories. You need to convince the jury that your jellyfish research was tightly connected to your mission plan that was disease-oriented, like you did on your original travel requests. Use all the right buzz words. Talk *only* about the medical relevance of your work. Stretch the truth a bit if you feel you must, although it may be less of a stretch than you think. Take advantage of the fact that the jury members are not scientists and impress them with your contributions to medicine, not with esoteric jargon about basic science. Why do you think the Vision Science Center supported you all these years? They're not stupid. My god, Ricardo, you've published—what ?—how many articles relevant to human disease?"

"A lot." Ricardo slumped. He knew she was right.

"Look, Ricardo, I don't think that this trial should ever have occurred. We're dealing with a philosophical issue, not a legal one, as I said the first time we met. Academic freedom can't be packaged in a set of rules and it gets twisted in the wrong hands. Why do you think the so-called 'intelligentsia' has been targeted in dictatorships? When Topping talks about moral responsibility—nonsense! What does 'responsible' even mean in academic research centered on knowledge?"

"So, you're saying that I should ignore my findings on jellyfish. How can I do that? It's the heart of basic research and what this trial is about."

Sophia looked frustrated. "The trial is *not* about jellyfish, or even about basic research. It's about money. Can't you understand that? Play the game! Convince the jury that your findings on jellyfish behavior and vision are byproducts, not the aim of your investigations, not what you intended or are going to pursue."

Ricardo started to look green, like Sophia's eyes. "You're right."

"Your personal interests and frustrations are another truth that fits a different puzzle. The jellyfish—and they are amazing—are part of your heart, not your job. I understand that. Benjamin knows that too. Pure jellyfish—the jellyfish in your scientific, if romantic heart—belongs to a different game. I think that's what Benjamin was trying to say. You did play the right game when you wrote your travel requests to go to La Parguera. You need to stick to the rules of *that* game during this trial. You can't win if you play the wrong game. Get it?"

Sophia's hands waved back and forth, and her expression glistened with sincerity. Ricardo felt embarrassed to be scolded, but yes, he got it. He had done a lot to benefit taxpayers and his professional motivations were to get funded, so he had always played the correct political game. He needed to continue playing it. He needed to win the game.

Sophia paused to catch her breath, and then said, "I don't mean to be arrogant, Ricardo. I want us to succeed."

"So do I." Ricardo was exhausted.

With that common understanding, they put their heads together to prepare examples of how basic explorations led to major advances in medicine, starting with the discovery of penicillin from mold. "The jury needs simple examples of medical advances from basic research," she said, over and over again, "because they are not scientists."

The Sunday evening before the trial resumed, Ricardo and Benjamin had a quiet dinner together at a local Italian restaurant.

"So tomorrow is the big day. You're testifying."

"That's right. Sophia went nuts telling me that I need to stress how medically important my work is. She wants me to play the fashionable, political game and forget about how interesting jellyfish are."

"She's right. Jellyfish won't impress the jury. That's for an academic conference, not a court of law. The ivory tower has crumbled, Ricardo. Today no one cares about knowledge or ideas that spawn new ideas for their own sake. Parade your medical accomplishments and link your jellyfish stuff to relevant research, like you did in your initial travel request."

Benjamin was echoing Sophia. Ricardo felt like a black swan.

Benjamin gently placed his hand on Ricardo's arm. "Ricardo, this trial is not about Nature or even about you. It's about money."

Ricardo sighed. "That's precisely what Sophia said. I guess the truth is that I'm egocentric. I always wanted to cultivate my garden, as Voltaire would've said. I'm not even sure anymore what my work is about. Maybe my research is irrelevant to everyone but me. All those people in the audience judging me, accusing me when I just want to be—I don't know what the right word is—*virtuous?*"

"Aren't we all egocentric hypocrites, at least at times. At the heart of it all, 'career first' is the mantra for all of us—you, me, Jenkins, Topping, even Sophia. And you were right, Ricardo."

"How?"

"I do like Sophia."

"Me too. She's on the ball and lives in the real world. Do you think I've done anything wrong, Benjamin? Marcus implied that I've corrupted bright young scientists by *stealing* them away from doing relevant research. Jenkins even implied that I'm a *murderer!*"

Benjamin gazed into space, twirling spaghetti with his fork, and took a sip of Chianti. "Good."

"Good? The Chianti? Hello? Am I a thief and a murderer? Benjamin, are you there?"

"Socrates," said Benjamin.

"Not quite. Not even Einstein. Benjamin, wake up!"

"Have you ever read *The Apology* by Plato? It's Socrates' defense at his trial in Athens. He was accused of impiety and of corrupting young men by his teachings. That was 2500 years ago. Anything ring a bell or sound familiar?"

"Socrates? He was condemned to death, wasn't he?"

"Yes, but he ended up taking poison—hemlock—in prison and he died surrounded by his friends. Do you know what I remember he was striving to be?"

"Not a clue," said Ricardo.

"*Virtuous!*"

"You're kidding."

After dinner, Ricardo went home and retrieved a dusty copy of Plato's writings buried in his collection of books. Ricardo became increasingly distressed about the power of public opinion as he read *The Apology*. He copied a part of one sentence that he considered using for his defense: "...virtue comes not from money, but from virtue comes both money and all other good things for mankind, in private and in public," but making the jury understand that seemed as depressingly difficult for him as it had been for Socrates. Socrates' statement that "life without enquiry is not worth living" discouraged Ricardo even more, because Socrates ended that enlightening truth by saying, "you will believe me still less if I say that."

Ricardo had a serious dilemma and he knew it. He couldn't put his head in the sand this time. He wasn't an ostrich; he was a defendant in a criminal trial.

And he was going to be in the witness box tomorrow, fighting for his life.

Chapter 37

The next morning Ricardo, too nervous to eat breakfast, trimmed his beard and put on his most expensive tie. He entered the courtroom a few minutes before nine. Spectators filed into the courtroom until the seats ran out. So much fuss over an old scientist doing a few experiments on jellyfish, thought Ricardo. Sophia and Benjamin were right: jellyfish were irrelevant. Attempting to impress the jury with jellyfish or trying to define his concept of basic science was pointless. The spectators had come to guard their pocketbooks and vent their anger. If dwindling taxpayer dollars were the present God, then Ricardo was being tried for impiety, like Socrates and then Galileo after him.

Ricardo's thoughts floated from person to person. Sophia, smart as a whip, wanted him to turn into a politician and embrace cynicism. Tell them what they want to hear, she had said. Wow them with the right buzz words. He would try. Pearl wanted to be helpful, he knew that deep in his heart, but why hadn't she told him that her father was blind from macula degeneration? What else hadn't she told him? Ann Silvan, his favorite from years ago, also meant well, but she was focused on her own career and that was different from his. That son-of-a-bitch Marcus Topping lived to seduce Congress for funds. Loyal Benjamin, as much a brother as a friend and colleague, had compared him to Socrates, not the philosopher, but the doomed victim of public opinion. No, that wasn't fair. Thank goodness for Benjamin. Then there was the judge, supposedly neutral—but was he?—and the bloodthirsty spectators, with Randolph Likens and his poison pen lurking in the back row. And most importantly, the jury: were they on his side? He would find out soon.

Ricardo pleaded with himself to keep his cool and pretended to look confident—appearances count—when he heard the bailiff call him to the witness box. He walked to the front of the courtroom, took the oath with his hand on the Bible, and sat in the witness box. He ran his fingers through his thin hair. His face was drawn; his hands unsteady. He'd lost weight during this ordeal so that even the last notch on his belt wasn't tight enough.

The landscape of the courtroom appeared different from the witness box than it did from his seat by Sophia. Benjamin had faded into the distance. The spectators in front of him replaced the judge as the symbol of authority. The jury looked more threatening. He could smell the perfume of the lady with the white streak in her hair, hear the slight shuffle of feet hidden behind the polished wood barrier sequestering the jury, and even see a pimple on the closely shaved chin of the foreman. Ricardo found it peculiar—sad really, and ironic—that a dozen anonymous strangers who knew nothing about science would decide his fate based on his research.

Ricardo heard a dog bark outside. He imagined the chaos if the dog had barked inside the courtroom. Suddenly he felt like a dog in the courtroom: out of place.

Sophia walked up to the witness box, her stride more assured than Ricardo knew she felt. They had agreed that she would limit herself to simple issues that would allow him to stress the medical relevance of his research. The strategy was to convince the jury that prosecuting Ricardo was counter-productive to the advancement of science and not cost-effective in the long run. Money had to be part of the equation.

By answering Sophia's questions, Ricardo established, once again, that he was an eminent scientist who had received awards for his medically relevant research on the eye, that he had mentored many postdoctoral fellows who now held important positions in academia and industry, and that his trips to La Parguera had been approved by the Vision Science Center and justified as legitimate extensions of his previous research on the mammalian cornea. He also emphasized that basic research was crucial for progress in science. History had shown time and again that important medical advances came from unexpected sources. Despite Sophia's impassioned instructions, he couldn't resist promoting basic science and ended by saying, "My studies on jellyfish have opened new and exciting avenues of research with major evolutionary implications." This conclusion had not been rehearsed with Sophia, and she gave him a severe look after he said it. How many times did she have to tell him to end with medical implications of his research? Nevertheless, he said it calmly and with authority. Overall, Ricardo appeared in control.

"Thank you, Dr. Sztein. That will be all."

Sophia returned to her seat with her fingers crossed.

The prosecutor opened his cross-examination using his thin voice. "Dr. Sztein, let's cut to the chase. How have the taxpayers benefitted from your research on jellyfish?"

Without hesitation Ricardo gave his prepared answer on how basic research that seemed disconnected to medicine often turned out to have clinical and industrial importance. He mentioned antibiotics derived from bacterial cultures, and heat resistant enzymes in microorganisms that facilitated gene cloning and opened new industries. Even research on bioluminescent jellyfish led to a Nobel Prize because of its medical implications.

"Yes, we know all that, Dr. Sztein, but what about *your* research?"

Ricardo was ready. He listed the mouse model he'd developed for Fuch's dystrophy, the genes he'd associated with that disease, the mouse corneal hormone that he'd anticipated would help heal injured corneas, his studies on cataracts. Then, in his most authoritative, matter-of-fact voice he reminded the jury that he'd received the LeBlanc Prize and the Melon Medal and other recognitions for his medically relevant research. How much more confident he felt when he separated his heart from his head.

Sophia nodded her approval.

"As for my jellyfish studies," he continued, "I was trying to trace the evolution of the genes that I've linked to Fuch's dystrophy. Understanding evolution of specific genes and proteins provide vital clues for dealing with hereditary diseases, devise gene therapies and, hopefully, manage viral pandemics." It wasn't so difficult to tell them what they wanted to hear once he got into the swing of it.

"I assure you, Dr. Sztein, that your past contributions to medical science have been noted. Also, your original research plan on jellyfish for the first trip to La Parguera was accepted as a high risk project—very high risk I would say—yet potentially relevant research. But what of your second trip to La Parguera, when your research started drifting into the jellyfish mind? And then there was the third trip to La Parguera, that scuba diving resort..."

"Objection, your Honor!" Sophia was red-faced in anger. "The prosecutor's implication that Ricardo went to La Parguera on vacation is outrageous."

"Sustained. The jury must disregard the connection of La Parguera to a resort."

As if they could.

The prosecutor looked unperturbed. "As I was saying, Dr. Sztein, what about that third trip to La Parguera when you took advantage of Dr. Topping's absence to slip the travel request through?"

"I wasn't trying to 'slip' anything through!" Ricardo exclaimed, his temper heating up. "Dr. Topping was out of town and it was the right season to collect the jellyfish in La Parguera. What was I supposed to do? I went to the Acting Director for my travel request."

By the use of a simple four-letter word—'slip'—the prosecutor had succeeded to brew a hurricane within Ricardo. He needed to settle his nerves in order not to blurt out some foolish attack that he would regret the moment the words tumbled out of his mouth.

The prosecutor continued. "Dr. Sztein, could you please tell the court how you j-u-s-t-i-f-y using taxpayer dollars to go to a vacationland like Puerto Rico to figure out what jellyfish see?"

There was that unfair vacation implication again! The intensity of the prosecutor's threatening tone increased with each word and by the time he reached the final "see," the capillaries in his round cheeks protruded like strands of spaghetti soaked in tomato sauce.

"Objection again. Vacationland *must* be deleted from the record," Sophia said, her tone indicating her exasperation.

"Sustained," agreed the judge. "But the defendant still needs to answer how he justified his extended research on jellyfish."

Hadn't he done that? Ricardo looked at Sophia's worried expression, and then at Benjamin.

Ricardo imagined himself in a toga in ancient Greece before a crowd of accusing citizens. He shut his eyes briefly. When he opened them the audience appeared as a self-righteous clergy. He scanned the faces of spectators, looking in vain for Lillian. Why had he shied away from her plea for him to help others avoid the pain of intractable diseases? Why hadn't he listened to Benjamin's sober warnings not to stray from the narrow mission of the Vision Science Center? Dr. Topping was right. He was more passionate about jellyfish than compassionate about people. He wasn't misunderstood. It was he who didn't understand.

"Please, Dr. Sztein, we're still waiting," said the prosecutor. He twisted the sapphire ring on the little finger of his left hand with his thumb.

The low rumble of the prosecutor's sinister voice set Ricardo on fire. There was something wonderful in that blaze of emotion. How good it felt! Freedom at last! He lengthened his spine, squared his shoulders and gave the prosecutor a smile of tranquil confidence. Although unprecedented during a testimony, he decided to go on the offensive. He could be as crafty as the prosecutor.

"Tell me, sir, do you win all your cases? That is, are all the defendants that you prosecute found guilty?"

"What?" asked the prosecutor, appearing confused. "I don't need to answer you. I'm asking the questions."

"Objection," blurted Sophia.

"What are you objecting to?" asked the judge.

"My client is trying to make a point—I'm sure. Mr. Jenkins does need to answer him."

"Really?" said the judge. "You're sure?" The judge paused a moment. "As unusual as this is, the objection is sustained. I'm curious as to what Dr. Sztein does have in mind. Please answer the question, Mr. Jenkins. However, I won't allow this turn in protocol to proceed further."

The prosecutor shot a disapproving glance at the judge, and then glowered at Ricardo.

"This is bizarre, Dr. Sztein, but yes, *generally* the defendants are found guilty."

"I see," said Ricardo. "Well, that's my *general* answer to your question."

"How's that?" It was the prosecutor's turn to be curious.

"I justify my research on delving into the mysteries of Nature because *generally* the experiments yield new insights that benefit people. There's penicillin, recombinant DNA, genetic engineering, as I'd mentioned before. I won't bore you with repetitions and more examples. However, we scientists do have our failures, when our curiosity leads us into a blind alley, just as I assume prosecutors have when a defendant is judged innocent. You aren't asked to *justify* your work when a defendant is found innocent, are you?"

The prosecutor, stunned, turned to the judge and said, "I certainly don't have to answer *that*, do I, your Honor?"

Ricardo sensed the momentum shift as he switched from prey to predator in this ugly trial. Now, he thought, was the time to unleash his list of imaginative ways his jellyfish research could provide valuable benefits to taxpayers. His thoughts went back to that night in La Parguera when he had the epiphany that jellyfish visualized evolution. What a wonderful night that was!

"So now, sir," Ricardo said, feeling entitled, "that we agree that not all ideas are correct or all attempts successful, I'll suggest ways that my research on jellyfish *might* be useful. First, the ability of jellyfish to visualize evolutionary pathways, if that speculation turns out to be correct, could be invaluable for identifying the most suited animal models for medical research, not only for human disease, but for diseases of our beloved pets—dogs, cats, horses, cattle—as well as of fish, which would benefit fish husbandry to feed our growing population. Imagine also if we discovered how jellyfish store and retrieve memories of evolution, we might be able to learn how to download information into our own brains like information is downloaded into a computer. Putting all sorts of information into our brains would become quick and easy. Who knows, we might even be able to link our brain with an animal's brain and see the world as it does. The practical ramifications of my jellyfish research are potentially huge!"

Ricardo paused, remembering how Lillian often warned him to not get carried away and trespass the line between fact and fantasy. Then he continued speaking more slowly and with less animation. "Bacteria provided the first models for gene regulation, which set the stage for gene therapy. Sea slugs—snails without shells—revealed mysteries of memory. Birds have taught us that it's possible to rest half the brain at a time. Think how useful it would be if we could be asleep and active at the same time!" After a fleeting few seconds, he ended, "All of Nature's secrets must be exploited for our benefit, and this can be most effectively accomplished if we leave no stone unturned as we explore those secrets."

Ricardo felt vindicated; he had made his case eloquently. However Sophia was frowning. Had he gone too far? Probably. When silence prevailed with no noticeable response from the audience, not even from Benjamin, his heart sank. It seemed that his plight remained unchanged. He was still the defendant, the scapegoat and the victim. His imagination had failed to rescue him.

"Dr. Sztein, the question before us is about misuse of tax money, not fantastic stories of what might be. Do you truly *believe* that speculating about jellyfish vision and behavior can benefit the taxpayers and medicine *now*? Ideas are cheap, although it's true that science fiction novels on occasion stumble into future truths. It's always if, if, if. But each 'if' is expensive. I would think that you, of all people, who watched your beloved wife succumb to cancer, must understand the need to put people first *now*, not in the indefinite future. Where's your conscience?"

Sophia raised her hand about to object, but then lowered her hand and remained silent.

"Ms Lass, do you have something to say?" asked the judge.

"No. Excuse me, your Honor."

Ricardo was incredulous. How could Sophia allow the prosecutor to question his conscience without objecting? She'd objected when the prosecutor questioned Benjamin about the motivation behind the jellyfish research, but now she permitted *his* conscience to be questioned. It was she who kept saying that the use of government money was on trial, not his conscience.

Ricardo's stamina started slipping, but then he regained strength by thinking that if this was his Masada, the inevitability of death removed any need for caution. The floodgates opened.

"Where's my *conscience*? You question my *feelings* about disease?" Ricardo said, his nostrils flared, his hands accompanying his words like a conductor's baton. "Good grief, sir. I hate disease. Disease makes me sick. It's health that deserves serious attention. There are many more healthy people than sick ones on this earth." Ricardo's eyes darted around the room, spitting flames.

The spectators stared at Ricardo in disbelief. Benjamin squirmed. Sophia gulped. The judge looked bewildered.

The prosecutor twisted his sapphire ring on his finger. With his voice as calm as the eye of a hurricane, he asked, "So you are interested in health, Dr. Sztein? You like people to be healthy rather than sick?"

"Of course. I wish that no one would get sick and that my friends would live for a long, long time, even though that would contribute to overpopulation."

Ricardo's glance fell on a lady who resembled Lillian in her youth and his heart skipped a beat. He imagined her saying, "Poor baby. I'm so sorry."

"I'm the one who is sorry." Ricardo whispered.

"Excuse me?" asked the prosecutor.

"Nothing," said Ricardo.

"Dr. Sztein, this is a very serious matter. Please come down to earth," the prosecutor said sternly.

"Come *down* to earth, you say? If I were a jellyfish, you would have to say, please come *up* to earth. We know so little about these remarkable animals. If I were a jellyfish, I would see your evolutionary history when I look at you as dancing images from sponge to human. Jellyfish are way ahead of us in some ways. We must learn from these squirmy, slippery, squishy, mysterious, wonderful, complex creatures."

Ricardo suddenly stopped talking. He looked down at the floor with great sadness in his eyes. Lillian would have been shocked at his childish sarcasm, but it was too late to take it back.

Chagrined, but the sober scientist again, Ricardo looked at the prosecutor and said, "Who if not the government will fund basic explorations to learn the secrets of jellyfish, to let the mind wander freely and to delve into the many fundamental mysteries of biology? The research funded by industry is directed to make money, and the research funded by philanthropy is more often than not dictated by the specific interests of the donor." This critical question asked by Ricardo—who is better suited to support basic research than the government?—was swallowed as if trapped in quicksand, for it was too little, too late.

An eerie quiet filled the chambers. Sophia's body language transformed from sturdy wood to folding cloth. Benjamin looked crestfallen. Even the prosecutor's blue eyes seemed apologetic for a victory that was not quite what he'd hoped for. Randolph Likens stopped typing.

Benjamin jotted a note on a piece of scrap paper and asked the spectator in front of him to hand it to Sophia. The note read: Find a way to get a break. Ricardo must settle down!

She turned to Benjamin, nodded and raised her hand to catch the judge's attention.

"Yes, Ms Lass. What are you objecting to now?"

The prosecutor snickered. Sophia walked to the bench before the judge and said in a soft voice, "I know this is unusual, your Honor, but I'm feeling sick. Could we *please* have a short break so I could go to the rest room?"

The judge rolled his eyes but announced a fifteen-minute recess. The bailiff took Ricardo to a side room for the interval and told him to remain there until the trial resumed. Benjamin met Sophia in the hall and said what she and everyone knew: Ricardo was committing suicide as far as the trial was concerned. Could she do anything to calm him? After a moment of reflection, Sophia said that Ricardo always had his cell phone in his pocket, and it beeped and vibrated every time he received a message. She would text him from the ladies room. With luck he would read her text before the trial resumed.

Sophia's text was emphatic: **Stop it! No more self-indulgence. Wow them with your science. It's not too late. Benjamin agrees. I mean it!!!**

It worked. Ricardo texted back: **Okay. Couldn't help it. Prosecutor is a...you know what. Sorry.**

Fifteen minutes whizzed by quickly. Sophia thanked the judge when they returned to the courtroom. Ricardo appeared more composed. Benjamin looked green. Sophia prayed silently.

When the trial resumed, the prosecutor said in a sweet, non-threatening, patronizing tone he had never used before, "Please, Dr. Sztein, could you tell the jury about your jellyfish experiments in layman's language. I think it's important that you educate us so we can appreciate your science."

How unexpected this was, like a surprise attack smothered with kindness. Sophia glanced at Benjamin; both looked worried. The prosecutor seemed to be playing good cop and bad cop wrapped in one.

"Certainly," said Ricardo, determined to comply with Sophia's texted mandate. He knew he needed to highlight authoritatively the major findings of his work within the context of humans and disease, and avoid technical details. "Jellyfish are living creatures that have multiple eyes that surround their bodies and resemble, in numerous ways, human eyes, both anatomically and functionally. By using the most up-to-date NASA computer, I showed that jellyfish see images as we do. The computer data then provided compelling evidence, at least in my opinion, that jellyfish integrate images of species they look at with images of their ancestors. In brief, jellyfish see past evolution. This finding is astounding and, if correctly interpreted, exceeds the capability of the human eye. Finally, by analyzing sounds and digital data from the computer, I speculated that jellyfish recognize and interact with other jellyfish. Taken together these observations imply that a jellyfish has a type of brain, or organizing center which functions as a brain. Again, if correct, this means that jellyfish have a mind. I would like to point out that these discoveries —still speculations—would never have been made by targeted research. They required curiosity and free-wheeling, destination-free exploration."

The courtroom was quiet enough to hear a pin drop.

"Quite remarkable," the prosecutor said, still using his good-cop voice. "Now let's go back to how you envisage this information on jellyfish being used?"

"So, we're back to justification are we?" Ricardo responded with a sharp edge that made Sophia cringe. "As I said earlier, jellyfish visions of evolution might help us identify the most appropriate animal models for disease. Cracking the jellyfish code for memory of past events might improve computer programs or advance treatments for dementia and Alzheimer's disease. Application of new knowledge is limited only by imagination. How many times do I need to say the same thing?"

The prosecutor ignored Ricardo's rhetorical question and let him ramble on, leaving enough rope for him to hang himself.

Ricardo took the bait of silence. "If I were to ask anyone, scientist or layman, how a jellyfish records evolution, or even a much simpler question concerning how they integrate the visual information they absorb, they would have to admit ignorance, like I did, like I still do. And, if we don't know the answers to important questions concerning life on earth, it seems justified to try and answer them. There, I'm *justifying* my work. Isn't it self-evident that it is necessary and productive to learn more about eyes and vision and evolution? I thought it was important to learn from jellyfish."

Ricardo looked self-satisfied, but the prosecutor acted no more impressed than if someone had asked him to pass the salt at the dinner table.

"What did you *expect* to find in your jellyfish research, Dr. Sztein?" asked the prosecutor.

"I was seeking questions, not answers. I didn't have a destination. There was no *there*. I was looking for potential, you might say."

Ricardo became animated. The prosecutor took a step backwards and said nothing, giving Ricardo still more space to stumble.

"Most scientists ask questions to solve known problems which, I admit, is logical. I get sidetracked. Hardly anyone even knows that jellyfish have eyes. I don't believe that I ever solved anything useful in my life; I wish I had. I guess it's too late now. I was privileged, however, to enter the mind of jellyfish, even if for only a few isolated moments. I saw another universe that is parallel to ours. Who ever conceived of trying to enter into the mind of a jellyfish when no one even considered that a jellyfish had a mind? I'm a reverse scientist, I suppose. I don't provide solutions. I generate problems."

"Yes, indeed," said the prosecutor. He turned to the jury and paraphrased Ricardo's words, "You *do* generate problems."

The jury members nodded solemnly.

"Let's go back to your infamous publication on jellyfish that concluded that jellyfish 'see' the evolutionary history of the animals they are looking at, even of animals that evolved after them. You wrote that jellyfish see 'videos of evolution' in your article. How in the world do you imagine that could be?"

"That was my *speculation*, not my conclusion," Ricardo said, feeling exasperated at having to repeat himself so often. "I was interpreting, not fabricating data. I agree that of all my observations, the idea of videos of evolution is the most puzzling, but also the most intriguing. If you think about it there are other observations that suggest some kind of genetically inherited memory. Imprinting is an example. How do baby ducks know to follow their mothers at birth, or how do humpback whales know what song to sing? There have been a number of scientific articles written in the last fifty years analyzing DNA as a repository of digital information. That could provide a mechanism for such videos. Don't forget I was filtering the jellyfish signals through a new, highly advanced computer specifically designed to convert data into digital form. I think it's foolhardy to abandon a new idea because it's not fully understood yet. Wouldn't you agree?"

"Perhaps. I'm not a scientist, Dr. Sztein, but I imagine that when one punctures an animal and hooks it up to a computer one could get funny looking electrical signals on the screen that might be interpreted in various ways. Those sounds that you heard, the ones you could never figure out, more electrical noise perhaps? What were your controls that are necessary to draw rigorous conclusions? Did you ever poke a wire into the tentacle of the jellyfish to see what happens on your computer screen? Do the tentacles 'see' according to your criteria? Do the tentacles 'communicate' with each other? Did you ever penetrate *your* muscles with the electrodes from the computer?" asked the prosecutor.

"Uh, no, I never did that. I never thought that...maybe...well...no, I didn't conduct those *particular* experiments," stammered Ricardo. He suddenly felt inept. "That's very perceptive of you. I never stuck an electrode in my own muscles or jellyfish tentacles. But I didn't just do one set of experiments. All my observations were repeatable. Controls can lead one astray as well, especially when one knows so little about the phenomena under investigation."

"How do you mean?"

"I discussed this with Dr. Wollberg some time ago with respect to fertilization. Would you conclude that a sperm does not activate development of an egg if the egg can be activated by many other stimuli, which it can? Of course the sperm activates the egg, although other things can too, even a pinprick or temperature change or various chemicals, depending on the species and conditions. Or what about embryonic induction or double assurance?"

"You're getting technical, Dr. Sztein."

Wasn't that what Sophia wanted him to do? Wow them with his knowledge of science, be the irrefutable authority?

"Well, sir, you brought up the question of controls, not me, so let me explain in greater detail. For example, during development tissues contact one another, which induces them to differentiate, that is, to form specialized organs. A famous example is the out-pouching of the mammalian embryonic brain of vertebrates, which contacts and induces the surface of the head to form a lens in the developing eye. That outgrowth involutes and differentiates into the retina. Induction is a highly specific phenomenon, yet many non-specific stimuli can mimic the inducing tissue. It took myriads of controls and years of research to resolve induction. I don't think it's fully understood yet. Or take double assurance as another example. That complicates interpretations in a different way."

"Double assurance?" asked the prosecutor.

Ricardo had captured everyone's interest, including the prosecutor's. Even Benjamin didn't know what double assurance was and sat up for the answer.

"Okay," Ricardo said. "Double assurance involves a cooperative interaction of an inducing tissue and a competent reactive tissue. An example is leg development in certain amphibians. The developing limb bud pushes out through the surface skin to ultimately form a leg. That's the phenomenon. It turns out that the surface tissue directly over the buried limb bud thins whether or not the limb bud pushes against it. Under normal circumstances the thinning makes it easier for the growing limb bud to burst through the surface. So what's the more important mechanism: pressure from the limb bud against the surface or thinning of the surface? You see, sir, biology is tricky. To know anything in depth requires intense study, controls on the controls. But one has to begin somewhere. Phenomena have to be initially described. That's where my jellyfish work fits in. It pours a foundation, but the house still needs to be constructed. It opens a door, but now we need to go through that door to see what is on the other side."

Ricardo spoke authoritatively, the scientist replacing the defendant. Finally. Sophia and Benjamin both looked pleased.

The prosecutor avoided further questioning on biology. "I am not saying that your conclusions, excuse me, your speculations, are wrong, Dr. Sztein, but it sounds to me that you might have been trying to generate mystery rather than to just satisfy your curiosity at taxpayers' expense."

"Not at all. I wanted to explore Nature. No one knew what or how jellyfish see, or why jellyfish often congregate as a group, which I found striking. Relatively little was known about jellyfish, yet they have been among the most successful survivors on this planet if you consider their longevity and their ability to adapt to their environment."

"Isn't there more to this than curiosity?" continued the prosecutor, refusing to relinquish his probing. "Dr. Sztein, do you realize how serious all this is?"

Ricardo was perspiring heavily. "Research is intensely serious to me. These remarkable jellyfish *need* to be studied. I believe we will learn as much about solving practical problems by allowing our curiosity free expression as by answering questions that we already envision. We must explore new terrain, even if it's the taxpayers' grandchildren who will benefit."

Ricardo paused. He then asked, his eyes dancing in their orbits, "Where is the *conscience* of society if they neglect to learn all they can about our universe in order to make it easier and more comfortable for future generations?"

"Conscience of society?" the prosecutor said smugly.

Ricardo didn't notice the judge sipping water or the spectators whispering to each other; his mind was back in La Parguera. He looked at Benjamin and wanted to say, "You know what I mean, don't you?" Instead he just stared through the oceanic distance between the witness box and his friend.

The prosecutor moved toward the witness stand, closing in for the kill. "One more question, Dr. Sztein. When you stuck a wire in a jellyfish eye, did you ever worry that you might be hurting the creature? What about those terrible screeching sounds coming from the impaled jellyfish? How do you know that the jellyfish weren't screaming in pain?"

A murmur rippled throughout the courtroom. Ricardo's eyes widened with worry, not only of the consequences of this disastrous trial, but also of being exposed as a deficient scientist, without compassion, an amateur rather than the professional that he considered himself to be. Had he not performed enough controls, the most basic rule of experimental science? Had he hurt the jellyfish? Maybe. He had thought of that before. But the work was published. It was too late to recall or modify it.

"Why can't anyone understand that we scientists are artists too? Our work expresses our view of the world, not just data. We use our data to write narratives, and these narratives are molded as more data are obtained."

"Dr. Sztein. Relevance. Taxpayer dollars. Helping sick people. Benefiting mankind. Having compassion. I know scientists study flies and worms, but they do it to find out what's similar between these animals and people, and then they use the information to develop new treatments for diseases. It seems to me that you looked for what's different between jellyfish and humans and squandered public funds searching for mysteries."

"Searching for mysteries? How dare you! I was searching for questions that answered mysteries!" Ricardo said, confused, too flustered and exhausted to say any more.

The prosecutor raised his chin and turned his back to Ricardo. He looked at Sophia and then at the jury.

"Thank you, Dr. Sztein. That will be all," he said. "I rest my case."

He returned to his seat without looking at Ricardo or anyone else.

Chapter 38

The trial reconvened at two o'clock for the concluding arguments. Spectators crammed into the courtroom while the judge's bench loomed empty, waiting for his Honor to enter. The prosecutor was going over his notes, occasionally consulting with his assistant.

Sophia sipped water and modified phrases from her prepared remarks. Ricardo looked over her shoulder, trying to read what she was writing. "Just tell them the truth: I'm a serious scientist doing serious research." Ricardo couldn't understand why he wasn't more anxious. Whatever the outcome, it seemed less threatening than the black hole he'd been living in.

"Sure," she said, without looking up. "A serious scientist like Galileo, right?"

Everyone rose when the judge entered and took his seat.

"Time to begin the concluding arguments. Mr. Jenkins, please proceed," said the judge.

The prosecutor's delivery was cunningly effective. At first he dwelled, predictably, on the ailing economy and the runaway national debt. He then gave a dazzling display of statistics on individuals suffering from various debilitating diseases and the national cost for treating them. "Despite the depressing truth of these statistics, they remain abstractions. Let me tell you about little Frankie Dupart. He is only one of many victims," he said. The prosecutor showed the jury a photograph of twelve-year-old Frankie who had died recently of lymphoma. "Ladies and gentleman, we are living in hard economic times. And the incidence of disease is rising. Frankie falls within the ten percent increase in lymphomas in the last two years. We need to eradicate scourges like cancer now with *responsible research* efforts. No one has more reason to understand these realities than the defendant." The prosecutor reminded the jury of the millions of government dollars that supported Ricardo's laboratory and then asked rhetorically, "How can *anyone* heading a laboratory in the Vision Science Center justify playing around with jellyfish while Frankie dies of lymphoma before he is even a teenager?"

The prosecutor then moved to disparage Ricardo's judgment in addition to making his case for the misuse of government funds. He reminded the jury of Ricardo's rambling nonsense about how health was more important than disease because more people are well than sick (this caused some laughter in the audience), and his implication that helping people live a long time raised the danger of overpopulation. "Dr. Sztein talked facetiously about overpopulation," said the prosecutor, "but sadly he never addressed the serious problems of disease: cancer, neurological disorders, blindness. In these hard times we need critical judgment and moral priorities from our government-funded scientists."

Ricardo clenched his jaw and leaned towards Sophia and whispered, "I lack judgment and moral priorities?" Even the judge looked upset with the prosecutor's vicious attack on Ricardo's character.

But the prosecutor was not deterred. He spread his arms and spoke with heartfelt sincerity about the moral responsibility and profound obligation of government officials to spend every penny of taxpayers' money for the immediate benefit of the country's citizens. "The time is over to think that knowledge will be useful no matter what. We need to set an example now once and for all."

The prosecutor walked theatrically to his seat with a display of grandiose showmanship.

However, Ricardo thought that the prosecutor also looked sad when he sat down. His facial tic was more active than usual and he was perspiring in the air-conditioned courtroom. Ricardo suddenly saw the prosecutor as an individual, a middle-aged man with a job to do, rather than an enemy. He was part of the web of life along with Ricardo and jellyfish. Ricardo wondered what the prosecutor's wife looked like and how many children he might have, then he thought of the note from the grandchild tacked on the door of the woman in the room next to Lillian's in the hospital.

Now it was Sophia's turn to give her concluding statements. She began by repeating historical cases of basic research resulting in medically relevant advances and then referred to Benjamin's remarkable discovery of Cactein as an example of practical advances coming from curiosity-driven acquisition of knowledge for its own sake. She appealed to whatever creative and artistic streaks the jurors might have by referring to Ricardo's rich imagination and his ability to create new concepts. "Would science or society truly benefit by confining fertile minds or denying the proven value of the so-called Ivory Tower?" she asked. She pointed out that Ricardo's desire to reflect on mysteries and not just focus on practical solutions to known problems should be encouraged, not incriminated. "What can possibly be achieved by incriminating creativity?"

Sophia paused to let her comments sink into the minds of the jury just when a deafening clap of thunder stole everyone's attention. It was pouring outside and lightning flashes decorated the heavens.

The building lost electrical power. Indifferent Nature had broken Sophia's tenuous connection to the jury. The electricity was restored a minute later, and the trial resumed.

Sophia's eyes narrowed and her neck stiffened. Ricardo recognized her resolved, angry side that had surfaced when she lectured him about his self-indulgence and texted him to settle down during his testimony.

"If we turn our lens to the past we see despicable tyrants, or *persecutors*," she said in a firm tone. "Hitler, Mussolini, Mao. There are many more. You know their names. Thankfully those terrible days are gone. But I fear the *spirit* of persecution remains in our society, despite our stated goals to be morally responsible." She paused momentarily. "I propose that today's persecutors are camouflaged *relevancers*." She paused once again. "R-e-le-v-a-n-c-e-r-s," she repeated slowly and distinctly. "Individuals who undermine the soul, set the rules, define morality, command acceptability, substitute rituals for choices, insist on their version of goodness and compassion. Recognize anything or anyone? Religious leaders? Political figures? Neighbors? We should all be ashamed, except perhaps Dr. Ricardo Sztein." After a final pause she continued, "The concept of *relevance* that has been such a focus of this trial is an abstraction, a malleable term that the camouflaged Relevancers, with a capital R, bend to their own advantage."

Brilliance may emerge unexpectedly as a shout or a whisper or the stroke of a brush. Sophia's brilliance at this moment was neither summarizing facts nor pleading for mercy, but providing a novel concept. There it was: *Relevancers*, more than a word, a new weapon that changed the perspective. By switching the adjective 'relevance' to the proper noun 'Relevancer', Sophia had refocused the drama from actors to directors and shifted the incriminating finger from pointing at Ricardo to pointing at the prosecutor, at the audience, at the government. Sophia's innovative concept of Relevancers questioned the validity of the trial itself.

Sophia stood motionless. There was no mention of 'Relevancers' in her prepared notes. The idea had developed spontaneously by blending intellect with passion as she delivered her final comments. She ended in a soft-spoken voice, more alto than soprano: "I think it's reasonable—even healthy—to allow creative individuals to decide *relevance* for themselves and give history a chance to act as jury."

Her ovation: silence, the deepest form of respect.

A moment later thunder rolled again, drumming out the prosecutor's rhetorical question, "Then *anything* goes?" Raindrops splashed off the window; the electric lights flickered. The prosecutor muttered, "What sophistry, Ms. Lass," just loud enough for the jury to hear. The juror with a white streak in her hair gave him a sour look.

The jury members had severe expressions when they filed out of the courtroom to deliberate.

"Come on, Ricardo, let's go," Sophia said. "It's out of our hands now."

Ricardo nodded. His new definition of eternity was the time it took for the jury to reach a verdict.

Chapter 39

Ricardo paced in his living room and drank enough coffee to prevent sleep for a week when he returned home to wait for the jury's verdict. His dinner consisted only of yogurt to calm his churning stomach. Lonelier than ever, he clicked on the television and randomly flipped channels. Likens's pale, round face flashed on the screen. He was summarizing the day's event at Ricardo's trial in his popular program, Your Money/Your Health. Predictably, Likens tilted his report to favor the prosecution. He lingered on a picture of little Frankie Dupart dying of cancer and said, "When will researchers put an end to such tragedy?" Likens then showed a picture of a jellyfish to illustrate Ricardo's research "at the expense of taxpayer dollars." He was merciless. Likens called Sophia's 'Relevancer' closing argument "brilliantly complementing Dr. Sztein's science fiction story about jellyfish having minds." Ricardo turned off the television when Likens showed crowds outside the courtroom with anti-Sztein placards.

Ricardo called Sophia to vent, but found little comfort in her. She had not seen Likens on television and told him to stop indulging his masochistic streak. "Go to bed and wait for the verdict," she said.

Unsatisfied, Ricardo called Benjamin in his hotel room and expressed conflated anger, discouragement and fear to his friend.

"Take it easy, Ricardo," Benjamin said. "There's nothing to do but wait. Fretting won't change the jury's verdict."

"I know. That's easy for you to say, but..."

"...still we cross our fingers, right?" finished Benjamin. "Even if we're not superstitious."

"Right. What else can we do but hope? Remember when we waited for hours for jellyfish to come to the light at the dock?"

"That was a night I'll never forget."

"Me either. Well, guess what?"

"What?"

"Even when we were ready to call it quits empty-handed, I never gave up hope that at least one jellyfish would rush to the surface." It gave Ricardo some comfort to turn his attention to the past, especially to his golden days at La Parguera.

"I guess hope can work."

"That's right. You never know. And thanks, Benjamin. I really mean it.

"For what? I didn't text the jellyfish to come up."

"You know what I mean...for being there for me, for sitting

through the trial, for supporting me, for putting up with all my whining and everything else all these years. For giving me advice to be careful, even if I wasn't smart enough to take it."

"It wasn't charity, Ricardo. My life wouldn't be the same without you."

There was a short lull in the conversation. Then Benjamin asked, "I never understood why you didn't pay for the trips to La Parguera yourself. You knew how tight government money was and what the political climate was like. You could have taken a leave of absence instead of official duty."

"Obviously I made a political mistake. Scientifically, the jellyfish research was as serious a project as anything I've ever done. I know you didn't feel the same way. I really thought it was a legitimate expense for the Vision Science Center. I still do."

"And also it was a little like giving your buddy Marcus Topping the finger, right?"

Ricardo smiled. "You said it, not me."

Ricardo replayed the trial in his thoughts as he tossed in bed. Marcus said that Ricardo was a fine scientist and the Vision Science Center was proud of him. His students, Ann and Pearl, praised him and were both devoted to biomedical research. Would an irrelevant scientist produce relevant students? And then there was Benjamin, his loyal colleague and esteemed scientist: he had stressed the value of curiosity-driven basic research. Shouldn't that help persuade the jury that Ricardo's jellyfish research was money well spent? And, Sophia's 'Relevancers' argument must have impressed the jury. He'd seen how intently they had listened and had nodded in agreement. How in the world had she come up with such a smart twist? It wasn't the era of Socrates (thank goodness), so conviction wasn't a foregone conclusion. There were many arguments to acquit him. He may not have been a Galileo (too bad), but he was a serious, acclaimed scientist and the jellyfish work was interesting and conceptually new. Wouldn't the jury recognize its importance?

After a late snack, Ricardo called Benjamin still again for support. "I'm sorry to disturb you so late, Benjamin. I've been going over all the reasons for why I should be acquitted. What do you think? Is there any hope for me? How long do you think it will take the jury to decide?"

"I don't know the answers to any of your questions." Benjamin hemmed and hawed, said that he was optimistic, but one never knows. Whatever happens, he said, he knew that Ricardo was a first rate scientist. "Try to get some sleep. We can talk again in the morning."

Ricardo slept little that night.

The phone rang midmorning the next day, sooner than expected. "The jury's reached a verdict," Sophia said. "The judge told me that we should be at the courthouse at one o'clock this afternoon." She didn't offer any encouragement. "See you there, Ricardo."

Ricardo hesitated for a few seconds before replacing the receiver, trying to figure out whether or not such a quick decision was in his favor.

After calling Benjamin to tell him the verdict was in, Ricardo met Sophia at the courthouse amid a flock of vultures. Photographers buzzed like hungry mosquitoes. Blinding mini-explosions from overactive cameras sparkled like fireflies. The reporters hovered like sharks smelling blood.

Handwritten signs with questions such as "Did You Enjoy Your Paid Vacations in the Sun?" and "What do Jellyfish Think about this Trial?" carried by angry taxpayers littered the block. There were also scattered signs supporting Ricardo. His eyes fixed on one that said, "Long Live Free Enquiry." Another said, "God Help the Ignorant." However, these glimmers of hope were swamped by the tide of disaffection.

"What do you think your chances are, Dr. Sztein?" asked one reporter.

"Don't say a word!" commanded Sophia. She grabbed Ricardo's arm and guided him into the courthouse.

Ricardo and Sophia went to their usual seats in the courtroom, which was filled to capacity. No one spoke in anticipation of the verdict about to be delivered. Everyone rose as one, and a great hush followed when the judge entered at one o'clock sharp. The spectators sat when the judge did and then there was a heavy moment of silence.

"Has the jury reached a verdict?" the judge asked.

"We have, your Honor," the foreman replied.

Ricardo stared straight ahead, his face pale, his hands shaking. He had a pit the size of the Grand Canyon in his stomach.

The bailiff handed the judge the slip of paper that the foreman gave him. The judge pondered the verdict for a few seconds and asked the defendant and his counsel to rise. Ricardo steadied himself by placing his hands on the edge of the table in front of him.

"The jury finds the defendant, Dr. Ricardo Sztein, guilty of irresponsibly misusing taxpayer dollars." Applause flooded the courtroom.

Ricardo blanched. Benjamin shook his head. The news traveled instantly on the Internet and the throngs outside cheered and waved their banners.

Due to sentencing guidelines, the unanimous vote for guilty obligated the judge to sentence Ricardo to ten years in a low security prison. The sentence could be appealed but not delayed. Ricardo was the first scientist to be convicted of this crime, a warning for all other researchers to take heed. The judge pronounced the ten-year sentence and pounded the gavel as if hammering shut a coffin. Case closed.

Ricardo looked like he was about to vomit. He imagined himself a jellyfish yanked from his natural habitat.

Randolph Likens slithered out of the courtroom. The prosecutor showed no emotion: business as usual. The traffic outside went on as if nothing had happened. Drivers honked their horns. Pedestrians waited for a green light to cross the street. The demonstrators returned to their regular life and left their hand-made signs scattered by the side of the street like road kill. The show was over.

Sophia's eyes overflowed with tears, smearing her makeup. Ricardo put his arm around her shoulders and gave her a quick squeeze. "Not your fault," he said. "I'm not Galileo. Sorry. Anyway, he was convicted too."

Despite having lost, there was something quieting about the battle being over. He could rest now. Of course he didn't want to go to jail, but there was no one to go home to. One place was as good as another. He had no desire to face his colleagues at the Vision Science Center, certainly not Dr. Topping. Enough was enough. A colleague would mentor Pearl until she found a job.

"We'll appeal." Sophia gritted her teeth, gathering her wits.

"It's no use," he answered.

Ricardo was placed in handcuffs and led away.

"Is that necessary, to handcuff him?" Benjamin asked the lady next to him.

"Absolutely," she said.

"Why?"

She glared at him. "My husband has cancer," she retorted and turned away to leave the courtroom.

PART IV

The low security prison for white-collar criminals was going to be Ricardo's home for the next ten years if he was lucky enough to live that long. It resembled a large, cheap motel. Each inmate was assigned to one of a series of equally spaced small rooms lining three narrow hallways. There was a communal bathroom at the end of each hall. Meals with the texture of boiled cardboard were served three times a day in a separate building. An eight-foot high chain link fence with barbed wire enclosed the compound. Few cars traveled on the country road in front of the facility. The landscaping within the prison consisted of two tulip poplars, a crepe myrtle and an aging weeping willow. A basketball hoop with a torn net was clamped onto a rusty metal pole that stood at the edge of a patch of concrete near the fence. The prison was a dreary scene, an insult to human dignity.

Ricardo's cell/room had a reasonably comfortable spring bed, an armchair and a small desk with an electric outlet. He was grateful that there was an Internet connection for his laptop computer. There was a shelf attached to the wall for books. A tungsten light bulb dangled at the end of a short wire attached to a broken fixture on the ceiling. During the day Ricardo was allowed to walk freely in the compound, although there wasn't much to see or do. The bored guards paid scant attention to anyone. The warden locked Ricardo's door at night.

Ricardo befriended his neighbors, who were small-time tax evaders. Occasionally he regretted not being in a high security prison with hardened criminals. What did he have to lose? At his advanced age he didn't consider himself a likely rape target and he imagined that mixing with serious offenders might be enlightening. Given the luxury of time without responsibilities, Ricardo thought about his diverse demons and secret desires. He lived many lives in his imagination: sometimes that of a lumberjack in the wilderness; sometimes that of a poet who managed a rural bed and breakfast; sometimes that of an intimate confidant in a brothel. There was a paradoxical freedom in jail with only his body confined. He regretted that his single-minded focus on science had prevented him from experimenting with other lifestyles, even superficially. He saw his life as a collection of activities not done, goals not reached, and sadly, a lineage not continued.

Although Ricardo missed Lillian greatly and was comforted by her picture next to his bed, on occasion he dreamed of Monique's lithe body and the subtle curl of the left corner of her upper lip. He never imagined her older than she was when he knew her that one night. In his dreams Monique always had sad eyes. Often Dr. Salisbury was in the background looking disappointed, adding another layer to his sense of dreams not realized, those of his kindly old mentor.

Ricardo read extensively, however what he treasured most was the desk in his room, where he wrote every day and kept his imagination fertile. He deflected questions on what he was writing about by saying, "This and that, nothing serious."

Lillian's ghost remained the cornerstone of his stability. He wrote her letters on his computer or in longhand, depending on his mood. He described his meals, discussed the weather, detailed the gossip among the inmates, and apologized for not having more to say. He sealed each hand-written letter in an envelope addressed to Lillian Sztein in the Grand Universe of Space and Time, then torched it with a match. He did keep the computer-written letters in a special file.

In the evenings alone in his room, Ricardo reflected on fate and compared his life with the apparent movement of the sun. The guard rescued a discarded poem from the trash basket in Ricardo's room:

The Path of Life

The brilliant golden-yellow midday sun
shines proudly, steady in the sky,
future darkness a mere abstraction.
Suddenly, it seems,
the fiery ball plunges downward,
reddens, dims,
becomes a diminishing sliver
as it retreats beneath the horizon.
Daylight disappears,
black night prevails.
There is nothing to be done.

Chapter 41

Days flowed into weeks, then months into years. Mundane details filled the void. He ate, chatted nothings with the prisoners and guards, read, watched television with little interest, wandered around the premises and used the exercise room from time to time. Mainly he wrote at his desk, his private sanctuary. No trespassing! Others lost interest in Ricardo's literary efforts, like commoners accept exclusion from royalty.

The most difficult day of each year for Ricardo was the anniversary of Lillian's death. He would relive the night in the hospital when he held her limp hand and kissed her dry lips, and often cried. The note taped on the door next to Lillian's in the hospital—"Git wel soone grama"—remained engraved in his mind. He felt so badly that Lillian had died without the satisfaction of being a mother. It was his loss as well as hers.

On the anniversary of Lillian's death during the eighth year of imprisonment, the guard knocked on Ricardo's closed door and barked, "Hey, Ricardo, there's a phone call for you." Ricardo couldn't imagine who it was. Sophia? Unlikely. Their communication had faded after the election of an administration even more conservative than the one that had been in power during the trial, making it pointless to appeal the verdict. Could it be Benjamin? Perhaps. They had stayed in touch by email, which Ricardo preferred because it was easier for him to hide his sadness. But their emails dwindled with time.

"Hello, Dr. Sztein?" said a woman's voice on the other end of the line.

"Speaking."

"You don't know me. I'm Juliette Levin. This is a little clumsy."

"What's this about? What do you want?"

Ricardo castigated himself for being curt, almost dismissive, because in truth he was excited about having something new happen in his life. Who was she? Did she bring good news or more heartbreak? Had something happened to Benjamin? He didn't recognize her voice, yet there was a distant ring of familiarity, an intonation that wasn't completely foreign.

"I'm doing some research and would like very much to talk to you. It would mean a lot to me," she said.

"Research? Are you a scientist? Do you study jellyfish by any chance?"

Suddenly Ricardo's hopes rose. Had she read his jellyfish article? Had she discovered something supporting his speculations? Maybe all was not lost.

"No, nothing like that. I'd rather not discuss it over the phone. Could I come by this weekend, or the next?"

"Yes, okay," he said, curious to know what she wanted to talk about. "This weekend would work. My calendar's not too booked and I could slip you in," he added sarcastically.

"Saturday at ten? They told me that visitors could come Saturday mornings."

"Perfect. See you then."

Suddenly everything seemed different in anticipation of Juliette Levin's visit—he had something to look forward to and could replace the dull present with an abstract future. Life had a pulse again.

At precisely ten o'clock on Saturday morning the guard stuck his head into Ricardo's room. "You have a visitor, Ricardo. Nice looking too."

Ricardo had slicked back what was left of his hair and trimmed his beard. He checked his appearance in the mirror.

"Look at you!" said the guard as Ricardo made his way to the visitors' room. Ricardo ignored the guard, yet he couldn't hide a self-conscious smile.

Ricardo was nervous. He hadn't had a visitor in years. His daily life had a certainty that created stability and safety. Each day was like the one before. Now that certainty was in jeopardy. What would he say to Juliette Levin? Tell her about the tough pork dinner he ate last night? Talk about the weather? No. Whoever she was, she wanted to speak to him. His job was to listen. What could she possibly want?

"Dr. Sztein?" said an attractive young woman.

He nodded. "Yes."

She didn't have a computer or pad and pen with her, so she probably wasn't a reporter. He figured she was approximately thirty-five years old, maybe younger. With her high heels they were about the same height.

"Juliette Levin." She held out her hand. "Very glad to meet you." Her eyes bore into him as if she were mining for gold.

They shook hands. Her soft skin and firm yet gentle grip resurrected him from a sexual grave. It had been so long since he had felt the tenderness of a woman's touch.

"Nice to meet you too," he said. He looked into her large brown eyes, the color of rich soil, and then was drawn to the glow of pink lipstick and slight curl of the left corner of her mouth. His heart skipped a beat.

She smiled and fidgeted.

"Shall we sit down?" she asked.

"Yes, let's."

They sat at the table by the window where the golden waves of her hair reflected the sunlight. She was something; blond hair, brown eyes and smooth skin. He had forgotten there was such loveliness in the world.

She rubbed a tear away with the back of her hand. "Dr. Sztein..." She hesitated, like she had on the telephone the other day. "May I ask you a few questions?"

"Certainly." He wondered what was sad enough to make her cry.

She regained her composure. "Did you go to Nice, France a long time ago?"

"Nice? Did we meet there?" No, he thought. That's impossible. She's too young. "Yes, I was there about thirty-five years ago."

"And you gave a keynote lecture there at a science conference?"

"Yes."

"And went to a discothèque after your lecture and ...met someone?"

He watched Juliette's cheeks redden. Pink lipstick! An upward curl at the left corner of her lips! His mind was racing now.

"You can't be...you're too young."

"Of course not," she said. "She was my Mom."

Neither knew what to say. Was it possible?

"Monique is your mother?" He was incapable of asking her if she was his daughter. It was too unnatural, strange and unlikely.

"Yes," she said. "I think so."

"Think so? You don't know who your mother is?"

"Yes, of course. Monique was my mother. I mean..."

"Was?"

"I think you're my father."

Ricardo said nothing for a few long seconds. "How could you possibly know? Your mother... I just saw her one night...I mean...she must have known other men, that is. I'm sorry. I'm just trying to be honest and make sense of what you're saying."

"I was born nine months after she returned from Nice."

Monique's image filled his mind. Her blond hair, like Juliette's but shorter and curlier, her blue-gray eyes, not brown like Juliette's, her moist pink lipstick and, especially, the upward curl of the left corner of her lip. He had never seen anyone but Monique with an asymmetry like that, except now in Juliette.

"My mother was *not* a whore," she said. "No, no, no." She clenched her jaw.

"I didn't mean...Sorry. She just disappeared after...she was gone in the morning."

"She was embarrassed."

"Is that what she told you?"

"Yes."

"How is she," Ricardo asked. "I've thought of her often. She had a curl at the left corner of her mouth just like you. She looked so sad."

"Dead. Hit and run."

"Oh. That's why you said 'was'. I'm so sorry."

"She was back in Paris visiting a friend five years ago, trying to cross that crazy circle at the Arch of Triumph. She should have used the tunnel. They never found who hit her. When it happened, I was in New York with my husband, Frank. He's a lawyer."

Ricardo barely heard Juliette say anything more. Monique was dead. Did he really have a daughter?

"You don't have a French accent," he said.

"My mother and I moved to Boston when I was two years old. I barely speak French. She wanted to leave France. It was easy for her to get a job as a nurse here since she was one in France."

"What do you do?"

"Cancer research for a pharmaceutical company."

"Really?"

"My mother always felt so sorry for the cancer patients in her ward. And, believe it or not, she was so impressed with your scientific work, admired it so much, that I sort of put the two together and here I am, a biomedical researcher."

"You have a PhD?"

"Yes, from the University of Chicago. Five years ago."

What irony, thought Ricardo, to have fulfilled Lillian's last plea through his illegitimate daughter with another woman. Did life ever move in straight lines?

"That's wonderful," he said. "Did your mother ever marry?"

"Never. She was in love once, hopelessly so. He broke her heart. She met you a few months later. She was struggling to get back on her feet. Her friends begged her to get out of Paris, to go somewhere warm and sunny for a while after the guy left her. She had buried herself in her nursing and sick people. She was depressed. So, she went to Nice for a couple of weeks and went to the discotheque just for company, nothing else, and that's where you met her. She met you the day before she returned to Paris."

Ricardo's eyes were wide with wonder.

"Yes, go on,'" he said.

"There is really nothing else. She liked the way you looked and she just jumped off the cliff, at least that's how she put it. You were a once in a lifetime, spontaneous adventure. It just happened. She knew it was wrong, but she never regretted it. And I'm the result. You *are* my father."

Ricardo was speechless. No fiction or scientific insight had the power of such a simple statement. "You are my father."

I have a daughter, he kept repeating in his mind.

"I have a daughter, a wonderful, beautiful daughter," he said aloud this time. He tried to hide his tears.

"We're quite a pair," she said, wiping her cheeks and laughing awkwardly. She offered him Kleenex.

Ricardo thought of Lillian and was relieved that she didn't know that the child she craved belonged to another woman. How strange that was! He repeated in a quiet voice, more to himself than to Juliette, and with greater joy than he could remember having ever experienced, "I have a daughter; I have a daughter." He then imagined seeing his traits in her: the narrowing of her dark brown eyes when she was nervous, her high cheekbones. Everyone in Ricardo's family had brown eyes like his—like hers. But her yellow hair was from her mother, although her mauve complexion seemed a blend of Monique's ivory and his earthy tone.

"How did you find me?"

"I've known about you for many years. My mother knew your name, of course, told me about you when I was five or six years old. Then, your trial was reported in the newspapers. I figured that you must be my father. I even went to your trial the day that you testified. I suffered with you."

"Really?"

Juliette's expression dampened. "I think the government has gone nuts."

"Why didn't you ever look me up before now?"

She hesitated and lowered her eyes, almost as if she were still hiding from him. "I don't know," she said. "I guess I was scared, or maybe...I don't know. You were my abstract father and time just passed."

'Abstract father', Ricardo thought, overjoyed, yet upset that she had kept away for so long. But he was grateful that Lillian never knew. He felt disloyal even now in front of his daughter, with Lillian dead. There were always reasons to keep secrets.

"How long have you been married, Juliette?"

"Four years." Then she hesitated. "There's more."

"Is that possible?"

"You have a granddaughter. Rachel. She's two years old and, you won't believe this, she looks like you! She has your dark coffee-brown eyes, though she has a lot more hair than you."

Ricardo rubbed the top of his head.

Juliette opened her purse and took out a photograph of the most adorable little girl he had ever seen.

"You can keep the picture if you want. I brought it for you."

He took it with a trembling hand and kissed his granddaughter's cheek, feeling embarrassed and entitled at the same time. He had no idea how to be a parent, much less a grandparent.

They were both self-conscious. The scene seemed unnatural, forced, and yet appropriate at the same time. He was a father and had been for many years, and now a grandfather as well. He had a lineage. It felt perverse to be so happy under the conditions: he was in prison; Lillian was deceased; Monique, the mother of his daughter, was dead. But Juliette was his daughter and he was holding a photograph of his granddaughter. It was a surreal moment, another curveball in the happenstances of life.

"I need to go now," she said suddenly straightening up. "We'll be in touch. I'm so glad that I finally came. It wasn't scary at all."

Juliette gave him her phone number and email address. She looked back at him and waved when she went out the door.

Ricardo returned to his room and taped Rachel's picture on the wall next to his bed. He looked for a curl of her upper lip, but it wasn't there. Her mouth was symmetrical, like his. He was happy to see his genes expressed in her.

"Who was that?" asked the guard when Ricardo passed him in the hall going to lunch.

"Pretty, isn't she? I'll tell you about her one day."

It was a beautiful day.

Chapter 42

Nothing made sense to Ricardo anymore. Lillian and he had struggled for years without success to have a child. However, a few hours with Monique, a transient encounter in a foreign country while he was away on business—the only infidelity in his marriage—resulted in a daughter and a granddaughter. And then his daughter—not he—fulfills Lillian's dying wish for him to do medically targeted research, on cancer no less! What was the point of planning anything? What was the role of intent in a human life? Monique had said, "Ça ne fait rien," when he'd told her that he didn't speak French. How right she'd been. And then there was his career. Honest devotion to science had landed him in jail for misuse of taxpayers' money, while Benjamin's tinkering with cactus led to his being elected to the American Academy of Sciences. It could have been that Cactein was useless and jellyfish secreted a miracle substance. It all boiled down to luck—bad luck in his case.

At about four in the morning Ricardo finally fell asleep and dreamed of Rachel playing in a schoolyard with other children. He stood alone outside a chain-link fence. Rachel looked in his direction but didn't see him. She ran and put her little arms around Juliette. Lillian watched in the distance behind the fence opposite Ricardo. She was crying. Ricardo awakened, his pillow wet with tears.

5:30. Breakfast wasn't until 7:30. He drifted off to sleep again and dreamed some more. This time Ricardo found himself in the courtroom surrounded by jellyfish. The prosecutor and Benjamin were shaking their heads and whispering to one another. Lillian was in the distance watching him. He wanted to speak to her but she was too far away. He started to move in her direction...

"Breakfast." announced the guard, banging on Ricardo's door.

"Go away. I don't feel well and I'm skipping breakfast."

"Suit yourself."

Ricardo lay on his back, his head cradled by the pillow. His mind slid backwards to his childhood. What was his mother like? Papi's paintings portrayed her in many ways: long-haired and thoughtful in one portrait, short-haired and playful in another; sometimes with a mermaid's tail, other times with legs and feet solidly planted on land; once with three eyes as if she noticed everything, once with big ears as if she heard everything; and once with a smile, but tears as well, as if she'd foreseen her fate. Ricardo imagined how sad she would have been to see him end his life in prison.

"Who am I?" he asked the air. "An Argentinean or an American, a loyal husband or an adulterer, a scientist or a storyteller, an honest man or a criminal? Am I compassionate?" There were no single answers to these questions. Each merited a 'yes' and a 'no', a 'maybe' and a 'sometimes'.

As he nodded off, his mind drifted to jellyfish and their unique ability to visualize the grandeur of evolution—remarkable and all-encompassing! He felt he was awake and turned his head to see the clock, but it had no dials. Where was the time?

Juliette asked as if from outer space, "Can I call you Dad?"

"Oh, yes. Please do," he said.

A child's high voice said, "Grandpa." She nuzzled against his chest. He remained absolutely still to not disturb the scene. How good it felt to have such loving innocence against him. If only he deserved it. Family was everything. Why did it take so long for him to understand that?

"I'm sorry, Lillian. I love you so much." He saw her ghost beside him.

"I know," she said.

"I wish you could have been with me the night that I entered the mind of a jellyfish. They live in such a mysterious world. I'm convinced they think and feel and interact."

She listened.

"I'm confused, Lillian. Am I a thief and a murderer?"

"Poor baby." She caressed his cheek. And then the left corner of her lip curled upward, and she was Monique, and then Juliette.

This moment, asleep and yet not asleep—these illusions and contradictions, this love and pain—was his reality. He rocked gently side to side as if carried by the advancing and receding tide. Familiar screeches echoed in his mind. He didn't know their meaning, but he no longer cared. The sounds dissolved into the purring of a cat, and then the purring switched to a sweet melody he'd never heard. Suddenly he found himself in murky waters. Jellyfish swam by like he was one of them, like they were family. A bright light from above clarified the water. The jellyfish transformed into sponges and other species, some with spines, some with scales, even some with fur. And then the jellyfish were just jellyfish again, pulsing calmly in the sea, like him, for he too was now a jellyfish—and that was fine with him.

Then Papi spoke. "You are who you are and that's all anyone can be, Ricardo."

Was Papi right? Was that all anyone could be? Ricardo thought of what he might have done, whom he might have helped if he'd followed Lillian's plea. Who he might have been.

"Being you is quite enough," his mother said. It was the first time he had ever heard her voice in his mind. How sweet it was. "Because," she added, "you are the person you are now and who you were and who you will become, all at once."

Yes, he thought, a person really has no borders.

Finally, in that tender, loving tone he knew so well, Lillian whispered, "You're enough for me."

She had forgiven him. That's who he was: a forgiven man, with a family.

Chapter 43

Less than a week later Ricardo was browsing the Internet when a headline on the front page of the New York Times leaped out at him. Not believing what he'd read he restarted the computer as if to try to reset reality itself, but he could no more change the news than he could retract his article on jellyfish.

US/Israeli Scientist, Benjamin Wollberg, Wins Nobel in Medicine and Physiology

Ricardo raced through the article. The report summarized Benjamin's first inkling of Cactein and his immigration to the United States, carrying a bundle of his treasured cactus. The reporter praised Benjamin's tenacity to pursue his passion despite having two grant proposals for this work rejected. The article quoted the Chairperson of Benjamin's department saying, "It took the rare imagination of a Benjamin Wollberg to foresee the importance of his observations on cactus and go on to isolate a polypeptide that has become the most effective treatment for clinical depression." The President of the American Academy of Sciences, a neurophysiologist, stated, "Wollberg has opened a new field of psychiatry by his revolutionary work that is helping to close the gap between the mind and the brain." Even the Senate majority leader, an internist reincarnated as a politician, chimed in, "Wollberg brings deserved honor to this country for his novel work that significantly lowers the cost of medical treatment for depression."

Basking in the limelight, Benjamin was quoted as saying, "I'm overwhelmed. If this wonderful recognition shows anything, it's that one must trust one's intuition and never give up." There was no mention of Ricardo in the article. Why should there be? Benjamin had not included him in his cactus work. He hadn't included anyone.

Ricardo was livid. Benjamin was a hero while he was in jail. Benjamin sure as hell didn't pay for all his Cactein experiments with his own money! Didn't he "misuse" taxpayer dollars as much as Ricardo had? But Benjamin's experiments had turned out to have a medical application. What good were jellyfish? Wasn't it as "revolutionary" to help close the gap between humans and jellyfish as it was to help "close the gap between the mind and the brain"?

Ricardo noted the author of the article: Randolph Likens! Hypocrisy had no limits.

Ricardo could do no right while Benjamin, the golden boy, could do no wrong. Benjamin had everything that Ricardo had ever dreamed of. Ricardo toyed with thoughts of suicide, but he lacked the courage. He yearned to be a jellyfish that could pulse freely without judging others or being judged. If only that were possible.

Ricardo checked whether the door to his room was shut, and then he sat on his bed and sobbed like a little boy. He thought of Juliette and looked at Rachel's picture, his new family. However, he couldn't erase Lillian's image from his mind, making him lonelier having a family of strangers than having Lillian, his true and everlasting love, dead.

Chapter 44

Ricardo moped around for two days after learning that Benjamin had received the Nobel Prize. He ate alone and spent long hours in his room licking his wounds and writing stories in which he traveled to imaginary worlds where judgment was suspended and all creatures, invertebrates and vertebrates, real and imagined, lived in harmony. What wonderful, fictional worlds they were! Innocence was presumed; good was rewarded. Yet he received little pleasure when he reread his stories. "Amateurish garbage!" he exclaimed, though he refrained from deleting the stories from the computer. No matter how pessimistic his mood, the old Ricardo, the ambitious scientist, the eternal optimist, the romantic dreamer and imaginative artist, refused to die. And when he thought of Juliette and of Rachel smiling at him, the thick fog lifted.

"How're you doing?" asked a fellow prisoner, who sat down next to him at lunch. He had often exchanged pleasantries with the inmate, a tax evader who had a kind face.

"I'm okay, I guess," said Ricardo. It was partly true.

"Nice day," the inmate said.

"Sure is. Sunny."

"Do you want to play a little basketball this afternoon? The warden put a new net on the hoop. I used to play in college, and I'd love to shoot a few baskets again."

"I'm too old for basketball," Ricardo said. "I'm 84. But I guess that I should work out more. It would do me good."

He thought of Lillian and his favorite picture of her in exercise clothes. If she had been with him now they would go to the gym together, like they used to, way back when.

"We all should. C'mon. You're never too old to throw the ball around a bit. We'll have some fun for a change."

"Maybe later this afternoon."

"No sweat. Take your time. I've no plans today!"

Ricardo smiled. "I'll find you later," he called out as he was leaving the dining room.

"I'll be waiting."

Ricardo went back to his room and started writing a new short story. It was about an Argentinean teenager with a bright future playing basketball. He didn't know yet how the story would end.

"Hey, Ricardo, you got a phone call," announced a guard knocking on his door.

A week ago receiving a phone call had been a momentous event. How quickly things change. Ricardo made his way down the hall to the telephone.

"Juliette?" he said into the receiver, assuming that it was she.

"Ricardo?" answered a man's voice.

"Benjamin?"

"Yes. It's been a long time, old friend. How are you?"

"All right." That's all Ricardo could force himself to say. What could a jailbird say to a Nobel Laureate? Then he thought of Juliette and Rachel, and said, "Not bad. Not bad at all, Benjamin."

"Who is Juliette?"

"Just someone I know."

"Good to hear your voice, Ricardo."

Once again, Ricardo did not know what to say.

"Ricardo, you there?"

"Sorry...yes...I'm here."

Ricardo's throat constricted. "My God, Benjamin. Congratulations. The Nobel Prize. I can't believe it."

"Amazing, no? I don't deserve it."

Benjamin's modesty didn't ring true. Ricardo changed the subject. "Anything new happening with jellyfish research? I suppose not, with funding being what it is."

"You're right. It's worse than ever. However, a graduate student in our department added Cactein to a bowl of jellyfish. He's too young to be intimidated by circumstances. I guess there's hope for the future."

"You've got to be kidding. Where did he get the jellyfish?"

"They were moon jellies from the Baltimore aquarium. When he added Cactein to the seawater, the jellyfish clumped together, and then a few minutes later they separated. His interpretation was that Cactein acted like a type of glue that made the jellyfish stick together, and then the Cactein dissolved in the seawater or broke down, allowing the jellyfish to separate."

"Really?" Ricardo asked. "He thinks Cactein sticks the jellyfish together like glue? Hmmm...there might be more interesting possibilities, don't you think?"

"What's that, Ricardo? I can hardly hear you. We must have a poor connection."

"I said there might be more interesting possibilities about how Cactein clumped the jellyfish," Ricardo repeated in a louder voice.

"I guess so. There always are more interesting possibilities," said Benjamin. "Sorry I haven't been in touch more. Life's so busy these days."

Ricardo couldn't say the same for himself. "I understand. Good luck in Stockholm."

"Thank you."

"Really. It's great about the Nobel. I mean it." Benjamin had been his friend for what—fifty years? That couldn't be erased.

Ricardo never mentioned Juliette or Rachel, or how he cried in despair when he first heard about Benjamin's Nobel Prize, or how he was writing every day, or how much he missed Lillian. His existence in prison brimmed with life after all, his private life, the one he lived in his head—the one that counted.

After speaking to Benjamin, Ricardo went to the cafeteria and found the inmate who had approached him earlier. "Ready to shoot a few baskets?" he asked.

"Sounds good to me," the inmate said.

After a failed attempt at a reverse layup, Ricardo turned to the inmate and said, "Please excuse this embarrassing question, but I've forgotten your name."

"No sweat, Ricardo. Just call me Billy. I hate William." Billy smiled.

"Okay. Billy it is."

Ricardo dribbled, turned in one direction and then another. His legs felt like springs, his joints moved freely. The ground felt solid under his feet. Suddenly he stopped.

"Are you okay?" Billy asked.

Ricardo looked at the chain link fence, which seemed lower than before, less confining. The air had a clean nip to it. He inhaled deeply. The oppressive humidity of summer was gone and the sharp sting of winter still distant. A gentle gust made the autumn leaves shimmer in the sunlight. Rachel's image floated in his mind. Would she be a dancer or an artist or a writer when she grew up, or a scientist, like her mother, like him? Would she give him great grandchildren? Would Juliette discover a cure for cancer?

"I'm fine, Billy. Just fine."

Ricardo bounced the basketball and darted to the left, leaving Billy flatfooted. He sprinted towards the basket and, with a little hop, released a jump shot. The ball arched towards the basket.

Swish.

Acknowledgements

I am deeply indebted to the Writer's Center in Bethesda for facilitating my transition from scientist to novelist. The following workshop instructors at the Writer's Center (in alphabetical order)—Robert Bausch, Kate Blackwell, Barbara Esstman, Catherine Mayo and Elizabeth Poliner—introduced me to the challenges and rewards of writing. In particular, Robert Bausch's story-telling ability and big—make that huge—humanity showed me how a writer can be a messenger from the heart, and Barbara Esstman's knack for identifying the gold within the clutter and expert editing of numerous drafts of this novel have been invaluable.

I gratefully acknowledge the Helen R. Whiteley Center at the Friday Harbor Laboratories, Puget Sound, University of Washington, where I spent three idyllic weeks beginning to write this novel, and thank Kathy Cowell, the Coordinator of the Center, who helped make my stay there pleasant and productive.

I thank each of the talented members of the workshops that I attended at the Writer's Center's and elsewhere who have contributed so much to my journey as a writer, and continue to do so.

I am grateful to the following for encouragement and for reading parts or entire drafts of this novel and providing very helpful insights (in alphabetical order): Charles Antin, Carol Arenberg, Robert Bausch, Frederick Bettelheim, Vera Bettelheim, John Burdick, Jo Buxton, Eve Caram, Jesse Coleman, Barbara Esstman, Michael Fisher, Neal Gillen, Jennifer Haupt, Roger Herst, Joseph Horwitz, Zdenek Kostrouch, Joyce Maynard, Ann McLaughlin, Stewart Moss, Leslie Nicholson, Anton Piatigorsky, Lona Piatigorsky, Warren Poland, Knud Ross, Beverly Ross, Stanton Samenow, Alan Schechter, Adele Siegal, Karen Solit and Babette Spaar. I apologize if I have inadvertently left out anyone.

I cannot thank enough my wife, Lona, for her patience, continual support and valuable suggestions upon reading and rereading various drafts of this novel.

I thank my long-time friend, Carolyn Feigelson, for introducing me to my publisher, Arnold Richards and IPBooks, and Kathy Kovacic for creating the cover of this book.

Finally, I am indebted to the National Eye Institute of the National Institutes of Health for supporting my scientific research and giving me the freedom to investigate the jellyfish eye.

About the Author

After receiving his Ph.D. degree from the California Institute of Technology in 1967, Joram Piatigorsky continued his research at the National Institutes of Health in Bethesda, MD. He established the Laboratory of Molecular and Developmental Biology in the National Eye Institute in 1981 and was its Chief until 2009, when he became an Emeritus Scientist. He has published approximately 300 scientific articles and reviews on the molecular biology of the eye. He served on the editorial boards of numerous professional journals, lectured worldwide, participated in national and international advisory and research funding panels and trained a generation of scientists in eye research. He received many awards for his research, the most recent being the Helen Keller Prize for Vision Research in 2008. Piatigorsky put forward the concept of gene sharing as a general strategy of evolution which is summarized in his book, *Gene Sharing and Evolution* (Harvard University Press, 2007). He is presently on the Board of Directors of the Writer's Center in Bethesda, Maryland. He has published a series of personal essays in the British Columbia journal, *Lived Experience*. *Jellyfish Have Eyes* is his first novel.

His email address is joramp@verizon.net